Introduction of the Mahabharata: A New Perspective

A Symphony of the Unseen and Untold

Aurobindo Ghosh

Ukiyoto Publishing

All global publishing rights are held by

Ukiyoto Publishing

Published in 2024

Content Copyright © Aurobindo Ghosh

ISBN 9789367959299

All rights reserved.

No part of this publication may be reproduced, transmitted, or stored in a retrieval system, in any form by any means, electronic, mechanical, photocopying, recording or otherwise, without the prior permission of the publisher.

The moral rights of the author have been asserted.

This is a work of fiction. Names, characters, businesses, places, events, locales, and incidents are either the products of the author's imagination or used in a fictitious manner. Any resemblance to actual persons, living or dead, or actual events is purely coincidental.

This book is sold subject to the condition that it shall not by way of trade or otherwise, be lent, resold, hired out or otherwise circulated, without the publisher's prior consent, in any form of binding or cover other than that in which it is published.

www.ukiyoto.com

I dedicate this book to Mr. Debasis Banerjee and his wife Mrs. Kakoli Banerjee of Champanagar, Bhagalpur, who is always with us. They are our backbone. They are Mahashay Deorhi's trouble shooter. They have profound knowledge of Mythology.

My heartfelt gratitude goes to my wife, Dr. Sharada Ghosh, whose discerning eye and unwavering commitment to excellence have been invaluable to this book. As a dedicated critic and meticulous editor, she has not only identified every flaw but has also painstakingly worked to make each story flow seamlessly. Her tireless efforts in editing, compiling, and organizing these narratives have been essential to this work.

I am also profoundly grateful to my children Dr. Dorothy, Dr. Gargi, and Aalap who form the foundation of my support system. Their encouragement and faith in my writing give me the strength to pursue this passion. To each of you, thank you for your patience, understanding, and belief in me. Lastly, let me take this opportunity to convey my gratitude to all the team members of Ukiyoto publishing for their maximum care to make this book a magnificent creation.

Foreword

Dr. Aurobindo Ghosh has become a household name in the literary world, captivating readers with his dazzling yet simple narration. A prolific writer, he burst into the limelight with his award-winning books Lily on the Northern Sky and Bimladadi's Dream, both universally acclaimed for their depth and storytelling brilliance. His books, cherished like treasures, have carved a permanent place in the hearts of his readers. For lovers of fiction or detective crime stories, his detective series stands unparalleled, offering gripping tales that showcase his boundless creativity and meticulous attention to detail. He has already contributed in 25 anthologies in different languages. He has already authored 11 books comprising Novels, detective stories, collection of short stories and poetries.

With Mahabharata-A New Perspective, Dr. Ghosh invites readers to embark on a transformative journey through one of the greatest epics of all time. The book delves into the Mahabharata, not just as a historical or mythological narrative but as a living testament to the complexities of human emotions, relationships, and decisions. This fresh interpretation explores overlooked characters, reframes pivotal events, and examines the nuanced roles of fate, morality, and dharma. Dr. Ghosh's insightful analysis and compelling storytelling breathe new life into ancient tales, offering readers a lens to understand this timeless epic in a manner that resonates with contemporary life.

One of the most remarkable aspects of this book is its emphasis on the significant contributions of unsung heroes. Characters like Shalya, whose reluctant participation in the war subtly influenced its outcome, and Ekalavya, who epitomized unparalleled devotion and sacrifice, are brought to the forefront. The book examines the vital yet often overlooked roles played by Vidura, the embodiment of wisdom and righteousness, and others who shaped pivotal moments in the epic. Through these narratives, Dr. Ghosh unravels the rich tapestry of the Mahabharata, celebrating not just the heroes and villains but the seemingly insignificant figures whose choices and contributions echo through history.

What sets this work apart is its thematic conceptualization that bridges the Mahabharata's ancient wisdom with contemporary relationships and challenges. Dr. Ghosh draws thought-provoking parallels between the strained bonds of Pandavas and Kauravas with modern familial conflicts, where rivalry and ambition often test the limits of kinship. The loyalty of Karna, torn between friendship and familial ties, mirrors the dilemmas faced by individuals balancing personal values against societal expectations. Similarly, Draupadi's resilience amidst adversity serves as a powerful symbol of the strength required to combat injustice, resonating with contemporary struggles for equality and dignity.

By weaving philosophy, history, human psychology, and modern relevance seamlessly, Dr. Ghosh opens the Mahabharata to a broader audience, making its themes universally accessible and meaningful. Mahabharata – A New Perspective is not merely a retelling but an invitation to rethink and rediscover an epic that continues to inspire, challenge, and guide humanity. This work is a tribute to every character, celebrated or unsung, and to the timeless wisdom embedded in their journeys, making it a must-read for scholars and enthusiasts alike.

Subha Singh,

Historian and Critic

Bhagalpur, 1.12.2024

Contents

Preface and Introduction to the Mahabharata

A New Perspective

The Mahabharata, an epic of unparalleled grandeur, has traversed millennia as a cornerstone of Indian literature, philosophy, and culture. Written by the sage Vyasa and encompassing over 100,000 verses, it is far more than a tale of war, heroism, and divine interventions. It is a profound exploration of human emotions, relationships, ethics, and the interplay of destiny and free will. Despite its vastness, much of the attention has been centered on iconic figures like Krishna, Arjuna, and Bhishma. However, beyond the epic's dominant narrative lies a treasure trove of overlooked perspectives and unexamined threads that weaves together its complex tapestry.

This book is an attempt to unravel the untold stories, unnoticed characters, and underexplored dynamics of the Mahabharata. By delving into these dimensions, the work aspires to provide a holistic and enriched understanding of the epic while challenging conventional interpretations.

The Significance of Insignificant Characters

Every epic rests on the shoulders of its unsung characters, and the Mahabharata is no exception. While the grand exploits of warriors and kings dominate its pages, numerous minor figures serve as crucial cogs in the narrative machinery. Characters like Shalya, Ekalavya, and even Vidura—despite his wisdom—are often relegated to the margins.

What would the epic have been without Shalya's subtle sabotage of Karna's chariot? Or Ekalavya's unparalleled commitment to mastery, which raises profound questions about the ethics of mentorship and caste hierarchies? These so-called minor characters often serve as mirrors, reflecting society's complexities and the ethical dilemmas faced by more prominent figures. This exploration aims to give them their due, shedding light on their pivotal roles and the lessons they impart.

Krishna's Friends: The Silent Support System

The divine persona of Krishna as a strategist, philosopher, and guide is a focal point of the Mahabharata. Yet, what about his friends who shared his journey as the cowherd of Gokul, the prince of Dwarka, and the ally in battle? Figures like Sudama, Arjuna, and Uddhava illustrate the various facets of Krishna's relationships, showing him as a friend, confidant, and nurturer.

Sudama's humble visit to Krishna offers a glimpse into the profound friendship rooted in equality, transcending material wealth. Arjuna, as Krishna's dearest companion and disciple, unveils a dynamic relationship based on trust and enlightenment. These relationships, explored in depth, reveal the humanity within divinity, making Krishna's character even more relatable and inspiring.

The Sages: Custodians of Dharma

Sages like Vyasa, Narada, and Parashurama are not merely bystanders in the Mahabharata; they are the architects, catalysts, and conscience keepers of its events. Their interventions, guidance, and sometimes cryptic actions shape the course of the narrative. Vyasa, as the composer of the epic, provides a meta-narrative perspective, blurring the lines between the creator and the characters. Narada's role as a celestial messenger and Parashurama's interactions with warriors like Karna highlight the sages' multifaceted contributions.

Through these explorations, this book delves into the role of sages as custodians of dharma and their struggles with the moral ambiguities that the epic frequently presents. Their presence emphasizes the importance of wisdom, foresight, and the often-overlooked burden of knowledge.

Friendship: A Bond Beyond Politics

The Mahabharata is replete with examples of enduring friendships that transcend the chaos of politics and war. The bond between Karna and Duryodhana is a poignant testament to loyalty and gratitude. Despite being on the "wrong" side of the war, Karna's unwavering commitment to Duryodhana demonstrates the depth of human connection, even when it defies moral judgment.

Similarly, the camaraderie between the Pandavas reflects a blend of duty and affection, tested by the trials of exile, betrayal, and war. Krishna's role as a friend to both the Pandavas and the Kauravas further complicates the notion of friendship, highlighting its capacity to bridge ideological divides.

This section examines these bonds to illuminate how the Mahabharata portrays friendship as a vital force that sustains individuals in the face of adversity.

Disastrous Decisions and Their Ripples

The Mahabharata is a saga of choices—some noble, others disastrous. The dice game, Draupadi's public humiliation, Bhishma's vow of celibacy, and Duryodhana's refusal to compromise are decisions that set off a chain of irreversible events. By analyzing these turning points, the book explores the fragile interplay between human agency and destiny.

Each disastrous decision holds a mirror to the characters' flaws, ambitions, and egos. Yudhishthira's addiction to gambling contrasts sharply with his otherwise virtuous demeanor, while Bhishma's vow exemplifies the dangers of misplaced loyalty. These choices serve as cautionary tales, reminding readers of the consequences of unchecked emotions and the weight of responsibility borne by leaders.

Most Suffered Women in the Mahabharata

The Mahabharata's sweeping narrative presents several women who endure immense suffering, embodying resilience amidst patriarchal norms and societal constraints. Their stories are a poignant reminder of the emotional toll of war, power struggles, and dharma.

•	**Draupadi:** Perhaps the most iconic figure among the wronged women, Draupadi endured relentless humiliation. Married to five brothers, her polyandrous marriage itself was a subject of societal judgment. However, her greatest suffering came during the dice game where she was staked and lost by her husbands. Her disrobing in the Kuru court was a gross violation of her dignity, and her cry for justice became a pivotal moment that led to the great war of Kurukshetra. Despite her agony, she remained steadfast in her pursuit of justice, symbolizing the fight against adharma.

•	**Kunti:** As the mother of the Pandavas, Kunti's life was marked by sacrifices and secrets. She bore Karna before her marriage and had to abandon him, a decision that haunted her throughout her life. Later, she bore the weight of raising her sons in exile and navigating the complexities of dharma during the

Kurukshetra war. Her suffering was internal, stemming from guilt, loss, and the burden of her decisions.

• **Gandhari:** The queen of Hastinapura and mother of the Kauravas, Gandhari suffered due to her unwavering loyalty to her husband, Dhritarashtra. Choosing to blindfold herself to share her husband's blindness, Gandhari lived a life of self-imposed darkness. Her greatest suffering came from witnessing the downfall and death of all her hundred sons, leading her to curse Krishna for allowing such destruction.

• **Amba:** Rejected by Bhishma, who abducted her during her swayamvara but refused to marry her due to his vow of celibacy, Amba's life was consumed by a quest for vengeance. Her suffering culminated in her rebirth as Shikhandi, driven solely by the desire to end Bhishma's life.

These women symbolize endurance in the face of betrayal, loss, and societal constraints, adding layers of depth to the epic.

Most Sinister Plans in the Mahabharata

• **Duryodhana's Attempt to Burn the Pandavas in the Lakshagriha:** Duryodhana, driven by envy and fear of losing the throne, orchestrated one of the earliest sinister plans in the epic. He conspired with his uncle Shakuni to build a palace made of lac, a highly flammable material, and invited the Pandavas and Kunti to reside there. The plan was to set it ablaze while they were inside, ensuring their death. However, the Pandavas, warned by Vidura, managed to escape through a secret tunnel. This act of treachery underscored the lengths Duryodhana was willing to go to secure power.

•	**The Game of Dice:** Shakuni's manipulation during the dice game is another notorious act of deceit. Using loaded dice, Shakuni ensured that Yudhishthira lost everything—his kingdom, wealth, brothers, and Draupadi. This event not only humiliated the Pandavas but also planted the seeds for the eventual war.

•	**Karna's Killing of Abhimanyu:** In a coordinated and unethical attack during the Kurukshetra war, Karna, Duryodhana, Drona, and others conspired to trap and kill Abhimanyu, the young and valiant son of Arjuna. They broke the warrior code by attacking him collectively and denied him the chance to defend himself, symbolizing the extremes of their desperation.

•	**Ashwatthama's Night Raid:** After the war was technically over, Ashwatthama, consumed by vengeance for his father Drona's death, launched a night raid on the Pandava camp. Using deceit, he slaughtered the sleeping sons of Draupadi and the Pandavas, an act that stands as one of the darkest moments of the epic.

Most Neglected Family Members

•	**Nakul and Sahadeva:** The twin brothers, sons of Madri and Pandu, often stand in the shadows of their elder brothers, Yudhishthira, Bhima, and Arjuna. Despite their remarkable qualities—Nakul's unmatched beauty and skills in horse management, and Sahadeva's wisdom and mastery of astrology—they rarely receive the recognition they deserve in the epic.

o **Nakul** is portrayed as a gentle and loyal warrior, proficient with the sword. However, his contributions in the war are often overshadowed by his elder brothers' exploits.

o **Sahadeva**, the wisest among the Pandavas, played a critical role in advising Yudhishthira during the war. It was Sahadeva who suggested that they seek Krishna's help. His predictions were accurate, yet his voice was rarely prioritized.

Their relative neglect highlights the hierarchical nature of familial relationships in the Mahabharata, where the elder siblings often dominate the narrative.

• **Vidura:** A bastion of dharma, Vidura was the son of Vyasa but born to a maid, which placed him in a subordinate position in the Kuru family. Despite his wisdom and foresight, Vidura's advice was often ignored, particularly by Dhritarashtra and Duryodhana. His warnings against the dice game and the war went unheeded, emphasizing the tragic neglect of righteousness in favor of ambition.

• **Ulupi and Chitrangada:** These wives of Arjuna are significant yet overlooked figures in the epic. Ulupi, a Naga princess, and Chitrangada, a Manipuri princess, contributed to Arjuna's journey and lineage (through their son Iravan and Babruvahana, respectively) but are often relegated to the margins of the narrative.

By shedding light on these neglected characters and themes, the Mahabharata reveals the complexity of human relationships and the consequences of overlooking wisdom and potential in the pursuit of power and glory.

Reimagining the Mahabharata

This book is not an attempt to rewrite the Mahabharata but to reimagine its stories through a contemporary lens. It seeks to explore the moral and philosophical dilemmas of its characters while examining their relevance to modern times. The epic's layered narrative offers timeless insights into leadership, justice, and human nature, which are as pertinent today as they were in Vyasa's era.

By shifting the focus to lesser-known aspects and perspectives, this work aspires to make the Mahabharata accessible to a broader audience while encouraging deeper introspection. Through these explorations, the book celebrates the epic's universality, showing how it transcends its historical and cultural context to resonate with readers across generations.

The Everlasting Relevance of the Mahabharata

The Mahabharata is not just a story of ancient India; it is a mirror reflecting humanity's eternal struggles, aspirations, and dilemmas. It challenges readers to grapple with questions of morality, identity, and the nature of truth. By venturing into uncharted territories of the epic, this book seeks to honor its complexity while offering fresh perspectives.

Whether through the lives of insignificant characters, the quiet strength of sages, or the disastrous decisions that reshape destinies, the Mahabharata teaches us that every voice matters, every action has consequences, and every perspective contributes to the whole. This exploration invites readers to rediscover the epic, not as a relic of the past but as a living, breathing testament to the human spirit.

Chapter One - Bhakti in the Mahabharata

Bhakti in the Mahabharata is intricately woven into its narrative, offering profound insights into devotion and its transformative power. While the epic primarily revolves around dharma (righteousness) and the complexities of human relationships, it also emphasizes Bhakti as a path to spiritual enlightenment and liberation.

Key Aspects of Bhakti in the Mahabharata:

Devotion to Krishna:

Krishna, as an incarnation of Vishnu, embodies divine love and grace. Arjuna's relationship with Krishna exemplifies the highest form of Bhakti, marked by trust, surrender, and a deep bond. In the Bhagavad Gita, Krishna reveals that devotion (bhakti yoga) is a direct and accessible path to liberation, transcending other spiritual practices like knowledge (jnana yoga) or action (karma yoga).

Draupadi's unwavering faith in Krishna, especially during moments of despair, such as the infamous disrobing incident, highlights the protective and compassionate nature of the divine when called upon with pure devotion.

Universal Accessibility:

Bhakti is portrayed as inclusive, transcending caste, gender, and social status. The Mahabharata emphasizes that devotion is based on sincerity and love, not on rituals or birthright. Krishna declares in the Gita that anyone, even the most humble, can attain the divine through devotion.

The Bhagavad Gita:

The Bhagavad Gita serves as the spiritual core of the Mahabharata, where Krishna explains Bhakti as a means to unite with the divine. He assures Arjuna that those who surrender their ego and dedicate their actions to him with unwavering love will be liberated from the cycle of birth and death.

Examples of Bhakti:

Vidura: His devotion to dharma and the divine is unwavering, showcasing Bhakti through righteous living.

Kunti: Her prayer to Krishna, asking for suffering so she can constantly remember him, reflects the selfless nature of Bhakti.

Yudhishthira: Despite his trials, Yudhishthira's dedication to dharma and Krishna underscores his quiet devotion.

Philosophical Insights:

The Mahabharata conveys that Bhakti transcends intellectualism and material pursuits. It is an emotional, heartfelt connection to the divine that provides solace, guidance, and ultimate liberation.

Through its characters and teachings, the Mahabharata positions Bhakti as a powerful force that transforms lives, offers protection, and leads to spiritual fulfillment. It highlights that devotion, combined with righteousness and selfless action, is the ultimate path to attaining divine grace.

Chapter Two - Most Influential Communicator: Krishna's Role as the Mentor and Orator

In the vast narrative of the Mahabharata, Krishna emerges not only as a divine figure but also as an unparalleled communicator. His eloquence, strategic thinking, and ability to adapt his message to his audience make him one of the most influential characters in the epic. Krishna's words shape destinies, resolve conflicts, and offer profound philosophical insights that continue to resonate through the ages.

Krishna's Communication in Key Moments

1.   The Bhagavad Gita: The Pinnacle of Persuasion

Krishna's most iconic role as a communicator unfolds on the battlefield of Kurukshetra. When Arjuna is paralyzed by doubt and moral conflict, Krishna's discourse in the Bhagavad Gita not only reawakens Arjuna's sense of duty but also lays down the philosophical bedrock of Hinduism.

Krishna's brilliance lies in tailoring his message to Arjuna's predicament, addressing not only his immediate concerns but also the universal dilemmas of existence, duty, and self-realization. The ability to transform a moment of despair into an eternal guide for humanity underscores Krishna's exceptional influence.

2. Diplomatic Negotiations: The Peacemaker's Voice

Before the war, Krishna attempts to mediate peace between the Pandavas and Kauravas. His carefully chosen words during his visit to Hastinapura reflect his skill in balancing diplomacy with assertiveness. Krishna appeals to Duryodhana's reason and pride, seeking to avoid war while subtly preparing for its inevitability. This episode highlights Krishna's ability to wield words as weapons, persuading allies and opponents alike to align with his vision of dharma.

3. Friendship and Mentorship

Krishna's role as a communicator is not confined to public orations; his private conversations with friends like Draupadi, Bhima, and Yudhishthira reveal his sensitivity and wisdom. Whether comforting Draupadi after her humiliation or advising Bhima on defeating Duryodhana, Krishna's words are always precise, empathetic, and purposeful.

Lessons from Krishna's Communication

Krishna's effectiveness as a communicator stems from several key traits:

- **Empathy and Understanding**: Krishna tailors his message to the needs and temperament of his audience.

- **Clarity and Vision**: He communicates with unwavering clarity, always aligning his words with the ultimate goal of establishing dharma.

- **Adaptability**: Whether addressing a warrior, a ruler, or a commoner, Krishna adjusts his tone and approach without compromising his message.

- **Strategic Thinking**: Krishna's communication is never impulsive; it is always calculated to maximize its impact.

Through Krishna, the Mahabharata teaches us that effective communication is as much about listening and understanding as it is about speaking.

Sanjaya: The Visionary Communicator of the Mahabharata

Among the myriad characters of the Mahabharata, Sanjaya stands as a unique figure, celebrated for his extraordinary ability to narrate events unfolding far beyond his physical reach. Gifted with divine vision by the sage Vyasa, Sanjaya serves as the eyes and ears of King Dhritarashtra during the Kurukshetra war. His role transcends that of a mere messenger; he becomes a philosopher, a counselor, and a moral guide, delivering profound insights into the nature of war, duty, and life itself.

Sanjaya's Divine Vision: A Boon of Vyasa

Before the Kurukshetra war began, Vyasa offered Dhritarashtra the gift of divine sight so he could witness the battle directly. Dhritarashtra, burdened by the sorrow of anticipating the destruction of his sons, declined the offer but requested that Sanjaya, his trusted charioteer and counselor, be granted this power instead. Vyasa blessed Sanjaya with the ability to see events as they unfolded on the battlefield, regardless of distance, and to comprehend the emotions, motives, and intentions of those involved.

This divine vision elevated Sanjaya's role from a passive observer to an active interpreter of events. He became the medium through which Dhritarashtra—and, by extension, the audience—could experience the epic war with unparalleled clarity and depth.

The Art of Sanjaya's Communication

Sanjaya's narration is not merely a recounting of events but a masterclass in effective communication. His role highlights several key aspects of his skill as a communicator:

1.   **Clarity and Detail**

Sanjaya's descriptions of the battlefield are vivid and precise, painting a mental picture for Dhritarashtra. He conveys not just the physical details of the war but also the emotional and psychological states of the warriors, providing a holistic view of the unfolding drama.

2.   **Impartiality and Objectivity**

Despite being in the service of Dhritarashtra, Sanjaya maintains an unbiased perspective. He does not shy away from narrating the defeats and moral failures of the Kauravas, even when it might upset the king. His commitment to truth makes him a credible and reliable narrator.

3.   Philosophical Insights

Sanjaya's narration goes beyond mere reportage; it delves into the deeper meanings of the events. For instance, he frequently reflects on the futility of war, the transient nature of life, and the importance of adhering to dharma. These reflections elevate his communication transforming it into a moral and philosophical discourse.

4.   Empathy and Sensitivity

While narrating the gruesome realities of war, Sanjaya exhibits remarkable sensitivity toward Dhritarashtra's emotions. He balances the need to convey the truth with the need to cushion the king from unbearable grief, demonstrating his emotional intelligence.

Key Moments in Sanjaya's Narration

1.   The Bhagavad Gita

Sanjaya's narration includes Krishna's discourse to Arjuna, the Bhagavad Gita. His retelling of this divine dialogue reflects his capacity to comprehend and articulate profound philosophical concepts, making him a crucial link between the divine and the mortal.

2.   Duryodhana's Fall

Sanjaya narrates Duryodhana's defeat and the subsequent destruction of the Kaurava army with a mix of sorrow and inevitability. His words convey the tragic consequences of pride, ambition, and enmity, serving as a poignant reminder of the cost of war.

3.   The End of the War

Sanjaya's account of the war's aftermath, including the deaths of the Kaurava and Pandava princes, underscores the emptiness of victory in the face of such immense loss. His narration becomes a lamentation for humanity, highlighting the universal themes of suffering and redemption.

Illustrations:

1. The Bhagavad Gita

Sanjaya's narration of the Bhagavad Gita is one of the most pivotal moments in the Mahabharata, not just for its philosophical depth but also for the profound responsibility it places on him as a divine intermediary. Blessed with the gift of divine sight by Vyasa, Sanjaya recounts the exchange between Krishna and Arjuna to the blind King Dhritarashtra. This discourse, set on the battlefield of Kurukshetra, transcends the immediate war to address universal truths about duty, righteousness, and the eternal soul.

As Arjuna hesitates to fight, burdened by moral dilemmas and familial bonds, Krishna's teachings become a beacon of clarity. Sanjaya vividly describes Arjuna's anguish, portraying him as a warrior torn between his dharma as a Kshatriya and his compassion as a human being. Sanjaya's words encapsulate the scene: Arjuna, with his Gandiva bow slipping from his hands, his body trembling and mind clouded by doubt, kneels before Krishna, seeking guidance. This imagery allows the blind Dhritarashtra, and by extension the audience, to experience the gravity of the moment.

Through Krishna's voice, Sanjaya articulates profound metaphysical concepts such as the immortality of the soul, the transient nature of life, and the importance of selfless action (karma). He narrates Krishna's revelation of the Vishwaroopa (Universal Form) with awe, describing a cosmic vision where time itself appears as a devouring force. His words bring alive the terrifying beauty of the form, a spectacle of infinite faces, blazing suns, and all-consuming jaws. Sanjaya's ability to convey this extraordinary moment underscores his unique role as the witness of divine revelation.

By the end of the Gita, Sanjaya's narration shifts subtly, reflecting Arjuna's transformation. He captures Arjuna's renewed resolve and clarity, emphasizing the transformative power of Krishna's teachings. For Sanjaya, the Bhagavad Gita is not merely a philosophical discourse but a testament to the eternal struggle of the human spirit to align with righteousness amidst chaos. His narration bridges the divine wisdom imparted by Krishna with the moral dilemmas faced by humanity, immortalizing the Gita as a timeless guide.

2. Duryodhana's Fall

Sanjaya's narration of Duryodhana's defeat marks the climactic unraveling of the Kaurava dynasty. His account combines vivid imagery with a profound understanding of the tragedy of unchecked ambition and pride. The duel between Duryodhana and Bhima on the blood-soaked battlefield becomes a microcosm of the larger war, encapsulating its brutality and futility.

Sanjaya describes the duel in vivid detail: the ground trembling under the warriors' feet, the clash of maces ringing like thunder, and the sheer intensity of Bhima's rage. Duryodhana, despite his arrogance and moral failings, fights valiantly, displaying the skill and courage befitting a Kshatriya. Sanjaya's narration captures this complexity, portraying Duryodhana not merely as a villain but as a tragic figure whose hubris has led him to this inevitable moment.

When Bhima driven by vengeance for Draupadi's humiliation, strikes Duryodhana's thigh, Sanjaya's tone shifts. He narrates the shattering of the rules of war with a mix of sorrow and inevitability. The blow, forbidden in mace combat, symbolizes the collapse of dharma amidst the chaos of war. Duryodhana's fall is not just physical but emblematic of the downfall of an entire lineage. His once-proud form, now lying broken and bleeding, evokes pity even in his enemies.

Sanjaya's narration also delves into Duryodhana's reflections in his final moments. He recounts how Duryodhana, despite his defeat, clings to his pride, declaring himself victorious for having fought to protect his kingdom. Sanjaya's words reveal the duality of Duryodhana's character—his unyielding arrogance juxtaposed with a certain tragic dignity. Through this portrayal, Sanjaya conveys the futility of ambition devoid of righteousness, leaving Dhritarashtra and the audience to grapple with the consequences of misplaced priorities.

3. The End of the War

The war's aftermath, as narrated by Sanjaya, transforms his role from a chronicler of events to a lamenter of humanity's collective failure. The decimation of both the Kaurava and Pandava armies leaves behind a haunting silence on the battlefield, and Sanjaya's narration poignantly captures the desolation and grief that follow.

Sanjaya describes the scene with heart-wrenching detail: mangled bodies of warriors, shattered weapons, and blood-soaked earth bearing mute testimony to the cost of war. His words convey the profound emptiness that engulfs the battlefield, where once-proud warriors now lie indistinguishable in death. He reflects on the irony of victory—the Pandavas have won the war but at the expense of nearly everyone they hold dear. The throne of Hastinapura, for which countless lives were sacrificed, now stands as a hollow symbol of power.

The deaths of the Kaurava and Pandava princes form the emotional core of Sanjaya's narration. He recounts the heartbreak of Gandhari, whose curse on Krishna stems from her immeasurable grief. Sanjaya's narration highlights her pain as a mother who has lost all her sons, embodying the universal sorrow of those left behind in the wake of violence.

Through Sanjaya's words, the war's aftermath becomes a meditation on the human condition. He reflects on the cyclical nature of suffering and redemption, emphasizing that true victory lies not in conquest but in the adherence to dharma. His lamentation serves as a stark reminder of the destructive potential of unchecked ambition and the need for wisdom and restraint.

In his narration to Dhritarashtra, Sanjaya does not shy away from the bitter truths of the war. He forces the blind king, both literally and metaphorically, to confront the consequences of his partiality and inaction. In doing so, Sanjaya's account transcends mere storytelling to become a moral reckoning, compelling the audience to reflect on the enduring cost of human folly.

Sanjaya's Legacy as a Communicator

Sanjaya's unique role in the Mahabharata offers valuable lessons in communication and leadership:

- **The Power of Truth**: Sanjaya's unwavering commitment to truth, even in the face of potential backlash, underscores the importance of honesty in communication.

- **Balancing Emotion and Logic**: His ability to empathize with Dhritarashtra while maintaining his objectivity demonstrates the need for balance in delivering difficult messages.

- **Vision beyond Sight**: Sanjaya's divine vision is symbolic of the ability to see beyond the surface, to understand the underlying causes and implications of events—a skill that remains essential for effective leadership and decision-making.

Sanjaya as the Voice of Conscience

In many ways, Sanjaya serves as the Mahabharata's voice of conscience. Through his narration, he not only informs but also educates, urging readers and listeners to reflect on the ethical and philosophical dimensions of the epic's events. His role reminds us that communication is not just about transmitting information; it is about inspiring understanding, introspection, and growth.

In the epic's grand tapestry, Sanjaya may appear as a secondary character, but his influence as a communicator with divine vision makes him a central figure in the narrative. His words bridge the gap between the battlefield and the throne room, between action and reflection, and between human frailty and divine wisdom.

Chapter Three - Significance of apparently insignificant characters

The Mahabharata, an epic of grand scale features not just central heroes and villains but also numerous seemingly insignificant characters who contribute subtly to its narrative. Here is a life sketch of fifteen such characters:

1. Yuyutsu

• **Parentage**: Son of Dhritarashtra and a Vaishya woman.

• **Role**: Known as a "half-Kaurava," Yuyutsu switched sides to join the Pandavas during the Kurukshetra war, showcasing his integrity.

• **Fate**: One of the few survivors of the war, Yuyutsu's allegiance to righteousness ensured his survival, and he later ruled Hastinapur after the Pandavas' departure.

2. Uttara

• **Parentage**: Daughter of King Virata of Matsya.

• **Role**: Married to Abhimanyu, Uttaraa's role is significant for bearing Parikshit, the sole heir of the Kuru dynasty.

- **Fate**: Widowed during the war, she lived a life of sorrow but ensured the continuity of the Kuru lineage by raising her son with the Pandavas' guidance.

3. Satyavati's Fisherman Father

- **Role**: He secured his daughter's position as queen by striking a deal with Shantanu, ensuring her children would inherit the throne.

- **Fate**: Though he fades from the narrative, his ambition indirectly paved the way for the rise of Bhishma, who shaped the course of the epic.

4. Chekitana

- **Parentage**: A Yadava warrior and ally of the Pandavas.

- **Role**: Chekitana fought valiantly for the Pandavas in the Kurukshetra war and is often overshadowed by more prominent warriors.

- **Fate**: He died during the war, his bravery a silent contribution to the Pandava cause.

5. Kripa (Kripacharya)

- **Parentage**: Son of Sharadvan and Janapadi.

- **Role**: An acharya of the Kuru princes and a neutral party in the war. His role as a teacher and survivor adds depth to the narrative.

- **Fate**: One of the few survivors, Kripa becomes a tutor to Parikshit, maintaining continuity in Kuru traditions.

6. Ekalavya

• **Parentage**: A Nishada tribal prince.

• **Role**: His story highlights the caste and social inequalities of the time. Despite his devotion to Dronacharya, he was denied the chance to formally train and was forced to offer his thumb as guru dakshina.

• **Fate**: Though marginalized, his self-sacrifice and skills made him an enduring symbol of dedication and injustice.

7. Chitrangada

• **Parentage**: Elder son of Shantanu and Satyavati.

• **Role**: His life was brief, as he was killed in battle against a Gandharva with the same name. His death allowed his brother Vichitravirya to inherit the throne.

• **Fate**: His early death had long-lasting consequences, creating a vacuum in the Kuru lineage.

8. Sudeshna

• **Parentage**: Queen of Virata.

• **Role**: Played a minor role during the Pandavas' incognito exile, where Draupadi served her as a maid. She inadvertently facilitated Draupadi's near-assault by Kichaka.

• **Fate**: She fades from the narrative after the Pandavas reveal themselves.

9. Rukmi

- **Parentage**: Brother of Rukmini, Krishna's wife.

- **Role**: A skilled warrior, Rukmi's arrogance cost him a place in the Mahabharata war. He sought vengeance against Krishna but ultimately allied with neither side.

- **Fate**: Rukmi's life serves as a cautionary tale of pride leading to isolation and irrelevance.

10. Vidura's Mother

- **Parentage**: A servant woman in the Kuru palace.

- **Role**: The mother of Vidura, whose wisdom often guides the epic's narrative. Though unmentioned directly, her existence highlights the caste and class dynamics of the time.

- **Fate**: She remains a background figure, her identity overshadowed by Vidura's contributions to dharma and justice.

These characters, though seemingly insignificant, add layers of complexity to the Mahabharata, emphasizing its portrayal of every spectrum of human life from the grand to the overlooked. Let us explore these characters in detail.

1. Yuyutsu: The Half-Kaurava with a Conscience

Yuyutsu occupies a peculiar position in the Mahabharata as the son of Dhritarashtra, the blind

Kuru king, but born to a Vaishya maid rather than Gandhari. While Gandhari gave birth to her 100 sons, Yuyutsu's birth often went unnoticed in the grander Kuru narrative. Despite being Dhritarashtra's son, he was never fully embraced by the Kuru family and grew up with a unique perspective, observing the privileges of the Kaurava princes and the moral dilemmas they often ignored.

As a young man, Yuyutsu became known for his uprightness and sense of justice, which starkly contrasted with the often unruly and immoral behavior of Duryodhana and his brothers. His upbringing, though rooted in the Kuru palace, gave him insights into the lives of the commoners, especially since his mother came from a lower caste. This dual identity likely shaped his values, making him a man of integrity.

Yuyutsu's pivotal moment came during the Kurukshetra war. On the eve of the battle, Krishna offered everyone the choice to join either the Pandavas or the Kauravas, emphasizing that dharma (righteousness) should guide their decision. Yuyutsu made a morally courageous choice: he defected from the Kaurava side to fight for the Pandavas. His decision symbolized the triumph of conscience over loyalty to family, a theme deeply woven into the Mahabharata's narrative fabric.

During the war, Yuyutsu fought valiantly for the Pandavas. Though not a prominent warrior compared to Bhima, Arjuna, or Karna, his presence on the battlefield was a testament to the ethical dilemmas faced by individuals caught in the web of familial and societal obligations. His defection also served as a moral indictment of Duryodhana's actions and highlighted the growing cracks in the Kaurava camp.

Yuyutsu's survival at the end of the Kurukshetra war marked him as one of the few remaining members of the Kuru family. After the Pandavas left for their final journey, Yuyutsu stayed back to help Parikshit, Arjuna's grandson and the sole heir of the Kuru dynasty, govern Hastinapur. In many ways, Jujutsu's life came full circle: from being an outsider in the Kuru household to becoming a custodian of its legacy.

Jujutsu's story is a quiet but powerful reminder of the importance of moral courage. Unlike many other characters in the Mahabharata, his choices were not driven by personal ambition or vengeance but by a commitment to righteousness. While he may not enjoy the same level of recognition as other characters, his role in upholding dharma during a time of great moral confusion remains significant.

2. Uttaraa: The Young Queen Who Saved the Kuru Lineage

Uttaraa, the princess of Matsya, is one of the understated yet crucial characters in the Mahabharata. She is remembered primarily for her role as the wife of Abhimanyu and the mother of Parikshit, the future king of Hastinapur. However, her life story is interwoven with tragedy and resilience, making her an essential figure in the continuation of the Kuru dynasty.

Uttaraa was the daughter of King Virata of Matsya, whose kingdom provided refuge to the Pandavas during their final year of exile in disguise. During this period, Arjuna, under the guise of a eunuch named Brihannala, served as a dance and music teacher to Uttaraa. Her respect for Brihannala and the Pandavas grew immensely during this time, particularly when they helped her father defend Matsya from Kaurava forces.

As a gesture of gratitude, King Virata offered Uttaraa's hand in marriage to Arjuna. However, Arjuna, considering her his disciple, declined the proposal and instead suggested she marry his son, Abhimanyu. The marriage between Uttaraa and Abhimanyu was celebrated with great joy, symbolizing the alliance between the Matsya and Pandava families. Uttaraa's life seemed promising and filled with hope as she became a part of the illustrious Kuru lineage.

However, her happiness was short-lived. Abhimanyu, despite his youth, was one of the most valiant warriors of the Pandavas. His death in the Chakravyuha formation during the Kurukshetra war was one of the most heart-wrenching episodes of the epic. Uttaraa, who was pregnant at the time, was left widowed at a young age, her dreams shattered by the brutality of the war.

The depth of Uttaraa's sorrow was further compounded when Ashwatthama, seeking vengeance after the Kauravas' defeat, unleashed the Brahmastra weapon on the Pandava camp. This weapon targeted her unborn child, threatening to end the Kuru lineage. In a desperate plea, Uttaraa approached Krishna for help, begging him to save her child. Moved by her devotion and the need to preserve dharma, Krishna intervened and revived her unborn son, who was stillborn due to the weapon's impact. This child, Parikshit, became the sole heir to the Kuru dynasty.

Despite her personal losses, Uttaraa exhibited remarkable resilience. She raised Parikshit under the guidance of the Pandavas, ensuring he grew up with the values of dharma and justice. Her dedication to her son's upbringing reflected her understanding of her pivotal role in sustaining the Kuru legacy.

Uttaraa's life is a poignant tale of love, loss, and duty. As the last queen of the Kuru dynasty, her sacrifices and maternal devotion played a crucial role in shaping the future of Hastinapur. Though her name is often overshadowed by the grander narratives of the Mahabharata, Uttaraa remains a silent yet significant force in the epic, embodying the strength and resilience of women in times of immense turmoil.

3. Satyavati's Fisherman Father-The Catalyst of Dynastic Change

Satyavati's father, often referred to as the Fisher King, is a character whose ambitions subtly yet profoundly altered the course of the Kuru dynasty. Though he occupies a brief role in the Mahabharata, his decisions played a pivotal part in shaping the epic's events.

The Fisher King was the chief of a small community of fishermen living near the Yamuna River. A man of modest means but sharp intellect, he recognized the extraordinary destiny of his daughter, Satyavati, who was born under mysterious circumstances. Satyavati, also known as Matsyagandha due to her fish-like odor, later acquired the divine fragrance of musk thanks to the blessings of the sage Parashara, with whom she bore a son, Vyasa.

The turning point in the Fisher King's life came when King Shantanu, the ruler of Hastinapur, met Satyavati and fell deeply in love with her. Shantanu's desire to marry Satyavati presented the Fisher King with a rare opportunity to elevate his family's status. However, the Fisher King was aware of the complexities of royal inheritance and sought to secure a future for his lineage.

When Shantanu approached him for Satyavati's hand, the Fisher King agreed but imposed a bold condition: Satyavati's children would inherit the throne of Hastinapur, excluding Shantanu's son by his first wife, Ganga, Devavrata (later known as Bhishma). This demand created a moral and emotional dilemma for Shantanu, who loved both Satyavati and his son. Unable to reconcile the two, Shantanu left the matter unresolved, leading to his silent suffering.

It was Bhishma who eventually resolved the impasse. Out of deep filial devotion, he approached the Fisher

King and vowed to renounce the throne of Hastinapur, swearing lifelong celibacy to ensure there would be no challengers to Satyavati's descendants. This vow, known as the Bhishma Pratigya, became one of the most consequential oaths in the epic, defining Bhishma's life and altering the destiny of the Kuru dynasty.

Impressed by Bhishma's resolve, the Fisher King consented to the marriage of Satyavati and Shantanu. His ambition had been fulfilled, as his daughter became the queen of Hastinapur, and her lineage would eventually rule the kingdom. However, his seemingly pragmatic decision had far-reaching consequences. The absence of a direct successor after the deaths of Satyavati's sons, Chitrangada and Vichitravirya, led to the complex web of events that culminated in the Kurukshetra war.

The Fisher King's actions embody the interplay of personal ambition and societal dynamics in the Mahabharata. While he is a minor character, his decisions highlight how individuals, regardless of their perceived significance, can profoundly influence the course of history. His insistence on securing Satyavati's future underscores the importance of agency and foresight in a world dominated by fate and dharma.

4. Chekitana: The Forgotten Warrior of the Yadavas

Chekitana, though a minor character in the Mahabharata, is a figure of courage and loyalty. He was a Yadava prince and a close ally of the Pandavas. His name may not evoke the grandeur of Arjuna or

Bhishma, but his unwavering support during the Kurukshetra war highlights the importance of steadfast allies in a righteous cause.

Chekitana was born into the Vrishni clan, the same illustrious lineage as Krishna and Balarama. As a Yadava warrior, he was trained in the arts of warfare from a young age, excelling in archery and hand-to-hand combat. Unlike Krishna and Balarama, who played pivotal roles as strategists and advisors, Chekitana's life was rooted in the battlefield, embodying the warrior spirit of his clan.

When the Kurukshetra war loomed, Chekitana aligned himself with the Pandavas, following Krishna's lead in supporting dharma. His allegiance stemmed from both familial ties and a firm belief in the Pandavas' just cause. Despite being overshadowed by other Yadava heroes like Satyaki, Chekitana was a fierce and dependable fighter, serving as a pillar of strength for the Pandava army.

During the eighteen-day war, Chekitana displayed remarkable bravery. On several occasions, he held his ground against formidable Kaurava warriors, including Duryodhana and his brothers. Though his duels lacked the dramatic flair of Bhima or Arjuna's battles, his determination and tactical prowess contributed significantly to the Pandavas' victories in skirmishes. One of his notable achievements was his defense of the Pandava camp when it came under attack during the night raids orchestrated by Ashwatthama and other Kaurava allies.

Chekitana also played a crucial role in protecting Yudhishthira, the eldest Pandava and the symbol of righteousness. Yudhishthira, though skilled in combat, was more vulnerable compared to his brothers and relied heavily on warriors like Chekitana to ensure his safety. Chekitana's loyalty to Yudhishthira extended beyond the battlefield; his advice and unwavering presence often uplifted the morale of the Pandava camp during moments of despair.

Despite his heroics, Chekitana's life came to a tragic end. Like many valiant warriors on both sides, he fell in battle, succumbing to the relentless carnage of the Kurukshetra war. His death, though largely uncelebrated in the epic's grand narrative, symbolizes the sacrifices made by countless warriors in the pursuit of dharma.

Chekitana's character represents the unsung heroes of the Mahabharata. He lacked the divine interventions that favored Krishna or the legendary status of Arjuna, yet his contributions were vital. His story is a reminder that the epic's success was not merely built on the exploits of its central figures but also on the collective efforts of individuals like Chekitana, who fought selflessly for a cause they believed to be just.

5. Kripacharya

Kripacharya, or simply Kripa, holds a significant yet often understated role in the Mahabharata. His character stands out due to his unwavering neutrality, remarkable survival instincts, and the immense influence he had on the Kuru dynasty, both before and after the great war. Here's a detailed narrative on Kripacharya:

Parentage and Early Life

Kripacharya was born to Sharadvan, a sage of great renown, and Janapadi, who was a royal woman of Kuru lineage. His birth itself was unusual and surrounded by divine circumstances. Sharadvan, a Brahmin, had been performing a sacrificial yajna, when Janapadi, who had been childless, approached him. After a period of penance, Janapadi's wish was fulfilled, and Sharadvan blessed her with a child, who was later named Kripa.

Kripa's birth was significant as he was not only a royal descendant through his mother but also a learned sage through his father's influence. This blend of royal and spiritual heritage shaped his character profoundly, making him both a warrior and a scholar.

Role as a Teacher and Mentor

Kripa is primarily known in the Mahabharata as the teacher and mentor to the Kuru princes, especially the sons of Dhritarashtra, Duryodhana, and Yudhishthira, as well as the Pandavas and Kauravas. In this role, Kripa is portrayed as a highly skilled instructor, imparting knowledge not just in martial arts, but also in statecraft, archery, and the intricacies of dharma (righteousness).

Kripa's role as a teacher was not limited to just the Kauravas or the Pandavas. His neutrality allowed him to serve both factions, imparting his wisdom without any bias. As a result, Kripa became one of the most trusted figures in the Kuru court, respected by both Dhritarashtra and Pandu. He was particularly skilled in the use of weapons and military strategies, and his contributions were invaluable in the education of the young Kuru princes.

Neutrality and the Kurukshetra War

One of the most intriguing aspects of Kripa's character is his neutrality during the Kurukshetra War. Unlike other figures who took sides, such as Bhishma and Drona, Kripa remained neutral, despite his close ties to both families. His neutrality stemmed from his deep sense of duty to his role as a teacher and his understanding that his primary allegiance was to dharma, rather than any individual or faction.

However, it is important to note that while he technically stayed neutral, Kripa's actions during the war were still pivotal. He fought on the side of the Kauravas, but his personal feelings of attachment to the Kuru family made him a reluctant participant in the destruction. In battle, Kripa proved to be a formidable warrior. He was an expert archer, and his fighting skills were comparable to some of the greatest warriors of the time, including his teacher Drona and his mentor Bhishma.

Despite his prowess on the battlefield, Kripa's role was not solely that of a warrior. He remained a guide for the Kauravas, especially Duryodhana, in their political and military decisions. His influence was notable, though his neutrality left him in a precarious position, as he refrained from overtly interfering with the choices of the Kaurava leadership, despite knowing the righteousness of the Pandavas' cause.

Survival and Post-War Role

Kripa's survival after the war is a testament to his character. Among the many survivors of the Kurukshetra War, Kripa was one of the few who lived to see the aftermath. His survival can be attributed to his wisdom and spiritual strength, but also to the fact that he had not directly engaged in any action that could bring about his downfall. His survival contrasted sharply with the fate of the other warriors, many of whom perished due to their loyalty to one side or their involvement in the tragic violence of the war.

After the war, Kripa's role shifted towards being a guide to the next generation. He became the tutor to Parikshit, the grandson of Arjuna and the son of Abhimanyu. Parikshit's education, much like that of the Kuru princes before him, was shaped by Kripa's teachings. This continuity helped preserve the Kuru traditions and values that had been set by the elders, even though the Kuru dynasty itself had been decimated by the war.

Kripa's Legacy and Significance

Kripa's legacy is multifaceted. He was a key figure in the preservation of the Kuru dynasty's knowledge and traditions. As a teacher, he influenced generations of warriors and kings. As a neutral party in the Kurukshetra War, he remained true to his dharma, even if it meant remaining silent when the situation demanded action. His survival ensured the continuity of the Kuru bloodline, especially with his tutelage of Parikshit, who would eventually ascend the throne.

In many ways, Kripa's character embodies the idea of balance in the Mahabharata. He is a figure who is neither swayed by emotions nor political alignments. His wisdom, impartiality, and commitment to duty make him a symbol of integrity in the midst of a world torn by conflict and division.

Kripa's Limitations

While Kripa was revered as a scholar and warrior, he was not without limitations. His most significant limitation was his inability to act decisively during the war. His neutrality, though admirable from a philosophical standpoint, often led to inaction when his guidance and wisdom could have changed the course of the conflict. His deep attachment to his dharma as a teacher and mentor left him unable to intervene actively, even when he witnessed the destruction of the Kuru dynasty.

Moreover, his role in the war as a participant in the Kaurava camp suggests that, despite his neutrality, he was not entirely free from the consequences of the war. The very fact that he fought on the side of the Kauravas was a source of moral ambiguity. Kripa, like many other characters in the Mahabharata, is a complex figure who remains loyal to dharma, but his lack of active intervention against the atrocities of the war raises questions about the true meaning of neutrality.

In the end, Kripacharya's life is a study of balance, a teacher who stood by his principles but also recognized the weight of his limitations in times of war and chaos. His survival, wisdom, and the continuity of the Kuru legacy make him a central figure in the Mahabharata's broader narrative of dharma, duty, and the moral complexities of war.

6. Shikhandi: The Warrior of Transformation and Destiny

Shikhandi stands out as one of the most enigmatic characters in the Mahabharata. Born as a woman and later transformed into a man, Shikhandi's life symbolizes themes of transformation, revenge, and the breaking of societal norms. Despite being a minor character in terms of narrative space, Shikhandi plays a pivotal role in the downfall of Bhishma, the invincible grand-elder of the Kuru dynasty.

Early Life and Birth

Shikhandi was born as Shikhandini, the eldest child of King Drupada of Panchala. From birth, Shikhandini's life was tied to destiny. Drupada had prayed for a child who could avenge him against Bhishma, who had humiliated him during a previous conflict. However, when his firstborn was a daughter, Drupada was initially disheartened, unaware that this child would fulfill his prayers in an unconventional manner.

Shikhandini's birth carried a karmic burden. According to legend, Shikhandini was the reincarnation of Amba, a princess wronged by Bhishma. Amba had been abducted by Bhishma along with her sisters for the purpose of marrying them to his brother, Vichitravirya. However, when Bhishma learned of Amba's love for King Salva, he allowed her to leave. Salva rejected her, leading to Amba's humiliation and despair. Swearing vengeance against Bhishma, she performed intense penance and was granted a boon by Lord Shiva to be reborn as the instrument of Bhishma's death.

Transformation

As Shikhandini grew up, her inner turmoil became evident. She was deeply aware of her destiny but also conscious of the limitations imposed by her female body in fulfilling it. In an act of divine intervention, Shikhandini encountered a Yaksha (a nature spirit) named Sthuna in the forest. The Yaksha, moved by her plight, exchanged his male body with hers temporarily. This transformation allowed Shikhandini to become Shikhandi, a warrior capable of fulfilling the prophecy. This act of transformation not only empowered Shikhandi but also challenged traditional notions of gender in the epic.

Role in the Kurukshetra War

Shikhandi's moment of destiny arrived during the Kurukshetra war. Bhishma, the Kaurava general, was nearly invincible due to a boon that allowed him to choose the time of his death. However, he had sworn never to fight a woman. Krishna, the Pandava strategist, used this to their advantage. He placed Shikhandi in Arjuna's chariot during the battle against

Bhishma, knowing that Bhishma would not retaliate against Shikhandi due to the latter's past as Amba.

With Shikhandi as a shield, Arjuna rained arrows upon Bhishma, ultimately bringing the mighty warrior down. Shikhandi's presence was instrumental in Bhishma's defeat, marking a turning point in the war.

Legacy

Despite Shikhandi's critical role in Bhishma's fall, their life remains overshadowed by the epic's grander narratives. Shikhandi represents an individual who defied societal expectations, embracing transformation to achieve a higher purpose. Their story highlights themes of destiny, vengeance, and the fluidity of identity, challenging rigid gender roles and norms of dharma.

Shikhandi's journey is a reminder of the Mahabharata's depth, where even seemingly minor characters shape the epic's monumental events. Through Shikhandi, the epic addresses profound questions of justice, transformation, and the complexities of human existence.

7. Ekalavya: The Unacknowledged Archer

Ekalavya is one of the most poignant and tragic characters in the Mahabharata, embodying the ideals of perseverance, devotion, and injustice. Though his appearance in the epic is brief his story raises profound questions about societal hierarchies, the ethics of mentorship, and the cost of ambition.

Early Life and Aspirations

Ekalavya was the son of a Nishada chief, Hiranyadhanu, and belonged to a tribal community. Despite his humble origins, Ekalavya harbored an intense desire to master the art of archery. This aspiration brought him to the gates of Dronacharya, the royal teacher of the Kuru princes, who was renowned for his unmatched skills in warfare.

When Ekalavya approached Dronacharya and requested to be his disciple, he was met with rejection. Dronacharya, bound by the social norms of the time, refused to teach a tribal boy, focusing instead on training the princes of Hastinapur. However, this rejection did not deter Ekalavya. Instead, it fueled his resolve to achieve greatness through sheer determination.

Self-Learning and Devotion

Undeterred, Ekalavya built a clay idol of Dronacharya in the forest, symbolizing his unwavering faith in his teacher. Through relentless practice and meditation, he mastered the techniques of archery on his own. His dedication was so profound that he eventually became a formidable archer, equaling, if not surpassing, the skills of Arjuna, Dronacharya's most beloved student.

Ekalavya's self-taught expertise came to light when the Kuru princes, while hunting in the forest, encountered him. A demonstration of his skills left them astounded, and they reported his abilities to Dronacharya. Arjuna who had been promised by Drona that he would become the greatest archer in the world grew apprehensive upon learning about Ekalavya's prowess.

The Test of Guru Dakshina

Fearing that Ekalavya's exceptional skills might eclipse Arjuna's, Dronacharya devised a plan to curtail the tribal archer's potential. Visiting Ekalavya, Drona acknowledged him as a disciple, citing the clay idol as proof of their bond. Ekalavya, overjoyed by this recognition, considered it a moment of vindication for his devotion.

Seizing the opportunity, Dronacharya demanded a guru dakshina (teacher's fee) that would ensure Ekalavya could no longer threaten Arjuna's supremacy. He asked for Ekalavya's right thumb, essential for wielding a bow. Without hesitation, Ekalavya cut off his thumb and presented it to Dronacharya as an offering, demonstrating unparalleled respect and loyalty.

This act, while showcasing Ekalavya's devotion, effectively diminished his abilities as an archer. Despite this setback, he adapted to using his left hand, continuing to excel in archery, albeit not at the level he once could.

Legacy and Symbolism

Ekalavya's story is a powerful commentary on societal inequities and the rigidity of caste hierarchies. His unwavering determination and ingenuity exemplify the triumph of individual spirit over adversity. At the same time, his fate underscores the tragic consequences of systemic oppression and favoritism.

Ekalavya's life is a stark reminder of the ethical dilemmas faced by revered figures like Dronacharya, whose actions, while pragmatic, were morally questionable. Through Ekalavya, the Mahabharata highlights the untold sacrifices of those who remain in the shadows, unacknowledged and uncelebrated.

Ultimately, Ekalavya's tale resonates as a testament to the complexity of human ambition and the cost of greatness in a world fraught with inequality.

8. Uttara: The Young Warrior and Hero of Virata

Uttara, the son of King Virata of Matsya, holds a brief yet crucial place in the narrative of the Mahabharata. His life, though overshadowed by greater warriors and kings, symbolizes youthful bravery, unpreparedness in the face of great challenges, and the ability to grow under guidance. Uttara's story unfolds during the Pandavas' incognito exile at the court of his father, Virata, and his role during that period offers an intriguing subplot within the epic.

Early Life and Characteristics

As the prince of Matsya, Uttara was raised in the luxury and comfort of royal life. Despite being born into a Kshatriya family, his upbringing did not prepare him for the rigors of war or the responsibilities of leadership. Unlike his sister, Uttaraa, who was graceful and well-mannered, Uttara was impulsive, brash, and untested in the battlefield.

Uttara idolized the stories of legendary warriors like Arjuna and Bhishma, often dreaming of achieving similar fame. However, his inexperience and overconfidence made him more of a spirited dreamer than a grounded warrior.

Meeting the Pandavas

During the thirteenth year of the Pandavas' exile, they lived incognito at the court of Virata. Each Pandava adopted a disguised identity to conceal their true selves from the spies of Duryodhana. Arjuna, in particular, took on the role of a eunuch dance teacher named Brihannala. During this time, Uttara grew close to Brihannala, often treating the dance teacher as a harmless companion, oblivious to the warrior's true identity.

When Duryodhana discovered the Pandavas' whereabouts, he orchestrated a raid on Matsya's cattle herds, led by Kaurava generals like Bhishma, Drona, Karna, and Duryodhana himself. With Virata and his main army engaged elsewhere, the responsibility of defending Matsya fell on the young prince, Uttara.

The Battle of Matsya

Eager to prove his valor and make a name for himself, Uttara volunteered to lead the defense. However, his lack of experience and fear of confronting legendary warriors became evident as the Kaurava army approached. Realizing his inadequacy, Uttara panicked and fled the battlefield.

It was at this moment that Brihannala revealed his true identity as Arjuna, the greatest archer of the age. Encouraged by Arjuna, Uttara returned to the battlefield, albeit in a supporting role. Arjuna, using the charioteer skills of Uttara, single-handedly defeated the Kaurava forces, demonstrating the power of the celestial weapons he had acquired over the years.

Though Arjuna emerged as the hero of the day, Uttaraa's transformation from a cowardly prince to a determined ally marked a significant turning point in his character. The experience taught him humility, courage, and the importance of mentorship.

Legacy and Symbolism

Uttara's story is often overlooked in the larger narrative of the Mahabharata, but it serves as a valuable lesson on the transition from youthful recklessness to maturity. While he lacked the prowess and discipline of seasoned warriors, his willingness to learn and adapt under Arjuna's guidance symbolizes the potential for growth in even the most unpolished individuals.

Uttara's involvement in the defense of Matsya also underscores the theme of unity. It reflects how, during critical moments, unlikely alliances and hidden talents can emerge to overcome great odds. His relationship with Arjuna, first as a skeptical companion and later as a loyal charioteer, is a testament to the transformative power of trust and mentorship.

Uttara may not have become a legendary warrior, but his role as the young, flawed prince who found courage when it mattered most ensures that his contribution to the epic remains memorable.

9. Barbarik: The Unsung Warrior of the Mahabharata

Barbarik, the grandson of Bhima and son of Ghatotkacha, is one of the most fascinating yet underappreciated characters in the Mahabharata. Known for his unmatched archery skills, steadfast devotion, and a sense of fairness, Barbarik's story is both inspiring and tragic. Though his participation in the Kurukshetra war was brief, his role was crucial in illustrating the themes of sacrifice, destiny, and the true nature of heroism.

Birth and Early Life

Barbarik was born to Ghatotkacha, the mighty Rakshasa prince and son of Bhima, and Mauravi, a princess from the Nagas. Inheriting the strength of the Pandavas and the mystical abilities of his Rakshasa lineage, Barbarik displayed extraordinary talent from a young age. Under the tutelage of his parents and celestial beings, he became a master archer.

What set Barbarik apart was not just his skill but also his possession of three divine arrows, granted to him by Lord Shiva. These arrows, known as Teen Baan, had unique properties:

1.   The first arrow could mark all the targets the user wanted to destroy.

2.   The second arrow could mark all the targets the user wanted to protect.

3.   The third arrow, when released, would destroy all the marked targets and spare the protected ones, regardless of distance or obstacles.

With these arrows, Barbarik earned the title of Teen Baan Dhaari the wielder of three arrows.

Barbarik's Pledge

Barbarik grew up hearing tales of the impending Kurukshetra war and the unparalleled warriors who would participate in it. Determined to contribute to the cause of dharma, he vowed to take part in the war. However, his sense of fairness led him to make a unique pledge: he would always fight on the side that was weaker.

This vow demonstrated Barbarik's commitment to justice but also foreshadowed the complexities of his involvement in a conflict as morally ambiguous as the Kurukshetra war.

Encounter with Krishna

On his way to the battlefield, Barbarik encountered Krishna, who was intrigued by this young warrior's confidence and unique philosophy. Disguised as a Brahmin, Krishna tested Barbarik's abilities and asked about his intentions in the war.

Barbarik explained his pledge to fight for the weaker side. Krishna, realizing the implications of Barbarik's vow, saw that his participation would create an unending cycle. Each time Barbarik joined one side, his unmatched power would tip the balance in its favor, forcing him to switch allegiance. This perpetual oscillation would render the war meaningless.

Krishna, in his divine wisdom, decided to prevent this paradox. He revealed his true identity to Barbarik and asked for his head as a guru dakshina (offering to the teacher). Understanding the importance of Krishna's request, Barbarik willingly offered his head, demonstrating unparalleled devotion and selflessness.

Barbarik's Role in the War

Even after his sacrifice, Barbarik's story did not end. Krishna placed Barbarik's severed head atop a hill overlooking the battlefield, granting it the boon to witness the entire Kurukshetra war. Thus, Barbarik became the silent observer of one of history's greatest battles.

When the war ended, the Pandavas, filled with pride, asked Krishna who deserved the credit for their victory. Krishna directed them to Barbarik's head, which had watched every moment of the war. Barbarik declared that Krishna himself was the true architect of victory, as it was his divine strategies and interventions that ensured the triumph of dharma.

Legacy and Symbolism

Barbarik's story is a profound commentary on sacrifice, morality, and the complexities of war. His willingness to give up his life for the greater good underscores the idea that true heroism lies in selflessness. His perspective as an impartial observer also highlights the role of divine will in human affairs.

In certain traditions, Barbarik is worshipped as Khatu Shyam Ji in Rajasthan, where he is revered as a deity who grants blessings to his devotees. His tale continues to inspire generations, reminding us of the virtues of fairness, devotion, and humility.

10. Chitraratha: The Gandharva King

Chitraratha, the king of the Gandharvas, is a lesser-known yet significant figure in the Mahabharata. As the celestial ruler of the Gandharvas, Chitraratha embodies elegance, culture, and a strong sense of justice. His brief but impactful interactions with the Pandavas provide insights into the themes of humility, divine justice, and the responsibilities of power.

Chitraratha's Domain and Abilities

The Gandharvas are celestial beings associated with music, art, and dance, and Chitraratha stands out as their most prominent leader. His domain extends across heavenly realms, filled with unparalleled beauty and prosperity. As a Gandharva king, Chitraratha possesses remarkable abilities, including mastery over music, an ethereal chariot drawn by supernatural steeds, and combat skills enhanced by divine weaponry.

Chitraratha is closely associated with divine beings such as Indra, the king of gods, and is often seen as an enforcer of celestial law, ensuring that mortals and immortals adhere to cosmic justice.

Encounter with the Kauravas

Chitraratha's most notable appearance in the Mahabharata occurs during an incident involving Duryodhana. After the Pandavas' exile to the forest following the infamous dice game, Duryodhana, consumed by arrogance and schadenfreude, decided to visit the Pandavas in their misery. His intention was to mock them and gloat over their misfortune.

Accompanied by a lavish retinue, Duryodhana camped in the forest, unaware that the area was under Chitraratha's protection. The Gandharva king, viewing Duryodhana's actions as disrespectful and disruptive, confronted him and demanded that he leave. True to his nature, Duryodhana refused, underestimating the celestial power of the Gandharva king. This led to a battle in which Chitraratha and his forces easily overwhelmed the Kaurava prince and his army.

Duryodhana was captured by Chitraratha, marking a significant moment of humiliation for the arrogant prince. The incident underscored the Gandharva king's role as a protector of divine order, punishing those who acted out of hubris.

The Pandavas' Intervention

When the news of Duryodhana's capture reached the Pandavas, Bhima saw it as poetic justice and relished the opportunity to leave their cousin in his predicament. However, Yudhishthira, adhering to his sense of dharma, instructed his brothers to rescue Duryodhana. Arjuna, with his extraordinary archery skills, confronted Chitraratha and managed to secure Duryodhana's release.

Chitraratha, recognizing Arjuna's valor and the Pandavas' adherence to righteousness, expressed his respect for them. As a token of goodwill, he gifted the Pandavas celestial knowledge, including the secrets of the Gandharvas' divine weapons and their unique abilities. This gesture not only cemented the Pandavas' alliance with the celestial realm but also served as a reminder of their higher destiny.

Symbolism and Legacy

Chitraratha's story carries profound symbolic meaning within the Mahabharata. His interaction with Duryodhana serves as a lesson in humility, illustrating the consequences of arrogance and the importance of respecting cosmic laws. Conversely, his relationship with the Pandavas highlights the rewards of virtue and the strength of righteous action.

Chitraratha also represents the intersection of the mortal and divine realms, bridging the gap between human struggles and celestial order. His presence in the narrative reminds readers of the constant interplay between human actions and divine oversight, a recurring theme in the epic.

Though a relatively minor character, Chitraratha leaves an indelible mark on the story, demonstrating the importance of grace, justice, and the pursuit of higher ideals in a world often consumed by conflict and chaos.

This concludes the detailed narratives for the ten lesser-known characters from the Mahabharata. Let me know if you'd like any further elaboration or exploration of other characters or themes!

11. Vidura's Mother Parishrami: The Silent Pillar of Dharma

Vidura, one of the most revered and respected figures in the Mahabharata, is often seen as a symbol of wisdom, righteousness, and unwavering commitment to dharma. His counsel played a critical role in shaping the events of the epic, offering guidance to kings, princes, and warriors alike. While Vidura's wisdom and role in the epic are celebrated, the story of his mother—the servant woman of the Kuru palace remains largely unspoken. She is not mentioned directly in the Mahabharata, but her silent presence is crucial to understanding Vidura's character, his relationship with the Kuru family, and the social dynamics of the time.

Parentage and Birth of Vidura

As Vidura's mother was a servant woman who worked in the Kuru palace, and her humble background contrasts sharply with the noble lineage of Vidura's father Vyasdeva, King Vichitravirya of the Kuru dynasty. The specifics of her name and early life are not detailed in the Mahabharata, but she was an important figure in the palace due to her role in serving the royal family.

Niyoga

Vichitravirya was the son of King Shantanu and the queen, Satyavati. Vichitravirya had several queens but he was unable to become father. Amba and Ambalika were the senior queens. Vichitravirya died young without an heir, the responsibility of continuing the Kuru lineage fell upon Bhishma. The palace decided to adopt Niyoga rituals. Sage Vyasdeva was summoned. He was requested to undergo Niyoga procedure with both Amba and Ambalika. Amba was frightened during the process and she closed her eyes. A son was born but he was blind. Secondly, Ambalika was assigned to undergo the Niyoga ritual. But during the process she was so frightened that she became pale. She gave birth to a albino child. No other queen was ready to perform the ritual. However, in the process of fulfilling the royal duties of the palace, concubine of King Vichitravirya, a servant woman Parishrami by name sent to Vyasdeva. The ritual was normal and she bore Vidura through Vyasdeva using Niyoga ritual. The nature of this relationship whether it was a consensual union or one of exploitation, due to the vast differences in status is not elaborated in the epic, but Vidura's birth to a servant highlights the complex caste and class dynamics of the time.

Though Vidura's mother held a low status in the palace, she raised him with great care, imparting a sense of justice and moral integrity. Vidura's sharp intellect and his deep sense of dharma were influenced by the values taught to him by his mother, despite her lowly social standing. As he grew older, Vidura would be known for his wisdom, practicality, and an unwavering commitment to truth, which were likely reflections of the silent strength and principles instilled in him during his early years.

Vidura's Role in the Kuru Dynasty

Vidura's role in the Kuru court was that of an advisor, and his wisdom became a cornerstone of the kingdom's governance. He served as the right-hand counselor to Dhritarashtra, though his birth from a servant woman made him a target of discrimination and resentment within the palace. The highborn Kauravas, particularly Duryodhana, often looked down upon Vidura because of his origins, but his wisdom was undeniable. Vidura's keen understanding of the political and moral landscape of the world allowed him to navigate complex situations and offer advice that sought to uphold dharma, even when it meant going against his own family.

He was the first to recognize the evil intentions of Duryodhana, the eldest Kaurava, and warned King Dhritarashtra several times about the growing animosity between the Kauravas and Pandavas. Vidura's unflinching support for dharma made him a voice of truth in a palace rife with corruption. His counsel was often disregarded, especially by Duryodhana, who was bent on war with the Pandavas, but Vidura remained steadfast in his dedication to justice and moral principles.

His advice to Dhritarashtra during the dice game, where the Pandavas were humiliated, is one of the most poignant moments in the Mahabharata. Vidura had foreseen the catastrophe that would unfold from the game and its consequences. He warned Dhritarashtra about the grave injustice being done to the Pandavas, yet his words went unheeded, leading to the tragic exile of the Pandavas. Despite this, Vidura's sense of right and wrong never wavered, and he continued to counsel the Kaurava king, often at great personal cost.

Vidura's Mother: A Silent Influence

While Vidura's mother never appears directly in the epic, her influence can be seen in his unwavering adherence to truth and justice. Vidura's wisdom and sense of fairness were not solely products of his royal lineage; they were shaped by the values instilled in him by his mother. Though she was a woman of low caste, she imparted to Vidura the virtues of kindness, justice, and integrity traits that would make him one of the most revered characters in the Mahabharata.

The fact that Vidura's mother is not mentioned by name in the epic speaks volumes about the societal norms of the time. Her identity is overshadowed by Vidura's extraordinary contributions to the Kuru dynasty, but in a way, her lack of recognition also highlights the caste and class dynamics that prevailed in ancient India. Despite her lowly status, Vidura's mother played a crucial role in shaping the destiny of the Kuru family by giving birth to a son who would embody the highest ideals of dharma, even as he was marginalized by his own family due to his origins.

In many ways, Vidura's life reflects the silent struggles of those who are born into lower castes or oppressed backgrounds but who rise above their circumstances through their intellect, virtue, and character. Vidura's mother, though unmentioned and unseen, is the silent force behind his rise to prominence, and her teachings undoubtedly played a pivotal role in shaping Vidura into the wise and righteous man he became.

The Importance of Vidura's Mother Parishrami

Parishrami remains an unsung hero in the Mahabharata, but her existence is crucial in understanding the larger themes of the epic, such as caste, duty, and dharma. Her role reflects the story of many marginalized individuals who, though overlooked by society, make profound contributions to the world. She is a representation of the silent forces in the background whether mothers, teachers, or the often-ignored members of society who shape the future without seeking recognition.

Vidura's wisdom, which he applied in the Kuru court and in his counsel to the Pandavas, was deeply influenced by the values taught to him by his mother. Despite the rigid caste system and social hierarchies, Vidura rose to become a figure of moral authority, demonstrating that greatness is not determined by one's birth but by one's actions and adherence to righteous principles.

Conclusion

Though Vidura's mother remains a background figure in the Mahabharata, her influence is profound. She represents the unseen, unrecognized forces that shape individuals into leaders, advisors, and wise men. Her story is a testament to the power of nurturing, of wisdom passed down through quiet channels, and of the resilience and strength of those who live on the margins of society yet create ripples that affect the course of history. In understanding Vidura's legacy, we can glimpse the silent but powerful role of his mother—a woman whose contributions may never be fully acknowledged, but whose influence is felt throughout the epic.

Vidura's mother, a servant woman in the Kuru palace, remains an unnamed and largely forgotten figure in the Mahabharata, yet her role in shaping the epic's narrative is profound. Born into a lower social class, she served in the royal Kuru household, a backdrop to the world of kings, warriors, and sages. While her identity is not directly mentioned in the epic, it is understood that she bore Vidura, one of the most influential figures in the Kuru dynasty.

Vidura's birth, the result of a union between the servant woman and King Vichitravirya, is significant not only because it produces one of the most virtuous men in the epic but also because it highlights the rigid caste and class structures of the time. Vidura's mother, despite her low caste, played an instrumental role in shaping the character and wisdom of her son. While his birth to a servant might have led to his marginalization within the Kuru palace, it did not diminish his ability to rise above his circumstances.

Vidura's life was marked by his deep commitment to dharma and justice, principles likely imparted by his mother, whose wisdom and values shaped him in his early years. As an advisor to King Dhritarashtra, Vidura was known for his pragmatic and moral counsel, often standing up for what was right, even when it meant opposing his own family. His unwavering devotion to truth and righteousness can be traced back to the values instilled in him by his mother.

Though Vidura's mother remains a background figure in the narrative, her influence is undeniable, as she gave birth to the wise and just Vidura, whose actions would reverberate throughout the Kuru dynasty and the Mahabharata itself.

12. Shalya: The Tragic King of Madradesha

Shalya, the illustrious king of Madradesha, is a complex character whose story is woven with themes of loyalty, strategy, and tragedy. Though often overlooked, his role in the Mahabharata is critical, particularly in the

Kurukshetra war, where his conflicted allegiance and ultimate sacrifice mark him as a tragic figure.

Birth and Lineage

Shalya was born into the royal family of Madra, a kingdom renowned for its prosperity, cultural richness, and liberal customs. He was the son of King Ashvapati, a wise and noble ruler who upheld the traditions of his land, including Kanyashulka, the custom of a bridegroom paying a dowry. Shalya had a sister, Madri, who later became one of the queens of Hastinapura as the wife of King Pandu.

As a prince, Shalya was trained in the arts of warfare, statecraft, and charioteering. His lineage and upbringing instilled in him a strong sense of pride and adherence to the code of honor. Known for his charm, wit, and courage, Shalya grew into a formidable warrior and an able ruler.

Shalya's Relationship with the Pandavas

Through Madri, Shalya shared a familial bond with the Pandavas. He was particularly close to her twin sons, Nakula and Sahadeva, whom he treated with fatherly affection after Madri's untimely death. This kinship with the Pandavas formed the basis of Shalya's initial allegiance to their cause during the Kurukshetra war.

Deception and Forced Alliance

When the Kurukshetra war loomed on the horizon, Shalya set out with his vast army to join Yudhishthira and the Pandavas. However, Duryodhana, anticipating Shalya's potential impact on the war, devised a cunning plan. He instructed his men to offer Shalya lavish hospitality along the way, disguising it as a gesture from Yudhishthira. Shalya, impressed by the arrangements, vowed to grant a boon to his unseen host.

When Duryodhana revealed him as the benefactor and requested Shalya to fight for the Kauravas, the king of Madra was shocked but bound by his promise. Reluctantly, he agreed, becoming a reluctant yet dutiful ally of the Kauravas. This incident highlights Shalya's unwavering commitment to honor, even when it conflicted with his personal loyalties.

Role in the Kurukshetra War

Despite his allegiance to the Kauravas, Shalya's loyalty to the Pandavas remained intact at heart. This duality defined his actions throughout the war. One of his most notable roles was serving as Karna's charioteer during the latter's climactic battle with Arjuna. Known for his exceptional charioteering skills, Shalya was an invaluable asset to Karna. However, Shalya subtly sabotaged Karna's morale by constantly taunting and belittling him, highlighting his lower status and reminding him of his dependence on Duryodhana.

This psychological warfare, though indirect, contributed to Karna's eventual defeat. Shalya's sarcasm and wit served as a subtle nod to his true allegiance, showcasing his ingenuity even in a compromised position.

Commander-in-Chief and Death

Following the deaths of Drona, Karna, and other key warriors, Shalya was appointed as the commander-in-chief of the Kaurava army. This role, though prestigious, was a double-edged sword, as the Kauravas were already on the brink of defeat. On the 18th day of the war, Shalya faced Yudhishthira in battle. Despite his valor and unmatched skill, he was slain by the eldest Pandava, marking the end of the Kaurava leadership.

Significance of Shalya's Character

Shalya's life encapsulates the dilemmas of dharma, loyalty, and honor. His reluctant alliance with the Kauravas, driven by his commitment to his word, reflects the complexities of moral duty. His taunting of Karna and dual role in the war underscore the strategic and emotional intricacies of the epic.

As a warrior, a king, and a brother, Shalya's story is one of sacrifice, divided loyalties, and unshakable principles. His actions, though seemingly contradictory, reveal a man torn between duty and devotion, making him a deeply human and relatable figure in the grand tapestry of the Mahabharata.

13. Satyaki: The Loyal Warrior of Yadava Clan

Satyaki, also known as Yuyudhana, is a lesser-known yet significant character in the Mahabharata. A valiant warrior from the Yadava clan, he is remembered for his steadfast loyalty to Krishna and the Pandavas. Despite his relatively modest role in the larger narrative, Satyaki's courage, martial prowess, and unyielding devotion to dharma make him an important figure.

Birth and Lineage

Satyaki was born into the Vrishni dynasty of the Yadavas, a clan closely associated with Krishna. His grandfather was Sini, who played a pivotal role in securing Devaki's marriage to Vasudeva, Krishna's parents. This connection made Satyaki a kinsman of Krishna and a part of the extended Yadava family.

From a young age, Satyaki was trained in the art of warfare, specializing in archery. He studied under Dronacharya alongside great warriors like Arjuna, Bhishma, and Karna. This training equipped him with the skills and discipline necessary to stand shoulder-to-shoulder with the finest warriors of his time.

Satyaki and Krishna

Satyaki's relationship with Krishna was central to his identity. As Krishna's devoted disciple, Satyaki followed his teachings and shared his vision of dharma. This bond extended to the Pandavas, Krishna's staunch allies. Satyaki's unwavering support for the Pandavas throughout their trials reflects his deep respect for Krishna and his commitment to righteousness.

Role in the Kurukshetra War

Satyaki's prominence comes to the forefront during the Kurukshetra war. Fighting on the side of the Pandavas, he was one of their most trusted warriors. His allegiance was not merely out of kinship but rooted in his belief in their just cause. Throughout the war, Satyaki displayed exceptional courage and played a crucial role in several battles.

• **The Duel with Bhurisravas**: One of the most dramatic moments involving Satyaki occurred on the 14th day of the war. He faced Bhurisravas, a mighty Kaurava warrior, in a fierce duel. Despite being overpowered, Satyaki's determination did not waver. When Bhurisravas attempted to kill him, Krishna instructed Arjuna to intervene, leading Arjuna to sever Bhurisravas' arm with an arrow. Seizing the moment, Satyaki killed the incapacitated Bhurisravas. This act, though controversial, underscored the complexities of war and the lengths to which Satyaki would go to protect the Pandavas.

• **Key Contributions**: Satyaki played a vital role in protecting Arjuna during the mission to pierce the Kaurava formation and kill Jayadratha. His relentless defense against numerous Kaurava warriors, including Karna and Drona, showcased his strategic acumen and combat skills.

Loyalty and Valor

Satyaki's defining trait was his unwavering loyalty. Whether it was standing by Krishna, supporting the Pandavas, or fulfilling his duties as a warrior, he never faltered. His valor on the battlefield, coupled with his sense of duty, made him an indispensable part of the Pandava alliance.

Post-War Life and Legacy

After the Kurukshetra war, Satyaki returned to Dwaraka. However, like the other Yadavas, he met a tragic end during the internecine conflict that destroyed Krishna's clan. This demise reflects the overarching theme of the Mahabharata—the impermanence of life and the inevitable consequences of war.

Why Satyaki is Important

Satyaki's significance lies in his embodiment of loyalty and courage. Though not as prominent as Arjuna or Bhima, his contributions to the Pandava cause were vital. His unwavering support for Krishna and his fearless defense of dharma highlight the importance of steadfastness and integrity in the face of adversity.

Satyaki's story serves as a reminder that even seemingly minor characters can have profound impacts on the epic's events and themes, making him an enduring figure in the Mahabharata.

14. Hidimba: The Rakshasi Who Redefined Love and Sacrifice

Hidimba, a character from the Mahabharata often relegated to the sidelines, is one of the most intriguing figures in the epic. A rakshasi (demoness) by birth, her story is one of courage, devotion, and the breaking of societal barriers. Despite her brief appearance, Hidimba plays a crucial role in shaping the future of the Pandavas through her son, Ghatotkacha.

Origins and Lineage

Hidimba hailed from a clan of Rakshasas residing in the dense forests of Ekachakra. Her brother, Hidimb, was a fearsome Rakshasa known for his cruel ways. Unlike her brother, Hidimba possessed a noble heart and the ability to see beyond the violent ways of her lineage. She was gifted with extraordinary strength, intelligence, and the ability to transform her appearance, traits characteristic of her rakshasa heritage.

Encounter with the Pandavas

Hidimba's life took a dramatic turn when the Pandavas, accompanied by their mother Kunti, sought refuge in the forest during their exile after escaping the house of lac. The scent of human presence attracted Hidimb, who ordered Hidimba to kill the intruders and bring their flesh for a feast. However, when Hidimba saw Bhima, she was captivated by his strength and nobility.

Defying her brother's orders, Hidimba approached the Pandavas in the guise of a beautiful woman and proposed marriage to Bhima. Her transformation from a rakshasi to a gentle, love-struck maiden symbolizes her inner conflict and desire to transcend her demonic nature.

The Battle Between Bhima and Hidimb

Hidimb, enraged by his sister's disobedience, confronted the Pandavas. A fierce battle ensued between Bhima and Hidimb, showcasing Bhima's immense strength and Hidimba's courage. Ultimately, Bhima slew Hidimb, freeing Hidimba from her brother's oppressive shadow.

Hidimba's decision to stay loyal to Bhima despite the danger reflects her determination and unflinching love. Her defiance of her brother and her choice to align with the Pandavas exemplify her moral courage and individuality.

Marriage to Bhima

Moved by Hidimba's sincerity and recognizing her noble heart, Kunti and the Pandavas consented to her marriage with Bhima. However, Bhima stipulated that the union would last only as long as their stay in the forest. This condition, though harsh, did not deter Hidimba, who accepted it with grace, valuing her time with Bhima over the constraints of societal norms.

Motherhood and the Birth of Ghatotkacha

Hidimba's union with Bhima resulted in the birth of Ghatotkacha, a half-rakshasa warrior endowed with immense strength and magical powers. Ghatotkacha inherited his mother's noble qualities and became a loyal ally of the Pandavas. His pivotal role in the Kurukshetra war, particularly in subduing Karna, underscores Hidimba's enduring contribution to the Pandava legacy.

After Ghatotkacha's birth, Hidimba returned to the forest, dedicating her life to raising her son and preparing him for his eventual role as a protector of dharma.

Why Hidimba is Important

Hidimba's significance lies in her transcendence of societal and genetic expectations. As a rakshasi, she defied her violent lineage to embrace love, compassion, and righteousness. Her decision to ally with the Pandavas, despite the transient nature of her relationship with Bhima, underscores her selflessness and commitment to a greater cause.

Through Ghatotkacha, Hidimba's legacy lived on, proving that even those marginalized by society can play critical roles in the pursuit of dharma. Her story serves as a reminder of the transformative power of love and the importance of individuality in a world governed by rigid norms.

15. Sudeshna: The Queen Who Sheltered the Pandavas

Sudeshna, the queen of the kingdom of Matsya, is a lesser-known but pivotal character in the Mahabharata. Her role, though seemingly minor, becomes significant during the thirteenth year of the Pandavas' exile, the year of incognito living (ajnatavasa). As the wife of King Virata, Sudeshna provides refuge to Draupadi and indirectly facilitates the Pandavas' successful completion of their exile.

Birth and Lineage

Sudeshna was born into a noble lineage and became the queen of Matsya through her marriage to King Virata. She was known for her grace, wisdom, and adherence to dharma. As the queen of Matsya,

Sudeshna managed the royal household with poise and upheld the kingdom's prosperity and reputation.

Sudeshna's life was largely centered on her duties as queen and mother. She was the mother of Uttara, Uttaraa, and Shveta, each of whom played important roles in the Mahabharata.

Sudeshna and Draupadi's Arrival

During the Pandavas' thirteenth year of exile, they were required to live in disguise to avoid detection by the Kauravas. Draupadi, disguised as a maid named Sairandhri, sought employment in Sudeshna's palace. Draupadi introduced herself as a skilled hairdresser from a noble family who had fallen on hard times. Moved by her plight and impressed by her beauty and demeanor, Sudeshna accepted her into her service, unaware of her true identity.

Sudeshna's decision to employ Draupadi was a turning point in the Pandavas' journey, as it provided them with a secure base to fulfill their exile in Matsya.

Challenges in the Palace

Sudeshna's palace became a backdrop for some of the most dramatic events of the Pandavas' incognito period. Draupadi, despite her disguise, attracted the attention of Kichaka, Sudeshna's brother, who was the commander of King Virata's army. Kichaka, infatuated with Draupadi, began to harass her, leading to a series of confrontations.

Sudeshna's role during this period was complex. While she sympathized with Draupadi's plight, she was also torn between her loyalty to her brother and her sense of justice. Her inability to stop Kichaka reflects the limitations imposed on women, even queens, in a patriarchal society.

Kichaka's Death

When Kichaka's advances became intolerable, Draupadi sought Bhima's help. Bhima disguised as the palace cook Vallabha killed Kichaka in a fierce encounter. Kichaka's death caused turmoil in the Matsya kingdom, but it also ensured Draupadi's safety and upheld her honor.

Sudeshna's indirect role in this episode highlights her contribution to Draupadi's survival. By providing her shelter and later standing by her, Sudeshna became an unwitting ally of the Pandavas.

Significance in the Mahabharata

Sudeshna's importance lies in her quiet support of the Pandavas during a critical phase of their journey. Her acceptance of Draupadi into her household provided the Pandavas with a haven to complete their exile successfully. Despite being unaware of their true identities, Sudeshna's actions demonstrated her compassion and ability to recognize and protect virtue.

Her character also reflects the challenges faced by women in navigating power dynamics and family loyalty. As the sister of Kichaka, Sudeshna's predicament underscores the societal pressures that often forced women to balance personal morality with familial obligations.

Legacy

Though her role in the Mahabharata is brief, Sudeshna's actions had long-lasting consequences. By providing refuge to the Pandavas, she contributed to the fulfillment of their dharma and their eventual return to power. Her story serves as a testament to the impact of small but significant acts of kindness and courage in the grand narrative of the epic.

16. Ulupi: The Naga Princess and Arjuna's Guide

Ulupi, a Naga princess, is a fascinating and lesser-known character in the Mahabharata. Her story is one of love, wisdom, and redemption, making her an essential figure in Arjuna's journey. Though her role is brief, it profoundly impacts Arjuna's life and the epic's broader narrative.

Birth and Lineage

Ulupi was born into the Naga clan, a race of semi-divine serpent beings who lived in the subterranean realms. Her father, Kauravya, was a prominent Naga king. As a princess of the Nagas, Ulupi was endowed with supernatural powers, immense wisdom, and deep knowledge of dharma and the Vedas.

Her upbringing in the mystical Naga kingdom gave her a unique perspective on life and the world, blending the divine and mortal realms. This background made her one of the most enigmatic characters in the Mahabharata.

Meeting Arjuna

Ulupi's encounter with Arjuna occurred during his period of exile, imposed as penance for entering Draupadi's chamber while Yudhishthira was present. While wandering near the Ganges, Arjuna was pulled underwater by Ulupi, who had fallen in love with him.

Ulupi confessed her feelings to Arjuna and expressed her desire to marry him. Initially reluctant, Arjuna eventually agreed, understanding her sincerity and respecting her devotion. Their union, though brief, was a turning point in Arjuna's exile.

Role in Arjuna's Redemption

Ulupi's wisdom and understanding of dharma are evident in her guidance to Arjuna. She not only expressed her love but also provided Arjuna with spiritual and moral insights. Through their union, she blessed him with invincibility in water, a boon that proved crucial during the Kurukshetra war.

Their son, Iravan, born of this union, later became a significant figure in the Pandavas' battle against the Kauravas. Though Iravan's role is often overlooked, his sacrifice to ensure the Pandavas' victory highlights Ulupi's enduring influence.

Ulupi and Arjuna's Revival

Despite their brief marriage Ulupi's influence on Arjuna extended beyond. During the Kurukshetra war,

Arjuna was cursed by Bhishma to be slain for his actions against warriors who had laid down their arms. To nullify this curse, Ulupi used her divine knowledge and powers to restore Arjuna to life, showcasing her unwavering support and love for him.

Significance in the Mahabharata

Ulupi's importance lies in her role as a guide and protector. Through her wisdom and supernatural abilities, she aided Arjuna at critical moments, ensuring his survival and success. Her actions also symbolize the harmonious integration of different worlds—the mortal and the divine—emphasizing the interconnectedness of all beings in the pursuit of dharma.

Despite her brief appearances, Ulupi's contributions underscore her loyalty, selflessness, and wisdom. Her union with Arjuna and her role in his redemption reflect her profound understanding of duty and love.

Legacy

Ulupi's legacy is carried forward through Iravan's sacrifice and Arjuna's victories. She remains a testament to the importance of love, wisdom, and divine intervention in shaping the destinies of the epic's protagonists. Her story reminds readers of the unseen yet significant influences that shape great narratives.

17. Pratipa: The Grandfather Who Bridged Generations

Pratipa, a prominent yet understated figure in the Mahabharata, was the grandfather of Bhishma and a crucial link in the lineage of the Kuru dynasty. Known for his wisdom, piety, and adherence to dharma, Pratipa's decisions and actions set the stage for many events that would later shape the epic.

Birth and Lineage

Pratipa was born into the illustrious Kuru dynasty and was a descendant of King Kuru, after whom the dynasty was named. He ascended the throne of Hastinapura and became a just and virtuous ruler. Known for his unwavering commitment to dharma, Pratipa was revered by his subjects for his fair governance and profound understanding of righteousness.

Pratipa's marriage to Sunanda, a princess of the Shivi dynasty, further solidified his rule and legacy. Together, they had three sons: Devapi, Shantanu, and Bahlika, each of whom played distinct roles in the continuation of the Kuru lineage.

The Encounter with Ganga

One of the most significant episodes in Pratipa's life occurred when he was meditating by the banks of the Ganges. Ganga, the river goddess, approached him in human form and expressed her desire to marry him. Pratipa, adhering to his principles of dharma and loyalty to his wife, declined her proposal. However, he promised to facilitate her marriage to his future son, thus laying the foundation for the union of Shantanu and Ganga.

This decision highlights Pratipa's foresight and commitment to honoring divine will, even as he remained steadfast in his duties as a husband and king.

Role in Shantanu's Ascension

Pratipa's wisdom and understanding of dharma were evident in his guidance to his sons. Devapi, his eldest son, renounced the throne and retired to the forest to pursue spiritual practices, leaving Shantanu as the rightful heir. Pratipa ensured that Shantanu was well-prepared to assume the responsibilities of kingship.

By recognizing Shantanu's potential and entrusting him with the throne, Pratipa ensured the continuity of the Kuru dynasty. His blessings and counsel played a significant role in shaping Shantanu's reign.

Importance in the Mahabharata

Although Pratipa's role is brief, his actions have far-reaching consequences. By facilitating the union of Shantanu and Ganga, he set the stage for the birth of Bhishma, one of the most pivotal characters in the epic. Bhishma's vow of celibacy and his unwavering dedication to the Kuru throne were deeply influenced by the values instilled in the family by Pratipa.

Pratipa's life also serves as an example of dharma in practice. His decisions, guided by righteousness and foresight, demonstrate the importance of aligning personal choices with the greater good. As a king, father, and patriarch, Pratipa embodied the virtues of responsibility, wisdom, and selflessness.

Legacy

Pratipa's legacy is most prominently reflected in Bhishma, whose sacrifices and loyalty to the Kuru throne were inspired by the principles upheld by his grandfather. Pratipa's adherence to dharma and his role in bridging divine intervention with mortal affairs underscore his significance in the Mahabharata. Though often overlooked, his life is a reminder of the enduring impact of righteous leadership and foresight.

18. Barbarika: The Silent Witness to the Battle of Kurukshetra

Barbarika, a relatively lesser-known but significant character in the Mahabharata, is renowned for his extraordinary strength, his connection to Lord Krishna, and the tragic circumstances that prevented him from actively participating in the battle of Kurukshetra. His story is one of sacrifice, divine insight, and the tragic consequences of power.

Birth and Lineage

Barbarika was born to the warrior Ghatotkacha, the son of Bhima, and a woman named Maurvi, who belonged to the Kshatriya tribe of the Kiratas. His birth was marked by remarkable strength and divine blessings. From a young age, Barbarika was known for his unmatched skills in combat and his immense physical prowess. He was a true warrior at heart, inheriting the fierce battle instincts of his father

Ghatotkacha, and his maternal lineage added to his warrior spirit.

The Three Boons and Divine Powers

Barbarika's most significant trait was his unmatched power, which he had received as blessings from various deities. Through intense penance, he earned three boons from Lord Shiva, which made him virtually invincible. These boons were:

1. **The Ability to Change His Shape**: Barbarika could assume any form, making him virtually impossible to track or defeat in battle.

2. **The Power of the Three Arrows**: Barbarika was given three powerful arrows that could destroy anything they struck. These arrows were so potent that they could destroy entire armies.

3. **Immortality of His Head**: Barbarika's final boon granted immortality to his head, which, though separated from his body, would continue to live on.

These boons made Barbarika a force of nature, capable of wreaking havoc on any battlefield. However, they also posed a moral dilemma, as they gave him the potential to be an overwhelming force in the upcoming war of Kurukshetra.

Barbarika's Promise and His Role in the War

As the Kurukshetra war loomed, Barbarika prepared to support his cousins, the Pandavas, who were at war with the Kauravas. He decided to observe the battle from a distance, as his powers were so immense that he feared his intervention could tip the balance in favor of one side too easily.

However, his participation in the war would ultimately never take place. Barbarika's involvement in the battle was predicted by Lord Krishna, who foresaw the chaos his power could cause. Realizing the dangerous potential of Barbarika's strength, Krishna decided to test his resolve and wisdom.

The Encounter with Lord Krishna

On the eve of the battle, Krishna, in his usual playful and divine nature, approached Barbarika in disguise and asked him which side he would support in the war. Barbarika, displaying his characteristic honesty, vowed to support whichever side was weaker during the course of the battle, so as to ensure that the war remained fair and balanced.

Krishna, understanding the implication of this vow, knew that Barbarika's intervention could destroy the war before it had even started. Krishna then asked Barbarika to show him the full extent of his power, and Barbarika demonstrated his ability to shoot three arrows at once, each of which could destroy an entire army. Krishna, however, pointed out that Barbarika's boons made him too powerful and that his intervention would prevent the war from having its rightful course.

Krishna then asked Barbarika for a favor. He requested Barbarika's head, stating that it was necessary for the success of the battle. Barbarika, ever the devoted warrior, agreed without hesitation, offering his head to Krishna. In return, Krishna promised that Barbarika's head would witness the entire battle from a high vantage point, ensuring that his sacrifice would not go unnoticed.

The Tragic Sacrifice

Krishna, with his divine powers, severed Barbarika's head and placed it atop a hill where it could watch the entire war. From this vantage point, Barbarika saw the entire unfolding of the Mahabharata war, witnessing the death of warriors, the fall of friends and foes alike, and the eventual victory of the Pandavas.

Although he never participated in the war directly, Barbarika's silent presence served as a reminder of the cost of war and the importance of dharma. His sacrifice represents the principle that power, no matter how great, must be wielded with caution, wisdom, and in accordance with righteousness.

Significance in the Mahabharata

Barbarika's role in the Mahabharata is often overlooked due to his brief and indirect involvement in the events of the war. However, his story is profoundly significant, as it illustrates the consequences of unchecked power. Krishna's decision to prevent Barbarika from fighting serves as a reminder that, even the most powerful of warriors must act within the bounds of dharma.

Barbarika's selflessness, honesty, and ultimate sacrifice represent the warrior's code of conduct, which places the greater good above personal gain. His story also emphasizes the theme of divine will and how even the most powerful individuals are subject to the overarching fate determined by the gods.

Legacy

Barbarika's legacy lives on in the tales of his incredible sacrifice and his connection to Krishna. His story is a poignant reminder of the moral responsibility that comes with immense power and the necessity of aligning one's actions with the greater cosmic order. The sight of Barbarika's head, silently observing the Kurukshetra war, became a symbol of detachment, the painful cost of war, and the silent witness to the karmic consequences that ensue.

19. Vikarna: The Voice of Dharma in the Kaurava Clan

Vikarna, one of the lesser-known but crucial characters in the Mahabharata, stands out as a beacon of morality within the Kaurava clan. Unlike his brothers, who were largely embroiled in the pursuit of power and greed, Vikarna is often remembered for his unwavering adherence to dharma, even when it placed him in direct opposition to his family. His story reflects the theme of righteousness amidst overwhelming corruption and injustice.

Birth and Lineage

Vikarna was the tenth son of King Dhritarashtra and Queen Gandhari, making him one of the Kauravas, the hundred sons born to the blind king. While all of

Dhritarashtra's sons were born through Gandhari's womb, Vikarna was one of the more distinguished among them, particularly due to his moral compass. Unlike many of his brothers, who followed Duryodhana's lead in plotting against the Pandavas, Vikarna stood apart as a voice of reason, showing compassion and a sense of justice.

The Dice Game and Vikarna's Stand for Dharma

The most defining moment of Vikarna's life occurred during the infamous game of dice (Dyutakrida) that set the stage for the Pandavas' exile. This was the turning point of the entire Mahabharata, where the Kauravas' betrayal and the Pandavas' subsequent hardships began.

When Yudhishthira, the eldest Pandava, was coerced into gambling away his kingdom, his brothers, and even himself, Vikarna was present. As the game progressed, the Kauravas, led by Duryodhana, began to display extreme cruelty. The ultimate insult came when Draupadi, the wife of the Pandavas, was humiliated in the court by being stripped in front of everyone. The court was silent, many of the assembled kings and elders not daring to speak against the wrongful act, either due to fear or political convenience.

In this moment of great injustice, Vikarna rose to defend Draupadi. He spoke out boldly, criticizing the Kauravas for their sinful actions and the disrespect shown to a woman who was both their guest and a daughter-in-law. He declared, "It is a sin to humiliate a woman, especially one of noble birth. It is against dharma to let such an act go unchallenged."

His words were a rare and courageous stand for righteousness in the face of overwhelming opposition. He argued that Draupadi should not be subjected to such a disgrace, and he even suggested that the game was already unfair, as Yudhishthira had already lost his kingdom, his brothers, and himself.

However, Vikarna's voice was drowned out by the more powerful and influential figures, especially his elder brothers, Duryodhana and Dushasana, who were bent on furthering their cruel agenda. Despite his protests, the Kauravas proceeded with their plans, and Draupadi was humiliated.

Vikarna's protest, though unsuccessful in stopping the event, became a symbol of moral courage. It highlighted his awareness of dharma, his integrity, and his willingness to speak up even when doing so was dangerous and unpopular.

Vikarna's Role in the Kurukshetra War

Though Vikarna stood for justice and dharma during the dice game, his loyalty to his family kept him on the side of the Kauravas during the Kurukshetra war. Despite his strong sense of right and wrong, Vikarna felt bound by the ties of family and brotherhood. This internal conflict is a testament to his character—while he opposed many of his brothers' actions, his duty as a Kaurava prince kept him fighting for their side in the great battle.

Vikarna fought valiantly during the war, showcasing his prowess as a warrior. He was one of the few Kauravas who did not completely lose his sense of justice on the battlefield. In one of the most poignant moments of the war, he is noted for his deep sorrow and reluctance during the confrontation with his brothers and the Pandavas. However, his duty as a warrior compelled him to continue fighting.

Vikarna's Death and Legacy

Vikarna's tragic end occurred in the final stages of the Kurukshetra war. During the battle, he faced off with many of the greatest Pandava warriors, including Bhima. Despite his valiant efforts, Vikarna was eventually killed by Bhima. His death, however, was not without its share of tragic irony. Bhima, recognizing Vikarna's inherent goodness and nobility, deeply lamented the fact that such a righteous soul had been forced to fight for the wrong side.

In his final moments, Vikarna's legacy as the voice of dharma remained unshaken. His death was seen as a symbol of the tragedy that befalls those who are caught between their duty to their family and the higher call of righteousness.

Vikarna's legacy is significant in that he remains one of the few characters in the Mahabharata who upheld the principles of dharma without seeking personal gain or glory. His story serves as a reminder of the importance of speaking out against injustice, even when it seems futile, and remaining true to one's principles, even in the face of personal loss.

Significance in the Mahabharata

Vikarna's importance in the Mahabharata lies in his ability to represent the conflict between personal loyalty and universal righteousness. His moral stand in the court, his courage in the face of overwhelming opposition, and his unwavering commitment to justice, despite his familial ties, make him a unique and significant character in the epic.

While many characters in the Mahabharata are consumed by their desires and ambitions, Vikarna's story offers a valuable lesson in moral integrity. He stands as an embodiment of the righteous man who, though flawed in his loyalty, never wavered from the path of truth and justice.

20. Chitraratha: The Gandharva King

Chitraratha, the king of the Gandharvas, is a lesser-known yet significant figure in the Mahabharata. As the celestial ruler of the Gandharvas, Chitraratha embodies elegance, culture, and a strong sense of justice. His brief but impactful interactions with the Pandavas provide insights into the themes of humility, divine justice, and the responsibilities of power.

Chitraratha's Domain and Abilities

The Gandharvas are celestial beings associated with music, art, and dance, and Chitraratha stands out as their most prominent leader. His domain extends across heavenly realms, filled with unparalleled beauty and prosperity. As a Gandharva king, Chitraratha possesses remarkable abilities, including mastery over music, an ethereal chariot drawn by supernatural steeds, and combat skills enhanced by divine weaponry.

Chitraratha is closely associated with divine beings such as Indra, the king of gods, and is often seen as an enforcer of celestial law, ensuring that mortals and immortals adhere to cosmic justice.

Encounter with the Kauravas

Chitraratha's most notable appearance in the Mahabharata occurs during an incident involving Duryodhana. After the Pandavas' exile to the forest following the infamous dice game, Duryodhana, consumed by arrogance and schadenfreude, decided to visit the Pandavas in their misery. His intention was to mock them and gloat over their misfortune.

Accompanied by a lavish retinue, Duryodhana camped in the forest, unaware that the area was under Chitraratha's protection. The Gandharva king, viewing Duryodhana's actions as disrespectful and disruptive, confronted him and demanded that he leave. True to his nature, Duryodhana refused, underestimating the celestial power of the Gandharva king. This led to a battle in which Chitraratha and his forces easily overwhelmed the Kaurava prince and his army.

Duryodhana was captured by Chitraratha, marking a significant moment of humiliation for the arrogant prince. The incident underscored the Gandharva king's role as a protector of divine order, punishing those who acted out of hubris.

The Pandavas' Intervention

When the news of Duryodhana's capture reached the Pandavas, Bhima saw it as poetic justice and relished the opportunity to leave their cousin in his predicament. However, Yudhishthira, adhering to his sense of dharma, instructed his brothers to rescue Duryodhana. Arjuna, with his extraordinary archery skills, confronted Chitraratha and managed to secure Duryodhana's release.

Chitraratha, recognizing Arjuna's valor and the Pandavas' adherence to righteousness, expressed his respect for them. As a token of goodwill, he gifted the Pandavas celestial knowledge, including the secrets of the Gandharvas' divine weapons and their unique abilities. This gesture not only cemented the Pandavas' alliance with the celestial realm but also served as a reminder of their higher destiny.

Symbolism and Legacy

Chitraratha's story carries profound symbolic meaning within the Mahabharata. His interaction with Duryodhana serves as a lesson in humility, illustrating the consequences of arrogance and the importance of respecting cosmic laws. Conversely, his relationship with the Pandavas highlights the rewards of virtue and the strength of righteous action.

Chitraratha also represents the intersection of the mortal and divine realms, bridging the gap between human struggles and celestial order. His presence in the narrative reminds readers of the constant interplay between human actions and divine oversight, a recurring theme in the epic.

Though a relatively minor character, Chitraratha leaves an indelible mark on the story, demonstrating the importance of grace, justice, and the pursuit of higher ideals in a world often consumed by conflict and chaos.

Chapter Four - Five most crucial decisions which brought downfall of Kauravas

Each of these five decisions; the rigged game of dice, the refusal to share the kingdom, the betrayal of Dronacharya, the dishonorable killing of Abhimanyu, and the rejection of Krishna's peace offer were pivotal in bringing about the Kauravas' downfall. Duryodhana's arrogance, his refusal to see the bigger picture, and his obsession with pride and power led the Kauravas down a path of self-destruction. These decisions left the Kauravas with no options for reconciliation, and ultimately, the war they fought was not only one of battle but also of moral righteousness. In the end, the Kauravas paid the price for their blind adherence to pride and evil, while the Pandavas, despite their trials, were victorious due to their commitment to dharma.

The Kauravas, led by **Duryodhana**, made several crucial decisions throughout the Mahabharata that significantly contributed to their downfall. These decisions were marked by arrogance, greed, jealousy, and a refusal to heed wise counsel. Here are five of the most pivotal decisions made by the Kauravas that ultimately led to their defeat:

Let's delve deeper into each of the Kauravas' most crucial decisions and analyze them in detail, each decision contributing more context, background, and implications, with a focus on how these choices led to their ultimate downfall.

1. The Game of Dice (Dyutakrida)

The Game of Dice, also known as **Dyutakrida**, is widely considered the pivotal moment in the Mahabharata, marking the beginning of the irreversible conflict that culminated in the Kurukshetra War. The Kauravas, particularly **Duryodhana**, harbored a deep resentment towards the Pandavas, fueled by jealousy and a desire to rid themselves of the perceived threat posed by the Pandavas' claims to the throne of **Hastinapura**. They saw the Pandavas' virtues as a challenge to their own dominance and sought to find ways to undermine them.

The invitation to the game of dice came from **Duryodhana's uncle, Shakuni**, who was a master manipulator. Shakuni, who had a personal vendetta against the Kuru family, especially **King Dhritarashtra**, was eager to bring down the Pandavas. The game, however, was designed with treachery in mind. Knowing that **Yudhishthira**, the eldest of the Pandavas, was bound by his sense of dharma and would not refuse a request for a game, Shakuni rigged the dice and the entire setup to ensure that the Pandavas would lose. Duryodhana and Shakuni wanted more than just a game; they sought the humiliation and downfall of the Pandavas, aiming to not only strip them of their wealth but also their dignity.

Yudhishthira, adhering to the principles of kshatriya dharma and loyalty to his elders, accepted the challenge without suspicion, not realizing that the dice were fixed. As the game progressed, Yudhishthira, despite his best efforts, lost everything—his kingdom, his wealth, his brothers, and even himself. The final humiliation came when he was forced to wager **Draupadi**, their shared wife, who was then dragged into the court and insulted in front of the entire assembly. This moment was one of the most degrading episodes in the Mahabharata, and it solidified the Kauravas' reputation for cruelty and dishonor.

The decision to play the game was one of supreme arrogance on the part of Duryodhana and his family. They assumed that, with the Pandavas out of the picture, they could easily seize control of Hastinapura. But in doing so, they made an irreversible enemy of the Pandavas, particularly of **Arjuna**, who would become the fiercest of warriors in the subsequent war. **Krishna**'s intervention also marked the beginning of the divine providence that would guide the Pandavas to their eventual victory.

The consequences of this decision were far-reaching. First, it shattered any hope for peace between the Pandavas and the Kauravas. With their honor compromised, the Pandavas were pushed into exile for **13 years**, with the last year to be spent in disguise. This exile, while a time of suffering, also proved transformative for the Pandavas. It was during this time that Arjuna obtained divine weapons, **Draupadi** grew stronger in her resolve, and the Pandavas strengthened their alliances with the **nations** around them.

Moreover, the Kauravas' actions exposed their own inherent moral failings. They had gained power through deceit and dishonor, while the Pandavas, despite their hardships, held fast to their values and virtues. This stark contrast would resonate throughout the war. The Kauravas' decision to humiliate the Pandavas not only violated the sanctity of royal hospitality but also planted the seeds for a fierce and righteous battle where dharma would eventually triumph over adharma.

Duryodhana's refusal to consider the consequences of this action, combined with Shakuni's manipulative scheming, made the game of dice a critical turning point in the Kauravas' downfall. The war that followed was the inevitable result of the seeds of hatred and resentment planted during this fateful game.

2. Duryodhana's Refusal to Share the Kingdom

One of the most significant decisions that led to the Kauravas' downfall was **Duryodhana's refusal to share the kingdom** with the Pandavas. After the Pandavas completed their period of exile and returned to reclaim their rightful share of the kingdom, Duryodhana, whose desire for absolute power had only grown during their absence, chose to deny them even a small portion of land. This decision marked a major turning point, making war between the Kauravas and the Pandavas not only inevitable but also justified in the eyes of many.

The Pandavas, after their exile, were not only entitled to a portion of land by right, but they were also willing to make peace and avoid war. **Krishna**, the Pandavas' divine guide and friend, offered Duryodhana peace and reconciliation. Krishna went to Duryodhana with a proposal to divide the kingdom between the Kauravas and the Pandavas, a proposal that would have ensured peace and avoided the devastating war. He suggested that Duryodhana allow the Pandavas to rule a small tract of land, as this would preserve peace and the kingdom's integrity.

However, **Duryodhana**, emboldened by his unchecked power and arrogance, refused Krishna's offer. His reasoning was that he could not allow the Pandavas, whom he regarded as rivals, to have any power. His blind ambition and fear of losing his control over Hastinapura led him to reject all efforts at reconciliation. The idea of sharing the throne, even in a limited capacity, was unbearable for Duryodhana. Instead, he insisted that the Pandavas had no right to anything and demanded that they leave Hastinapura for good.

Duryodhana's refusal was driven not only by greed but also by his belief that the Pandavas were a threat to his own claim to the throne. Throughout the Mahabharata, he had been envious of their strength, character, and growing support. His actions, however, alienated **Krishna**, the **elders** of the Kuru family, and many other kingdoms who saw the Pandavas as just and worthy of their rights.

This decision was a monumental mistake. By refusing the Pandavas a rightful share of the kingdom, Duryodhana ensured that the Pandavas would have no choice but to go to war. **Bhishma**, the grand patriarch of the Kaurava family, tried to advise Duryodhana to accept a peaceful settlement, but Duryodhana ignored him. This stubbornness ultimately isolated him from the counsel of wise elders and led him down a path of destruction.

The consequences of Duryodhana's refusal were felt immediately. The Pandavas, feeling no recourse but to take up arms, gathered their allies. They were supported by **Krishna**, who chose to become Arjuna's charioteer and offered his divine assistance in the war. This created an unbridgeable gap between the Kauravas and the Pandavas, and soon, the entire Kuru dynasty was split into two warring factions.

By rejecting peace, Duryodhana committed himself and his family to a disastrous war that would eventually lead to their ruin. His decision reflected his inability to see beyond his own narrow ambitions and his refusal to compromise for the greater good, even at the cost of the kingdom and his family's future.

3. Murder of Dronacharya's Son, Ashwatthama

The killing of **Ashwatthama**, the son of the great teacher Dronacharya, was another moment in the

Mahabharata that demonstrated the Kauravas' willingness to forsake dharma in the pursuit of victory. **Duryodhana**, who had always been focused on achieving victory at any cost, made a decision to strike a grievous blow to the Pandavas by targeting Ashwatthama, who had become a fierce warrior on the battlefield. However, what made this act especially reprehensible was the manner in which the Kauravas attacked Ashwatthama.

As the war raged on, Dronacharya, who had been one of the most formidable leaders of the Kaurava army, began to show signs of weariness. The Pandavas had killed his son, **Ashwatthama**, or so they believed, which made Dronacharya emotional and devastated. His grief caused him to be less focused and more vulnerable. Duryodhana, in an effort to destabilize Dronacharya and break his resolve, chose to spread the false news that Ashwatthama had been killed in battle.

In a cruel act of deception, Duryodhana sent an elephant named **Ashwatthama** into the battlefield and had it killed. The soldiers then falsely proclaimed that Ashwatthama, Dronacharya's son, was dead. When Dronacharya heard this, he was overcome with sorrow and lost his will to fight. The Kauravas took advantage of this moment of vulnerability, and in the heat of the battle, **Dhrishtadyumna**, the commander of the Pandava forces, killed Dronacharya.

While this could be seen as a strategic military move, it was done with deceit and in violation of the rules of warfare, making it a morally reprehensible act. The

Kauravas had not only killed one of their greatest warriors but had also dishonored their teacher, whose lessons had shaped them into warriors. This act turned the tide of the battle against the Kauravas. It shattered Dronacharya's loyalty and commitment to his students and left the Kaurava army without one of its greatest leaders. The act demonstrated the Kauravas'

4. The killing of Abhimanyu

The valiant son of **Arjuna** and **Subhadra**, is one of the most tragic and infamous episodes of the **Kurukshetra War** in the **Mahabharata**. His death was not only a horrific moment of cruelty but also an act of blatant disregard for the codes of warfare, as the Kauravas conspired to trap and kill him in a manner that was both deceitful and dishonorable. To understand the context of Abhimanyu's killing, it's crucial to examine the planning, execution, and the roles of the various Kaurava warriors who participated in this malicious act.

The Plan to Kill Abhimanyu

The incident that led to Abhimanyu's death took place on the **13th day of the Kurukshetra War**, when the Kauravas, led by **Duryodhana**, decided to use the **Chakravyuha** formation to corner and kill the young Pandava prince. The Chakravyuha was a complex military formation, known for its concentric circular arrangement that would create a virtually impenetrable defense. It was famously difficult to break through, and only a handful of warriors knew how to enter and exit the formation safely. **Arjuna**, the greatest archer and warrior of the Pandavas, was the only one who knew the secret of breaking the Chakravyuha. However, **Arjuna** was not present on the battlefield that day because he was engaged elsewhere, protecting the **northern front** of the Pandava army. This strategic absence set the stage for the fatal trap that the Kauravas would lay.

Abhimanyu, though only a young warrior, was extremely skilled in warfare and had been trained in the art of fighting by his father, Arjuna. He knew how to break into the Chakravyuha, but he had not been taught the method to exit the formation. **Lord Krishna** had specifically warned **Yudhishthira** and others about the danger of the Chakravyuha, and how dangerous it could be if Abhimanyu were left alone to fight inside. However, the Pandavas, misjudging Abhimanyu's ability to hold his ground alone, allowed him to enter the formation, believing that the support from other warriors would be enough to ensure his safety.

The Execution of the Killing

Once inside the Chakravyuha, **Abhimanyu** fought bravely, as he single-handedly held off a large number of Kaurava warriors. His courage and skill were unmatched, and he killed many Kaurava soldiers. However, because of his age and limited experience, Abhimanyu was unable to break out of the formation once he had entered. He had been surrounded, and no one from the Pandava side could reach him in time to assist. As the day wore on, **the Kauravas decided to**

take advantage of the situation and orchestrate his death.

The first step in the plan was to ensure that Abhimanyu was cut off from any possible aid. The Kaurava commanders, including **Duryodhana**, **Dushasana**, **Karna**, and **Jayadratha**, conspired to trap the young warrior within the formation and prevent him from escaping. These leaders were not only determined to kill him but also intended to humiliate him. They knew that **Abhimanyu** was a formidable fighter, and they feared his potential to turn the tide of battle. Therefore, rather than allowing him to fight his way out honorably, they chose to ensure his death by unfair means.

As Abhimanyu continued to battle, **Jayadratha**, the king of Sindhu, played a crucial role in trapping Abhimanyu within the Chakravyuha. **Jayadratha** used his position and his warriors to block all the entrances to the formation, preventing any support from reaching Abhimanyu. The battle that ensued was a massacre. One by one, the Kaurava warriors began attacking Abhimanyu with increasing ferocity, and he was overwhelmed by the sheer number of them.

The first major violation of war rules came when **Karna**, **Duryodhana**, **Ashwatthama**, and others, who had witnessed the fight, decided to attack Abhimanyu in unison, even though he was outnumbered and already severely injured. **Abhimanyu** had already been knocked unconscious at one point, but still, the Kaurava warriors continued their relentless assault.

The cruelty of the attack grew as they employed every possible means to ensure his death. **Karna**, a seasoned warrior, and **Duryodhana**, the Kaurava leader, took part in attacking Abhimanyu when he was vulnerable.

The Specific Participants in Abhimanyu's Death

1.   **Jayadratha**: As the main blocker of Abhimanyu's escape route, **Jayadratha** played a pivotal role in ensuring that the Chakravyuha formation was maintained. He was the one who initially held back the rest of the Pandava army, preventing them from entering to help their son. His actions were cowardly, as he relied on the fact that Abhimanyu would be isolated and outnumbered.

2.   **Karna**: **Karna**'s role in the killing of Abhimanyu was deeply significant. As one of the greatest warriors on the Kaurava side, Karna used his skills to strike Abhimanyu with his weapons when the young prince was already surrounded and had no way to defend himself. Karna's actions were particularly egregious because, despite being one of the most respected warriors, he participated in the unfair killing of an unarmed young prince.

3.   **Duryodhana and Dushasana**: As the chief orchestrators of the Kaurava army's decisions, **Duryodhana** and his brother **Dushasana** were key figures in this cruel plot. They stood by and watched as Abhimanyu was killed, contributing to the sense of betrayal and dishonor that marked their leadership. Their approval of such ruthless tactics proved their

utter lack of scruples and the depths of their animosity towards the Pandavas.

4.   **Ashwatthama**: The son of Dronacharya, **Ashwatthama** was a mighty warrior, and his involvement in Abhimanyu's killing reflects the depth of betrayal within the Kaurava camp. He was not merely a passive onlooker but an active participant in the attack on the young prince. Ashwatthama later would go on to commit his own atrocity by attacking the sleeping Pandava army, but this event marked the start of his descent into villainy.

The Aftermath of Abhimanyu's Death

The killing of Abhimanyu was a turning point in the war. It was not just the death of a brave young prince but a blatant violation of the **code of dharma**, especially the rules of warfare. Abhimanyu was a young warrior who had fought with unparalleled courage, and yet he was attacked by multiple warriors who violated every principle of fair combat.

The **Pandavas**, upon learning of his death, were devastated. **Arjuna** was particularly struck with grief and anger, as he had always considered Abhimanyu a hero in the making, a successor who would carry on his legacy. His fatherly affection for Abhimanyu was profound, and he vowed to exact justice. This tragic loss fueled Arjuna's rage and determination to defeat the Kauravas. The death of Abhimanyu marked the beginning of a more brutal phase in the war.

Krishna, who had witnessed the entire event, was also deeply moved by the injustice of Abhimanyu's death. He reminded Arjuna that this was a consequence of the Kauravas' unchecked cruelty and that the moral failure of the Kaurava side had sealed their fate. Abhimanyu's death became a rallying cry for the Pandavas, who were now more determined than ever to win the war and avenge the loss of their beloved son and nephew.

Abhimanyu's killing is remembered as an act of dishonor, and it set the stage for the downfall of the Kauravas. It illustrated their cowardice and lack of respect for the very codes of war that governed their existence, marking the beginning of their inevitable defeat.

5.   Duryodhana's Refusal to Accept Krishna's Peace Proposal.

Very few people know about the entire episode of Krishna's approach to Duryodhana with the proposal. Who were the people involved in the decision making? Why this proposal was made? Why it was important? What were the expected pros and cons? Lastly, what was the lesson taken from this incident? From management point of view was it right decision?

The refusal of **Duryodhana** to accept **Krishna's peace proposal** is one of the most significant events in the **Mahabharata**, encapsulating the complexities of leadership, pride, and decision-making. Krishna's attempt to mediate a peace agreement between the **Pandavas** and the **Kauravas** is a crucial moment in the epic, and the decision to refuse Krishna's peace offer ultimately set the stage for the **Kurukshetra War**, a devastating conflict that resulted in the annihilation of the Kaurava clan. Understanding the circumstances behind Duryodhana's refusal, the people involved, and the consequences of his decision offers key insights into leadership, strategy, and human behavior.

The Proposal and Its Importance

Krishna's peace proposal was made as a final attempt to avoid the **Kurukshetra War**. He traveled to **Hastinapura** as a messenger on behalf of the Pandavas, offering **Duryodhana** a solution that could spare the lives of millions. The proposal was simple but powerful: the Pandavas were willing to live in peace with the Kauravas if they were granted at least a small piece of land to rule. This was not about taking the throne but simply securing a rightful share of the land that was theirs by birth. Krishna, as the divine messenger, knew that such a proposal was just and based on fairness.

Krishna's proposal was important for several reasons:

1.   **Preserving Life and Resources**: The war would result in the death of many, not only warriors but civilians too, leading to irreversible destruction. By accepting the peace proposal, the Kauravas could have avoided this bloodshed.

2.   **Upholding Dharma**: Krishna, though on the side of the Pandavas, recognized that the Kauravas were also entitled to rule, but not at the expense of the Pandavas' birthright. His proposal reflected a fair

solution based on the principles of **dharma** (righteousness).

3.   **Divine Intervention**: Krishna was not just a political envoy; as an incarnation of **Vishnu**, his approach to peace carried divine significance. Accepting his offer would have been seen as an acceptance of divine will, a chance for reconciliation and justice.

The Decision-Making Process and People Involved

The decision to accept or reject Krishna's proposal was not solely Duryodhana's. The key players involved in the decision-making process were:

1.   **Duryodhana**: The Kaurava prince, whose pride and sense of entitlement to the throne made him dismiss the proposal outright. He was deeply influenced by his ego, his jealousy of the Pandavas, and his blind loyalty to his elders.

2.   **Shakuni**: The maternal uncle of Duryodhana, and the mastermind behind many of the Kauravas' schemes, including the infamous dice game. Shakuni had a long-standing vendetta against the Pandavas and saw Krishna's proposal as a threat to the Kaurava clan's power.

3.   **Dronacharya and Bhishma**: These two were the senior-most figures in the Kaurava camp. While Bhishma was known for his commitment to duty, his **vow of celibacy,** and his loyalty to the throne of Hastinapura, Dronacharya was more of a strategist and

teacher. However, both had long struggled with internal conflict between their duty to Duryodhana and their sense of justice towards the Pandavas.

4. **Karna**: A close ally of Duryodhana, Karna was unwavering in his support for the Kaurava cause. Despite knowing that the Pandavas were just, his deep friendship with Duryodhana clouded his judgment, and he played a pivotal role in persuading Duryodhana to reject Krishna's offer.

5. **Vidura**: A voice of wisdom and reason within the Kaurava family, Vidura had consistently advised Duryodhana to reconcile with the Pandavas. However, he was often ignored by Duryodhana, whose decisions were swayed by his emotions and those of his advisors.

Why Was the Proposal Made?

The peace proposal was a final effort to prevent the inevitable war. Krishna, being aware of the Kauravas' growing aggression and the pride of Duryodhana, understood that only a divine intervention could prevent the war. Krishna's intent was to provide an opportunity for reconciliation, offering peace before the situation spiraled into a disastrous conflict. He hoped that the offer of a small piece of land for the Pandavas might appeal to Duryodhana's sense of reason and avoid further bloodshed. Krishna knew that the war, though destined, could still be postponed if the Kauravas accepted the offer.

Expected Pros and Cons of the Proposal

Pros:

1.　　**Prevention of War**: The most obvious benefit would be the avoidance of war, which would save countless lives and preserve the prosperity of Hastinapura.

2.　　**Maintaining Peace**: It would allow both the Kauravas and Pandavas to continue to rule their domains without conflict. The two parties could coexist, potentially leading to an alliance.

3.　　**Upholding Dharma**: By accepting Krishna's offer, Duryodhana would have preserved his reputation as a just ruler who values peace and righteousness.

Cons:

1.　　**Perceived Weakness**: For Duryodhana, accepting the proposal might have been perceived as a defeat, diminishing his claim to the throne and damaging his pride. He felt that agreeing to this would mean acknowledging the Pandavas' superior claim to the kingdom.

2.　　**Influence of Advisors**: Duryodhana's decision was heavily influenced by **Shakuni**, who was known for his cunning and manipulative nature. Shakuni's influence pushed Duryodhana towards war rather than peace, promising him that victory would lead to greater power.

Duryodhana's Refusal: The Lesson

Duryodhana's refusal to accept Krishna's peace proposal led to one of the most devastating wars in Indian history. The lesson from this episode is a powerful one, particularly in leadership and management. Duryodhana's decision was based on **pride**, **ego**, and **insecurity**. His failure to see the bigger picture, to recognize the opportunity to lead with wisdom, and to choose peace over war reflected poor leadership and decision-making. **Pride clouded his judgment**, and in his refusal to compromise, he brought about the annihilation of his family and the destruction of his kingdom.

From a **management perspective**, Duryodhana's decision was a classic example of **poor decision-making** driven by personal emotions and external influence. A true leader needs to make decisions based on **long-term benefits**, **rationality**, and **justice**, rather than impulsive reactions to pride or fear. Krishna's proposal was an opportunity to achieve peace, and rejecting it cost Duryodhana everything.

Krishna, on the other hand, exhibited the qualities of an effective leader by offering a solution that preserved the possibility of peace, highlighting that **leadership is about serving the greater good**, even when the situation seems dire. By offering peace, Krishna demonstrated his profound understanding of dharma and the importance of foresight in leadership.

In conclusion, Duryodhana's refusal of Krishna's peace proposal was not just a personal failure; it was a failure of leadership and vision. His refusal sealed the fate of the Kauravas; while Krishna's wisdom and foresight would go on to guide the Pandavas towards their ultimate victory.

Chapter Five - Ten Influential Sages of Mahabharata

1. Vyasa (Krishna Dvaipayana Vyasa)

Illustrious Career

Vyasa is one of the most revered sages in Hindu tradition. He is the author of the **Mahabharata**, **Puranas**, and is credited with composing the **Vedanta** texts. Vyasa's role is vast and transcends any one individual story or moment; his career is defined by his spiritual and scholarly contributions that span across generations. Vyasa is considered to be the "compiler" of the Vedas, as he divided the ancient Vedic texts into four parts to make them more accessible to society. This act of organizing the Vedas laid the foundation for the preservation and transmission of ancient knowledge. He was the son of the sage Parashara and Satyavati, and his life itself is enveloped in divine purpose.

Vyasa's role in the **Mahabharata** is even more profound. Not only is he the narrator, but he is also the father of **Dhritarashtra**, **Pandu**, and **Vidura**, all significant figures in the epic. Vyasa's birth is itself surrounded by extraordinary circumstances. His father Parashara was a great sage, and Vyasa's mother, Satyavati, was a fisherwoman, yet she was chosen by the divine to bear a son who would be the greatest compiler of knowledge and creator of epics. His intellectual contributions and the subsequent creation of the **Mahabharata** had a far-reaching influence on the Indian culture and the concept of dharma (righteousness), guiding kings, rulers, and common people alike.

Contributions to the Kingdom

Vyasa's contributions to the Kuru dynasty are notable not only in terms of his direct influence on the rulers but also through the lineages he established. His sons—Dhritarashtra, Pandu, and Vidura—were essential to the unfolding of the events in the Mahabharata. As the father of Dhritarashtra, the blind king of the Kuru dynasty, Vyasa established a ruler who would have to navigate the complicated politics and warfare of the epic despite his physical limitations. His son Pandu, though not a direct ruler due to his self-imposed exile, became the father of the five Pandavas, the central protagonists of the Mahabharata. Vidura, Vyasa's third son, was known for his wisdom and sense of justice. He became the Prime Minister of the Kuru kingdom and acted as an advisor during the crucial moments in the epic, even though he had no direct claim to the throne.

Vyasa's role as a teacher was also monumental. His advice and guidance were sought by kings and princes, both in the Kuru kingdom and beyond. His most significant contribution came during the time of the Kurukshetra War. When the Pandavas were exiled, Vyasa visited them and reassured them of their eventual return to power, showing the importance of patience, fate, and destiny in the journey of dharma. His words were deeply philosophical, urging the Pandavas to remain steadfast in their adherence to dharma, no matter the trials they faced.

Additionally, Vyasa provided counsel to both the Kauravas and the Pandavas during their moments of distress, helping them to navigate their complex roles in the impending war. This duality of teaching and wisdom demonstrated Vyasa's neutrality and sense of cosmic order, as he did not take sides, instead promoting the principles of righteousness above all.

Teaching and Preaching

Vyasa's teachings are primarily based on the eternal truths of dharma, karma, and moksha. His understanding of the divine order, human life, and its impermanence are evident in the philosophical underpinnings of the **Mahabharata**. He emphasized the importance of balance between personal desires and public duty. Throughout the Mahabharata, Vyasa encourages various characters to follow their dharma, no matter how difficult or seemingly unjust their circumstances may appear.

For example, when **Yudhishthira**, the eldest of the Pandavas, was deeply troubled by the moral complexities of the war, Vyasa's counsel was instrumental. He reassured him that the path of righteousness, even when surrounded by darkness, is always the right one. Vyasa's influence as a teacher was not just confined to the royal court; it permeated the entire narrative of the Mahabharata, giving the story its philosophical depth and relevance.

Moreover, Vyasa's greatest contribution was the **Mahabharata** itself, which is not merely a war story, but a **"Dharmashastra"** (book of dharma). Through the dialogues between various characters, Vyasa illustrates the moral ambiguities that define human nature, the importance of truth, the necessity of sacrifice, and the divine's role in human affairs.

Importance and Neglect

While Vyasa's importance in the Mahabharata is undeniable, he remains one of the most neglected figures in the epic in terms of personal narrative. While his wisdom shaped the actions of every major character in the epic, Vyasa is often seen as a remote and almost divine figure, whose influence is indirect rather than active. His own personal story—his troubled relationships with his sons (especially Dhritarashtra and Pandu) and his own emotional struggles—are often relegated to the background. Vyasa, as a character, is often overshadowed by his sons, the Pandavas, and the war itself, leading to a general underappreciation of his personal journey.

Moreover, Vyasa's neutrality during the war can sometimes be seen as indifference, as he refrains from taking sides in the conflict. Though this detachment is a reflection of his understanding of the larger cosmic order, it may be seen by some as a lack of engagement in the moral struggles of the time. His essential role in the cosmic design often takes precedence over his personal emotions or struggles, which leaves his character less explored compared to the more active warriors and kings.

Finally, Vyasa's role in the Mahabharata, as a sage and narrator, places him above the mortal realm, leading to a deification that limits his relatability to modern audiences. While revered, his character is often viewed more as an instrument for revealing universal truths than as a fully realized person in the epic. This might explain why Vyasa is frequently neglected in narratives centered around individual heroism, passion, or tragedy.

Conclusion

Vyasa, as the author, philosopher, and teacher in the **Mahabharata**, is irreplaceable. His wisdom transcends time and culture, offering profound insights into life, duty, and morality. Despite this, he is often overlooked as a character in his own right, with his role reduced to that of a divine narrator and neutral figure. Vyasa's contributions to the kingdom of Kuru and the broader moral landscape of the Mahabharata are unparalleled, yet his personal struggles and the depth of his character remain underexplored, making him a neglected figure in the epic's narrative. Nonetheless, his teachings remain central to the enduring relevance of the Mahabharata as a timeless guide to dharma and life itself.

2. Sage Narada

Illustrious Career

Sage **Narada**, often referred to as **Narada Muni**, is one of the most significant and multifaceted sages in the Hindu tradition. He is considered the eternal wanderer, the divine sage who is present in all three worlds—heaven, earth, and the underworld. Narada's illustrious career is defined by his role as a messenger of the gods, a devout sage, and a cultural and spiritual mentor to both celestial beings and mortals alike.

Narada is often portrayed as the embodiment of the **bhakti** (devotion) movement, a forerunner of the devotional philosophies that would later become prominent in Indian spiritual thought. He is most famously known for being a direct devotee of **Lord Vishnu** and is considered the first sage to have promoted the idea of **sankirtana** (the congregational chanting of the divine names), particularly the chanting of **Vishnu's name**. Narada is also closely associated with the spread of **knowledge** and **wisdom**, carrying with him the knowledge of the universe, its secrets, and divine will.

Narada is unique in that he is often depicted as an ever-present figure in various mythological narratives, moving from one place to another and shaping the course of events by inspiring individuals, both divine and human. He is considered the **Adhyatma Vidya** (spiritual knowledge) bearer and the one who bridges the gap between different worlds, disseminating divine messages, and often playing a crucial role in resolving conflicts.

In the **Mahabharata**, Narada's role is primarily that of a guide and counselor, although his presence is marked by both his wisdom and his playful, mischievous nature. He often intervenes at pivotal moments in the epic, imparting critical knowledge and advice to various characters, but he also orchestrates events from behind the scenes with his subtle influence.

Contributions to the Kingdom

Narada's role in the **Mahabharata** is far-reaching and influential. While he is not directly involved in the governance of any kingdom, his spiritual guidance and interventions had profound effects on the major characters, especially **Dhritarashtra**, **Vidura**, and **Krishna**.

• **Vidura**, who was both a son of Vyasa and a wise counselor to King Dhritarashtra, often received teachings from Narada. It was Narada who advised **Vidura** on the significance of righteousness and dharma. Vidura's own wisdom and role as an advisor were strengthened by his association with Narada, making him a key figure in upholding the moral order within the Kuru dynasty.

• Narada's influence also extended to **Dhritarashtra**, the blind king, as he delivered important messages about the unfolding events and divine justice. Though he was unable to see the physical world, Dhritarashtra often relied on Narada's wisdom to understand the deeper cosmic order and the reasons behind the impending destruction.

• Narada's contributions were more significant in shaping the political landscape of the Kurukshetra War through his interactions with **Lord Krishna**. It was Narada who foretold the great conflict, and his guidance helped Krishna navigate the moral and political complexities of the war. Narada's presence during critical moments, including his advice to the Pandavas and Kauravas, helped set the stage for the eventual rise of the Pandavas and the fall of the Kauravas.

While his direct influence was more spiritual than political, Narada's ability to shape the course of events by urging characters to remain steadfast in their devotion to dharma made him an invaluable figure in the epic.

Teaching and Preaching

Narada's teachings were based on the principles of **devotion (bhakti)**, **righteousness (dharma)**, and **spiritual wisdom**. He was a great promoter of **Vishnu bhakti**, encouraging individuals to focus on the divine and surrender to it wholeheartedly. Narada's most famous teaching was his emphasis on the importance of the **name of God**, particularly the chanting of **Vishnu's name**, which was said to free individuals from the cycles of birth and death. His propagation of **sankirtana** the collective chanting of divine names— was central to his teachings.

In the Mahabharata, Narada is often depicted as a spiritual guide who advises not just the kings and warriors, but also sages and gods. He preached that true victory lies not in material wealth or power, but in adhering to righteousness, devotion, and the ultimate surrender to the divine will. His teachings to the Pandavas, especially during their exile, were filled with wisdom on how to endure adversity and remain unwavering in their commitment to dharma, even when faced with overwhelming odds.

He also often acted as an intermediary between the gods and humans, transmitting divine knowledge to mortals. Through his interventions, he served to align the actions of various characters with divine will, ensuring that the ultimate victory of dharma would be achieved, even if the journey was fraught with struggle.

Narada's profound influence is particularly visible in his advice to **Yudhishthira**. When Yudhishthira faced the moral dilemmas associated with the game of dice, Narada's wisdom helped him understand the greater cosmic purpose behind the suffering, while urging him to stay focused on dharma and the larger picture.

Importance and Neglect

Narada's importance in the **Mahabharata** is immense, yet he is often an overlooked figure compared to the warriors, kings, and even the more dominant gods and goddesses in the epic. His role as a **spiritual catalyst**, rather than a direct participant in physical combat or politics, contributes to his often subtle presence in the narrative. Narada's importance is not as a physical warrior but as a spiritual one, whose actions guide characters through the murky waters of moral complexity and divine destiny.

While he remains a beloved figure in Hinduism—especially in devotional traditions—his full significance is often neglected in the grand scope of epic literature. His role in shaping the unfolding events and influencing key characters' decisions through divine wisdom sometimes makes his presence seem more like that of a behind-the-scenes orchestrator, thus reducing his visibility in the epic's popular narratives.

Additionally, the modern interpretation of Narada's character sometimes leans heavily on his playful and mischievous nature, which overshadows the depth of his philosophical contributions. His **Bhakti** movement, which laid the foundation for later spiritual philosophies, is often not given due credit in mainstream discussions, leading to a reduced recognition of his critical role in the epic and in the broader tradition of Indian spiritual thought.

Narada's preaching of **Bhakti**, his establishment of a deeper relationship with the divine, and his constant movement across realms can also be seen as a metaphor for the soul's journey toward spiritual liberation. In this context, his teachings are immensely important, though they often do not receive the attention they deserve in the broader, action-centric narratives of the Mahabharata.

Conclusion

Sage Narada's influence in the **Mahabharata** and his broader contributions to Hindu thought are undeniable. His role as a divine messenger, guide, and teacher to the great figures of the epic has shaped the spiritual and moral fabric of the story. Though his direct involvement in the epic's central events is limited, his indirect influence and his emphasis on **devotion** and **righteousness** are pivotal in shaping the course of history and providing the moral backbone for the tale. His character, which combines wisdom with a sense of divine playfulness, reminds us of the importance of devotion, humility, and surrender to the divine will, which are sometimes neglected in the rush of material pursuit.

3. Sage Vashistha

Illustrious Career

Sage Vashistha, one of the most revered sages in Hindu tradition, holds an esteemed position in both the **Mahabharata** and **Ramayana**. Vasishtha is often described as the **Kulapati (family teacher)** of the **Ikshvaku dynasty** and a primary **sage** of the **Brahma Rishi** category. He is considered one of the **Saptarishis** (Seven Great Sages) and is revered as a teacher of unparalleled wisdom and knowledge. His career spanned across multiple generations of rulers, and he was the spiritual guide to numerous kings, including **King Dasharatha** (the father of Lord Rama).

Vashistha's illustrious career began with his deep knowledge of the **Vedas**, the **Upanishads**, and **spiritual practices**, making him the highest authority on dharma (righteousness) and karma (actions). As a powerful sage, Vashistha was instrumental in shaping the political and spiritual landscape of ancient India.

His influence extended to not just earthly rulers, but also to gods and sages, bridging the gap between divine knowledge and human life.

One of the pivotal moments in Vashistha's career was his involvement with the story of **King Shantanu** and **Sage Vashistha's relationship** with him. Vashistha also plays a critical role in maintaining the balance of dharma and ensuring that the duties of kingship are carried out in alignment with divine law.

Vashistha's greatest contribution was in his role as the teacher of the ruling families, particularly his role as the mentor to **Lord Rama**'s family and his involvement in shaping the character of several royal dynasties in the Mahabharata, most notably the **Kuru dynasty**. He taught kings how to be just, compassionate rulers and how to govern with a strong adherence to **truth** and **justice**.

Contributions to the Kingdom

Sage Vashistha played a critical role in establishing the spiritual and moral framework upon which the kingdoms were run. His advice to kings such as **Dasharatha**, **Shantanu**, and others significantly impacted the governance and the moral direction of their kingdoms.

1.   **King Dasharatha**: Vashistha was the revered teacher and spiritual guide to King Dasharatha of **Ayodhya**. The King, who faced immense challenges in fulfilling his duties, relied on Vashistha's counsel to govern with wisdom and righteousness. One of the

most well-known stories involving Vashistha is when he helped resolve a dispute between the king and his priests, guiding Dasharatha in his decision to have **Lord Rama** crowned as the successor to the throne.

2.   **King Shantanu**: Vashistha's guidance was also pivotal during the reign of **King Shantanu**, the father of **Bhishma**. When the king's kingdom faced the challenge of choosing an heir, Vashistha stepped in and taught Shantanu about the value of dharma, particularly in relation to the responsibilities of a ruler. His insights helped ensure that Shantanu's decisions were just and in accordance with the greater good of the kingdom.

3.   **The Kuru Dynasty**: In the **Mahabharata**, Vashistha's contributions to the Kuru dynasty are notable. His influence on **King Dhritarashtra**, **Vidura**, and **Bhishma** helped guide the kingdom during critical periods of conflict, especially when the Kauravas and Pandavas were embroiled in the intense rivalry that led to the Kurukshetra War. He provided counsel on matters of **dharma**, the legitimacy of the throne, and the moral conduct of the royal family. Though he was not actively involved in the events of the war, his role as a moral compass for the Kurus cannot be overstated.

In addition to his direct influence on rulers, Vashistha is credited with many contributions to **spiritual teachings** and **sacred knowledge**, especially as a transmitter of the **Vedic traditions**. His teachings on the **nature of the self**, the **universe**, and the **path to**

spiritual liberation have left a lasting impact on the philosophical traditions of India.

Teaching and Preaching

Vasishtha's teachings were foundational to the formation of many spiritual practices and moral codes in ancient Indian society. His focus on **dharma, truth**, and **wisdom** was integral in shaping the conduct of both kings and sages. Some of the key themes of his teachings include:

1.   **Adherence   to   Dharma**:   Vasishtha emphasized that a ruler's duty is to protect and promote **dharma**—the ethical path of righteousness. He stressed that kings should always govern in accordance with the greater cosmic order and make decisions that are just, even if it requires personal sacrifice. This focus on dharma served as the moral foundation for the kingdoms and provided rulers with the tools to act wisely and compassionately.

2.   **Spiritual Knowledge and Self-realization**: In addition to his role as a teacher of kings, Vasishtha also imparted profound spiritual knowledge. His teachings on the **nature of the soul**, the universe, and the connection between all living beings are central to the Vedic tradition. His discussions of **Atman (self)**, **Brahman (the ultimate reality)**, and **Maya (illusion)** served to deepen the understanding of the cosmos and one's place within it. This knowledge is encapsulated in the famous dialogue between Vasishtha and **Lord Rama** in the **Yoga Vasistha**, a

text that explores the philosophy of **yoga** and **meditation**.

3.   **Ethical Governance**: Vasishtha's teachings were also focused on **ethical governance**. He promoted the idea that rulers should consider the welfare of all citizens, practice **non-violence**, and ensure the prosperity of the people. His focus on **sacrifice, non-attachment**, and **service to others** made his teachings a holistic guide to ruling justly and living virtuously.

4.   **The Power of Knowledge**: Vasishtha's commitment to **knowledge** was not just spiritual but also intellectual. He is credited with authoring several important works in the Vedic tradition, including teachings on **mantras, sacrificial rituals**, and **spiritual practices**. His vast knowledge of the universe and the metaphysical realm was deeply respected by both the gods and mortals alike.

Importance and Neglect

While Vasishtha's role in shaping the moral and spiritual direction of India cannot be overstated, he remains a somewhat overlooked figure in the popular retelling of epic tales, especially in comparison to more visible figures like Lord Krishna, Arjuna, or Bhishma.

The importance of Vasishtha lies in his foundational contributions to the moral and spiritual teachings that guided the royal families and sages of his time. He is the embodiment of wisdom and **spiritual enlightenment**, yet his significance is often overshadowed by more active protagonists in the epics. This neglect may be due to his quieter, more passive role in the epic events, as Vasishtha's power was not in physical action but in the guidance he offered behind the scenes.

Another reason for his neglect could be the fact that his teachings are often philosophical and spiritual in nature, making them more abstract and difficult for many to comprehend fully. This is in contrast to more tangible actions in the epics, such as the battles of the Kurukshetra War or the heroic feats of warriors.

Despite his seemingly understated role in the **Mahabharata**, Vasishtha remains a central figure in Hindu philosophy and spiritual teachings. His contributions to **Vedanta**, **yoga**, and **ethical governance** continue to resonate in the lives of those who seek wisdom and truth in the modern world. However, as with many great sages, his full significance is often recognized only by those deeply involved in spiritual practices and philosophical study, leading to a relative neglect of his contributions in the mainstream narrative of the epic.

Conclusion

Sage Vasishtha's contributions to the **Mahabharata** and the wider spiritual and political landscape of ancient India are profound. His teachings on **dharma**, **spiritual wisdom**, and **ethical governance** remain central to the Indian way of life. Despite his immense influence on kings, sages, and the very course of the epic, his role is sometimes overshadowed by other more active participants. Yet, his legacy as a guiding light for righteousness and his profound philosophical teachings continue to endure, making him one of the most important yet often neglected figures in Hinduism and in the Mahabharata itself.

4. Sage Bharadwaj

Illustrious Career

Sage Bharadwaj is one of the most respected and influential sages in the Mahabharata and in Vedic tradition. He is considered one of the **Saptarishi** (Seven Great Sages) and holds a unique position among the ancient sages for his profound knowledge in multiple fields, including **philosophy**, **medicine**, **astronomy**, and **military strategy**. Bharadwaj is often seen as an embodiment of wisdom and learning, revered for his intellectual capacity, spiritual insights, and contributions to various domains of knowledge. His life story is filled with accomplishments that not only shaped the spiritual landscape of ancient India but also left an indelible mark on various sciences.

Bharadwaj's career spanned many significant contributions to both **Vedic knowledge** and **worldly wisdom**. He was a pivotal figure in many important narratives in the Vedic texts, and his teachings were a source of guidance for kings, warriors, and spiritual seekers. His knowledge of **yajnas (sacrificial rites)** and **vedic hymns** was highly respected. Sage Bharadwaj's career is particularly noted for his contributions to the foundation of the **Vedic education system**, where he taught numerous disciples, some of whom became legends in their own right.

One of the significant episodes that highlight Bharadwaj's illustrious career is his involvement in the **Mahabharata**, where he plays a critical role in offering guidance to both the **Pandavas** and the **Kauravas**. Though he is not as prominently featured in the epic as figures like **Bhishma**, **Drona**, or **Krishna**, his contributions are still deeply impactful and reflect the underlying knowledge systems that shaped the epic's unfolding.

Bharadwaj's most famous disciples included figures such as **Drona**, who became the teacher of the Kuru princes, and **Kautilya**, the renowned scholar and strategist. It is believed that Bharadwaj's guidance influenced the development of the martial arts and military tactics that were later taught to the Kuru princes, including the Pandavas and Kauravas. Additionally, Bharadwaj's teachings on governance and leadership, which combined both spiritual and practical knowledge, were instrumental in shaping the future of the kingdoms he served.

Contributions to the Kingdom

Sage Bharadwaj's contributions to the kingdoms of his time were extensive and varied, particularly in the fields of **education**, **governance**, **military strategy**, and **medicine**. His teachings were not limited to spiritual matters but also had practical implications for rulers and military leaders.

1.   **Teacher to Kings and Warriors**: Bharadwaj was one of the foremost teachers to the **Kuru princes**, and his guidance shaped the future of both the **Pandavas** and the **Kauravas**. As a mentor, he was concerned with developing not only the spiritual and philosophical knowledge of his disciples but also their **physical training** and **strategic acumen**. Bharadwaj played a crucial role in shaping the military training of warriors like **Drona**, and his teachings were later passed on to the next generation of Kuru warriors. He was regarded as a well-rounded teacher who understood the balance between spiritual purity and the practicalities of ruling and fighting wars.

2.   **Strategist and Tactician**: Bharadwaj's knowledge of military strategy was highly regarded, and he is often associated with developing advanced techniques in **archery** and **battle tactics**. His strategies were used during the Kurukshetra War to outwit opponents and strategize the course of battles. Though Drona is more widely recognized for his direct involvement in training the Kuru princes, Bharadwaj's influence was profound in laying the groundwork for such teaching.

3.   **Advocate of Dharma**: One of the core aspects of Bharadwaj's teachings to kings and princes was the promotion of **dharma** or righteous conduct. He emphasized that rulers must be just, fair, and wise in their decisions, and their actions should always serve the welfare of their kingdom and people. Bharadwaj's wisdom was foundational in the development of the

Kuru dynasty's moral and ethical guidelines. In many ways, his teachings laid the philosophical groundwork that governed the actions of the heroes of the Mahabharata.

4. **Medicine and Healing**: Another area where Sage Bharadwaj contributed significantly was in the field of medicine. He is often credited with authoring medical treatises that addressed the **science of healing**, and it is said that his expertise in the **Ayurvedic tradition** led him to develop methods for curing various ailments and treating injuries. His influence in the medical field was significant enough that he is often regarded as one of the founding figures of the **Ayurvedic system of medicine**.

5. **Astronomy and Mathematics**: Bharadwaj is also revered for his contributions to **astronomy** and **mathematics**, disciplines that were vital to the governance and administration of kingdoms. His works on the **movement of celestial bodies** and the use of **mathematical principles** for accurate measurements were integral in the functioning of ancient India's timekeeping and navigation systems.

Teaching and Preaching

Sage Bharadwaj's contributions were not limited to theoretical knowledge; he was also a teacher who imparted practical wisdom in various fields of knowledge.

1. **Spiritual Wisdom**: Bharadwaj was an ardent devotee of **Lord Shiva** and imparted the knowledge of

Vedanta, Upanishadic philosophy, and **meditation**. His teachings emphasized the importance of inner peace, detachment, and the recognition of the ultimate **Brahman** (the ultimate reality). His spiritual teachings were not only directed toward spiritual aspirants but were also woven into his teachings for kings, helping them achieve not just political success but also personal growth and enlightenment.

2.   **Role as a Teacher of the Martial Arts**: Bharadwaj was instrumental in the training of warriors in various forms of martial arts, particularly **archery** and **swordsmanship**. His disciples, such as **Drona**, were among the best archers and warriors of their time. Bharadwaj's deep understanding of **military strategy** and his ability to pass on these skills made him a key figure in shaping the Kuru dynasty's martial prowess.

3.   **Teaching Dharma to Kings**: Bharadwaj is also known for his philosophical teachings on **kingship** and **dharma**. He taught rulers that their duty was to serve their people and uphold righteousness at all costs. He believed that a king's **dharma** was not merely to rule but to protect the people from harm, ensure justice, and preserve the welfare of the state. Bharadwaj's teachings on **equity**, **justice**, and **compassion** influenced many kings of his time, including the Kaurava and Pandava kings.

4.   **Teachings on Righteous Conduct**: One of the key themes in Bharadwaj's teachings was the importance of adhering to **righteous conduct** in all matters of life. He taught his disciples that actions

performed without selfish motives and aligned with **truth** and **dharma** were the true path to **spiritual liberation**. His teachings on **dharma** were especially relevant during times of conflict, such as the impending war in the Mahabharata, where righteous conduct was a central issue.

Importance and Neglect

While Bharadwaj's contributions are immense, his figure is not as celebrated in popular culture as other prominent characters of the Mahabharata, such as **Krishna**, **Bhishma**, or **Drona**. This relative neglect may be attributed to the fact that he played more of a behind-the-scenes role in the epic, providing guidance and knowledge to others rather than directly engaging in the conflicts of the Mahabharata.

Despite his immense wisdom and influence, Bharadwaj's contributions have been overshadowed by the actions of more visible characters. His teachings were foundational to the success of many key figures in the Mahabharata, yet he himself did not take part in the war or the central narrative.

However, the significance of Bharadwaj's teachings in shaping the moral and spiritual framework of ancient India cannot be denied. He continues to be revered by those who study the ancient sciences, philosophy, and the intricacies of royal governance. His legacy as a teacher, healer, and philosopher lives on, even if his name is less prominent in the mainstream narrative of the Mahabharata.

Conclusion

Sage Bharadwaj's contributions to the Mahabharata and ancient Indian knowledge systems are vast and varied. From spiritual wisdom to military strategy, his teachings shaped the trajectory of the Kuru dynasty and the kingdoms of ancient India. While his role may seem understated in comparison to the more prominent figures of the Mahabharata, Bharadwaj's legacy as a teacher, strategist, healer, and philosopher endures, making him an indispensable figure in the epic and in the spiritual and intellectual traditions of India.

5. Sage Agastya

Illustrious Career

Sage Agastya is one of the most revered sages in Hindu mythology, known for his immense contributions to both the **spiritual** and **practical** aspects of life. He is a prominent figure in the **Mahabharata**, as well as in other ancient texts such as the **Ramayana**, the **Vedas**, and various Puranas. Agastya is believed to be one of the **Saptarishi** (Seven Great Sages), the ancient seers who imparted wisdom that helped lay the foundation for Vedic knowledge and spirituality. He is known for his legendary intellect, deep spirituality, and unparalleled influence on the development of the spiritual and cultural landscape of ancient India.

Sage Agastya's career spans multiple domains: **spiritual teacher, warrior, sage-astronomer**, and **philosopher**. His name is synonymous with great learning and divine blessings, and he is often depicted as the **spiritual progenitor** of numerous dynasties and the author of several hymns in the **Rigveda**. Agastya's wisdom and teachings influenced not only kings, warriors, and scholars but also entire civilizations. His deep knowledge of the natural world, human nature, and cosmic order shaped the philosophical and scientific understanding of his time.

Among Agastya's most significant contributions was his involvement in the **spread of Vedic knowledge**, especially in the **south** of India, where he is credited with establishing several **spiritual centers** and spreading the knowledge of the **Vedas** to distant lands. His works and teachings have impacted multiple disciplines, including **medicine**, **astrology**, **linguistics**, and **music**.

Contributions to the Kingdom

Sage Agastya's contributions to the kingdoms of ancient India were profound, influencing both the spiritual and the material aspects of governance. His insights were sought by kings, warriors, and scholars who wished to understand the deeper laws of the universe and apply them to their rule.

1.   **Spiritual Teacher to Kings**: Agastya was not just a teacher of **Vedic** and **spiritual knowledge** but also a wise counselor to kings. His teachings were instrumental in the governance of various kingdoms, especially in terms of establishing a **moral code of conduct**. He emphasized the importance of **righteousness** (dharma) and **truth** in governance, and

many kings sought his guidance in making just and wise decisions. His teachings on **dharma** helped rulers ensure that their reigns were based on ethical and moral principles, fostering peace and stability.

2.   **Establishment of Spiritual Centers**: Agastya was not only a spiritual teacher but also a **pioneer** in spreading Vedic knowledge across different regions. He is credited with taking the Vedas to the southern parts of India, where his teachings and practices became the foundation of many **spiritual traditions** in South India. It is said that Sage Agastya traveled to places like **Kanchipuram** and **Tiruvannamalai**, where his presence significantly impacted local practices, promoting a synthesis of Vedic knowledge with the cultural traditions of the South.

3.   **Warrior Sage**: Sage Agastya was also a **warrior sage** who fought alongside the **Devas (gods)** to defeat the **Danavas (demons)**. His battle with the **demon Vritra** is one of his most famous exploits, where he helped the gods regain control of the world by defeating the forces of darkness. Agastya's dual nature as both a sage and a warrior highlights his unique position in ancient Indian society. His wisdom in strategy and warfare made him an invaluable ally to those who sought to maintain cosmic order, and his role in many battles, particularly against forces threatening the world's balance, made him a protector of dharma.

4.   **Teacher of Divine Knowledge**: In the Mahabharata, Agastya is portrayed as a teacher of

divine wisdom to **Pandavas** and other key characters. His teachings often involved not only the understanding of spiritual principles but also knowledge regarding **astronomy**, **alchemy**, **medicine**, and **architecture**. His contributions in these fields helped shape the development of **Ayurveda** and **astrology,** as well as the understanding of the universe and its workings. Agastya's wisdom also helped kings and warriors sharpen their decision-making and leadership skills.

5.   **Sage of Nature and Healing**: Agastya's contributions to medicine are legendary. He is often credited with authoring several texts on **herbal medicine,** and his knowledge of **Ayurveda** was passed down for generations. Sage Agastya was known for his ability to cure ailments through the use of natural remedies and healing plants, and his texts are regarded as foundational in the practice of traditional Indian medicine. His healing abilities were legendary, and he was often called upon to provide solutions for both physical and mental ailments.

Teaching and Preaching

Sage Agastya's teachings spanned a vast range of subjects, and his spiritual knowledge was vast and profound. As a teacher, Agastya emphasized not only the importance of **spiritual enlightenment** but also the practical application of that knowledge to daily life. His contributions to various fields were vast, and he provided teachings that were designed to help people achieve success and harmony in both the material and spiritual realms.

1.   **Spiritual Teachings**: Agastya's spiritual teachings emphasized the need for **self-discipline**, **meditation,** and **devotion** to the divine. His teachings were centered around the idea that inner peace could only be achieved through **righteous living** and a deep understanding of the self. Sage Agastya's message was one of devotion, simplicity, and respect for nature. He believed that understanding the **cosmic order** and **nature's laws** was the key to understanding one's place in the world and finding peace.

2.   **Teachings on Righteousness and Governance**: As a counselor to kings, Agastya's teachings on governance were based on the principles of **dharma** and **justice**. He emphasized that rulers must be fair and impartial, ensuring that their kingdom's welfare was the ultimate goal of their reign. He taught that a king's duty was not just to control the kingdom but to **uplift the people** by fostering righteousness, fairness, and social harmony. Agastya's teachings on kingship were foundational to many royal families of his time.

3.   **Role in the Mahabharata**: In the Mahabharata, Agastya plays a significant role in imparting important knowledge to both the Pandavas and the Kauravas. He is one of the sages who contributes to the **Bhishma Parva**, offering wisdom on various aspects of warfare and ethics. Agastya's role in the epic is less prominent in terms of direct action

but is vital in terms of the philosophical underpinnings he provides to the narrative. His teachings on dharma, meditation, and the principles of righteous warfare are critical in guiding the characters through their moral dilemmas.

4.   **Sage of Universal Knowledge**: Agastya's influence in the Mahabharata also extends to his teachings about the universe. He is regarded as one of the greatest scholars of ancient Indian cosmology and **astronomy**, and his teachings on the **creation of the world**, the movement of the **planets**, and the **laws of nature** continue to influence thinkers and scholars. His contributions to the understanding of the cosmos were foundational in shaping the worldview of ancient Indian thinkers and remain an integral part of Indian philosophical thought.

Importance and Neglect

Sage Agastya's importance cannot be overstated, yet, like many sages of his time, his contributions are often overshadowed by other more well-known figures in the Mahabharata. His teachings, though fundamental to the understanding of dharma and cosmic law, are sometimes overshadowed by the larger narratives of the epic, such as the **Bhishma** and **Krishna** stories.

One reason for this neglect may be Agastya's role as a **background figure** who imparts knowledge but does not directly influence the events of the Kurukshetra War. He is revered in **Southern India** and other parts of the Indian subcontinent, where his influence on the **spread of Vedic teachings** is immense. However, his role in the epic is somewhat subdued compared to more action-oriented characters like **Arjuna** or **Krishna**.

Nevertheless, Agastya's contributions to the **spiritual and intellectual heritage of India** are invaluable. His works on medicine, astrology, governance, and warfare continue to be part of the foundational knowledge in Indian culture. His teachings on the unity of all existence, the importance of righteousness, and the quest for self-realization resonate deeply in the hearts of those who seek wisdom.

Conclusion

Sage Agastya remains one of the greatest and most influential figures in Indian history. His **multidimensional contributions** to the spiritual, intellectual, and scientific fields have left a lasting legacy. Though his role in the Mahabharata may not be as central as that of other figures but his wisdom shaped the destiny of both kings and commoners. Agastya's life serves as a reminder of the enduring power of knowledge, dharma, and self-realization, making him one of the most significant sages in the history of ancient India.

6. Sage Kapila

Illustrious Career

Sage Kapila is one of the most celebrated sages in Hindu philosophy, known as the founder of **Samkhya philosophy**, one of the six orthodox systems of Indian philosophy. His teachings had a profound impact on the spiritual and intellectual development of ancient India. Kapila's **Samkhya** is considered one of the oldest and most influential schools of thought in Indian philosophy, and his approach to understanding the universe remains central to many streams of Hindu thought.

Kapila's life and contributions are shrouded in a blend of historical and mythological narratives. He is believed to have been born in **Tretayuga** as the son of the sage **Vishrava** and was thus a part of a divine lineage. Kapila's spiritual and intellectual pursuits began early, and he is credited with extensive teachings in philosophy, cosmology, and metaphysics. His work in **Samkhya** was revolutionary, as it sought to explain the nature of reality through a framework of **dualism** the division of the world into **Purusha** (consciousness) and **Prakriti** (material nature).

Kapila's contribution to the understanding of the human experience and the **liberation of the soul** is central to many spiritual teachings in Hinduism. His philosophy of **non-theistic dualism** was groundbreaking in its time and has influenced both later Hindu philosophies and other schools of Indian thought.

Contributions to the Kingdom

Though Sage Kapila is best known for his philosophical contributions, his influence also extended to governance and the development of societal norms. His teachings, particularly in the realm of **morality** and **dharma**, were respected by rulers and scholars alike.

1.   **Philosophical Contributions to Kingship**: Kapila's teachings on the nature of the universe and the soul influenced rulers in ancient India, especially in terms of their understanding of the self and how it related to governance. He believed that understanding the nature of **Prakriti** (the material world) and **Purusha** (the eternal self) was essential for rulers to govern with wisdom. His teachings on detachment and liberation also guided many kings in making decisions that prioritized the well-being of their citizens over personal gain.

2.   **Moral and Ethical Governance**: Kapila's philosophy also laid the groundwork for **ethical governance**. His ideas about the **nature of good and evil** and the pursuit of truth were instrumental in helping rulers navigate moral dilemmas. His teachings advised kings to avoid attachment to material wealth and power, encouraging them instead to govern with wisdom, justice, and compassion. This helped to establish a moral framework that sought to balance personal ambition with a duty to the greater good of the kingdom.

3.   **Influence on Social Norms**: Kapila's teachings had a significant impact on the social structure and practices of ancient India. His work emphasized the importance of the **individual's liberation** and the recognition of the soul's divine nature, which led to a more enlightened approach to

social order. By elevating the concept of the self, he encouraged people to transcend the rigid social structures of the time, fostering a society that valued individual knowledge and spiritual growth.

4. **Contributions to the Development of Yoga**: While **Patanjali** is often credited with systematizing the practice of **yoga**, Sage Kapila's Samkhya philosophy was foundational in shaping the philosophical underpinnings of yoga. His exploration of the **material world** (Prakriti) and the **spiritual world** (Purusha) set the stage for the development of **yogic practices** that seek to unite the two realms. Kapila's focus on **detachment**, **self-discipline**, and the nature of consciousness became key concepts in yoga practices, influencing later traditions of spiritual awakening.

Teaching and Preaching

Sage Kapila's teachings were far-reaching, with a focus on **philosophical inquiry** and **spiritual liberation**. As the founder of the **Samkhya school**, he advocated for an understanding of the universe based on a system of dualism, where **Purusha** (consciousness) is distinct from **Prakriti** (material nature). This distinction formed the basis for his teachings on human existence, the **nature of suffering**, and the path to **moksha** (liberation from the cycle of birth and death).

1. **Samkhya Philosophy**: Kapila's central philosophical system, **Samkhya**, posits that the universe is made up of two eternal principles: **Purusha** (consciousness) and **Prakriti** (material nature). The

interaction between these two forces gives rise to the entire universe and all its phenomena. According to Kapila, the soul (Purusha) is trapped in the cycle of birth and death due to its entanglement with the material world (Prakriti). The path to **liberation** involves realizing this distinction and seeking detachment from the material world. Kapila taught that true knowledge (Jnana) arises from recognizing the separation between these two realms, leading to the realization of the soul's eternal nature and the cessation of suffering.

2.   **Teaching on Suffering and Liberation**: Sage Kapila emphasized the **nature of suffering** and how attachment to the material world leads to bondage. According to his philosophy, all living beings experience suffering because they are attached to material things, which are temporary and transient. The key to overcoming suffering is through **detachment**, which can be achieved through the understanding of the true nature of reality. Liberation (moksha) is attained when an individual realizes that the material world is separate from the soul and that the ultimate goal of life is to achieve union with the eternal **Purusha**.

3.   **The Role of the Teacher**: Kapila's role as a teacher was not only to impart **theoretical knowledge** but also to provide practical wisdom for achieving spiritual liberation. He taught his disciples through discussions and dialogues, answering their questions on life, death, the universe, and the nature of the self.

His teachings were based on **logical analysis** and encouraged a deep inquiry into the workings of the world. This approach led his students to become **independent thinkers**, who were encouraged to find the truth for themselves through **reasoning** and **introspection**.

4.   **The Relationship Between Knowledge and Action**: Kapila emphasized that true knowledge leads to self-realization and that self-realization requires action. However, he clarified that the action should not be motivated by desire or attachment to the material world but by the desire for **spiritual growth**. This teaching reinforced the idea that one can live a life of purpose while also seeking liberation from worldly attachments.

Importance and Neglect

Sage Kapila's teachings remain among the most profound in Hindu philosophy, and his system of **Samkhya** continues to be studied by scholars and spiritual seekers alike. His philosophy of dualism, focusing on the separation between **Purusha** and **Prakriti**, has influenced numerous later traditions of thought, including **Vedanta** and **yoga**.

Despite his significant influence, Kapila's contributions are often overshadowed by other philosophical schools, particularly **Advaita Vedanta**, which has become the dominant philosophical tradition in modern times. While **Vedanta** focuses on the non-dual nature of reality, Samkhya's dualism presents an alternative approach that is less commonly discussed in mainstream philosophy.

Kapila's teachings on **detachment** and **liberation** are also sometimes neglected in favor of more accessible forms of spirituality or practical teachings that emphasize worldly success. His message of **non-attachment** and the understanding of the soul's true nature is profound but requires deep intellectual engagement, which may deter some from fully appreciating its value.

Conclusion

Sage Kapila remains one of the most important yet often neglected sages in the Mahabharata and the broader landscape of Hindu philosophy. His **Samkhya system** laid the groundwork for much of Indian metaphysics, and his ideas continue to influence spiritual seekers to this day. Kapila's message about the **separation between the material and the spiritual worlds**, the path to **liberation**, and the **nature of suffering** has a timeless relevance, offering profound insights into the human condition. His neglect in modern discussions reflects a wider trend of focusing on more accessible or dominant philosophies, but his work remains a cornerstone of ancient Indian intellectual and spiritual thought.

7. Sage Vyasa (Vedavyasa)

Illustrious Career

Sage Vyasa, also known as **Vedavyasa**, holds a prominent place in the Hindu epic narrative as the author and compiler of the **Mahabharata**, one of the two great epics of India, and the **Vedas**. Vyasa is considered a central figure not only in the Mahabharata but in the development of Hinduism itself, as he is credited with organizing and editing the Vedic texts, writing the **Puranas**, and establishing the philosophical and theological foundations of Hindu thought. Vyasa's career spans several lifetimes, with his most important work being the **Mahabharata**, which he narrates in his role as the narrator and central figure in the epic.

Vyasa is traditionally considered to be the **son of the sage Parashara** and **Satyavati**, a fisherwoman, who later became the queen of King Shantanu of Hastinapura. Vyasa's birth itself was miraculous, and his life and career were marked by profound wisdom and spiritual insight.

In the Mahabharata, Vyasa appears not only as the **author** of the epic but also as an important **character**. His interactions with the central figures of the Mahabharata, such as **Dhritarashtra**, **Vidura**, and **Bhishma**, place him in the heart of the epic's narrative, offering spiritual and philosophical guidance to many of the key characters. His wisdom and guidance are critical in shaping the events that unfold during the Kurukshetra War, as he provides counsel and foresight about the devastating consequences of the conflict.

Contributions to the Kingdom

1.   **Compiler of the Vedas**: Vyasa's role in compiling and organizing the **Vedic texts** is one of his

most enduring contributions to Indian civilization. The Vedas, which were initially passed down orally, were compiled and classified by Vyasa into four distinct collections: **Rigveda, Yajurveda, Samaveda,** and **Atharvaveda**. These texts form the foundational spiritual and philosophical guide for Hindus, covering everything from rituals to metaphysical speculation. Vyasa's systematic organization of the Vedas helped preserve ancient knowledge and ensured its transmission to future generations.

2.   **Mahabharata and Its Moral Teachings**: Vyasa's authorship of the **Mahabharata** is perhaps his greatest contribution. The epic is not just a story of war, but also a deep exploration of **dharma** (duty), **karma** (action), **bhakti** (devotion), and **moksha** (liberation). Through the **Bhagavad Gita**, Vyasa imparted critical spiritual wisdom that would influence not only the Kuru dynasty but the whole of Indian philosophy and religious thought. The epic itself, through the lives of the **Pandavas, Kauravas**, and key figures like **Bhishma** and **Krishna**, encapsulates the complexities of **human nature** and **moral dilemmas** faced by rulers, warriors, and citizens alike.

3.   **Teaching of Dharma**: Vyasa's influence on kingship and governance in the epic is profound. He taught the kings of the Kuru dynasty, particularly King **Dhritarashtra**, the importance of **righteousness** in governance and the heavy consequences of deviating from dharma. He also advised rulers on how to govern in a way that balanced justice and compassion, guiding

them through both moral and political challenges. His teachings, often communicated through his interactions with **Vidura** and **Bhishma**, emphasized the responsibilities of rulers to protect their citizens and uphold justice, even when personal stakes or familial ties were involved.

4. **Spiritual and Philosophical Influence**: Vyasa's philosophical insights in the **Mahabharata** were instrumental in shaping the ethical and spiritual landscape of India. He encouraged characters like **Yudhishthira**, **Arjuna**, and others to find their true path of dharma amidst the tumult of war. Through his teachings, Vyasa emphasized the idea that true knowledge comes not from external success but from **inner clarity**, and that the ultimate goal of life is to achieve liberation from the cycles of birth and death.

5. **The Founding of the Puranas**: Vyasa is also credited with authoring the **Puranas**, a genre of texts that preserves the mythology, history, and spiritual teachings of the ancient world. The **Vishnu Purana**, **Bhagavata Purana**, and several others are attributed to Vyasa, each of which has had a significant impact on the development of Hindu ritual and devotional practices. These texts tell stories of gods and heroes, serve as moral guides, and offer instructions on worship and philosophical contemplation.

Teaching and Preaching

Vyasa's teachings go beyond simple moral advice; they encompass the essence of **spiritual practice**, **righteousness**, and **cosmic wisdom**. His method of teaching was deeply **dialogical**, often involving conversations between students and sages, kings and ascetics. These dialogues provide a framework for understanding the complexities of human life and the divine.

1.   **Dharma and Karma**: At the heart of Vyasa's teachings is the concept of **dharma**—the moral law that governs the universe. Vyasa expounded on the idea that dharma is not a fixed set of rules but a dynamic force that changes according to time, place, and circumstance. His teachings on dharma emphasized **duty**, **compassion**, and the idea of following one's personal and social obligations without attachment to the outcomes. He urged rulers and warriors to act in accordance with their dharma, even in the face of difficult choices, as seen in the character of **Arjuna** during the **Bhagavad Gita** dialogue.

2.   **The Bhagavad Gita**: Perhaps the most famous of Vyasa's spiritual contributions is the **Bhagavad Gita**, a part of the Mahabharata, where Vyasa narrates the conversation between **Lord Krishna** and **Arjuna** on the battlefield of Kurukshetra. In this sacred dialogue, Vyasa presents the ideas of **selfless action, detachment, devotion,** and **the nature of the eternal soul**. Through the Gita, Vyasa teaches that the pursuit of **material success** and **attachment** to the fruits of action leads to suffering, while selfless actions performed with **dedication to God** bring liberation.

3.   **The Role of the Sage and Teacher**: Vyasa was also a key figure in teaching the importance of the **guru-shishya** (teacher-student) relationship in spiritual development. He exemplified the qualities of a true sage—wisdom, patience, and selflessness—and imparted teachings to the next generations. His wisdom was not just theoretical but practical, applying to real-life situations, as seen in the way he guided the characters of the Mahabharata through their struggles. His profound philosophical insights provided the foundation for later developments in **Vedanta**, **yoga**, and other schools of Indian thought.

4.   **The Importance of Knowledge and Self-Realization**: Vyasa stressed that the ultimate goal of life was **self-realization**—the knowledge of one's true divine nature. His teachings emphasize the **transience** of the material world and the **eternal nature of the soul**. Through his work in the Mahabharata, Vyasa encourages individuals to seek the **truth** of the universe and to live in harmony with the **divine**.

Importance and Neglect

Despite Vyasa's profound contributions, his teachings, particularly his philosophical and spiritual messages, are sometimes overshadowed by the more widely recognized figures like **Lord Krishna**, **Shankaracharya**, or **Ramanuja**. Vyasa's significance lies not just in his authorship of the Mahabharata but in his contribution to the shaping of Indian intellectual and spiritual traditions. His teachings on **karma**, **dharma**, and the **pursuit of liberation** are universal and timeless, yet they are often neglected in favor of more contemporary philosophical systems or practices.

Vyasa's unique role in Hindu tradition as the compiler of the Vedas, the author of the Mahabharata, and the composer of the Puranas cannot be overstated. Yet, his importance is often relegated to the background, especially in popular discussions that tend to focus on other characters and deities. His **teaching of the eternal truths** and the complex exploration of human nature through the Mahabharata remains an underappreciated treasure.

Conclusion

Sage Vyasa, through his monumental contributions, has shaped not only the spiritual landscape of India but also the intellectual, philosophical, and ethical frameworks that continue to guide individuals and societies today. His teachings on **dharma, karma**, and **liberation** remain a foundation for understanding the human condition. While his work is immensely important, it is often neglected in modern discussions, overshadowed by more contemporary figures or less accessible texts. However, Vyasa's legacy, as a sage and teacher, continues to influence millions of followers, ensuring his place as one of the most important figures in Indian spiritual and philosophical history.

8. Sage Bhrigu

Illustrious Career

Sage Bhrigu is one of the **Saptarishi** (seven great sages) mentioned in Hindu mythology. He is considered to be the most important among the **Brahmarishis**, the sages closest to the divine truth. Bhrigu's **career** and contributions to Hindu thought, spiritual wisdom, and his role in the Mahabharata epic make him a central figure in the tapestry of ancient Indian sages. His legacy spans across multiple texts, from the **Vedas** to the **Mahabharata** and the **Puranas**.

Bhrigu was born to the **sage Vasishtha** and **Arundhati** in a divine and noble lineage. He is renowned for his **immense penance** (tapas) and his role as one of the chief **contributors to the system of Vedic astrology** (Jyotisha). He is credited with authoring the **Bhrigu Samhita**, a famous text that deals with astrology and predictions. His influence in Indian spiritual and astrological circles has been monumental.

Contributions to the Kingdom

1.   **Astrological Contributions**: Sage Bhrigu's most important legacy lies in his development of **Vedic astrology**. The **Bhrigu Samhita**, attributed to him, is one of the oldest and most respected works on astrology. This text contains extensive details about human **karma**, the influence of celestial bodies on individual destinies, and the planetary movements' impact on personal and cosmic events. His astrological principles continue to guide modern practitioners of astrology in interpreting horoscopes and understanding the cosmic order of events.

2.   **The Creation of the Bhrigu Nadi**: Sage Bhrigu is credited with establishing a system known as **Bhrigu Nadi**, which focuses on using astrological charts to predict an individual's past, present, and future based on the positions of planets at birth. The system is said to have been compiled and preserved through generations and remains a significant tool in contemporary astrology.

3.   **Influence on Kings and Rulers**: Bhrigu's wisdom was sought by kings, rulers, and warriors. His astrological readings and **divine insight** helped them make decisions about matters of state, governance, and personal conduct. Notably, Bhrigu was instrumental in advising kings on choosing **auspicious times** for starting military campaigns, coronations, and other vital ceremonies. His association with kings like **King Yayati** and the rulers of **Hastinapura** highlights his importance in both spiritual and political affairs.

4.   **The Formation of the Triad of Deities**: Bhrigu is famously credited with being the sage who **tested the three principal deities** of the Hindu pantheon, **Brahma**, **Vishnu**, and **Shiva**—to determine their supreme status. The story of the **Bhrigu test** is significant in Hindu mythology and demonstrates Bhrigu's impartial wisdom. He went to Brahma's abode and found Brahma engrossed in meditation, which Bhrigu considered a lack of compassion, and thus deemed him unworthy of being the highest deity. He then went to Lord Vishnu's abode, where Vishnu was lying on a serpent bed,

appearing to ignore him. Bhrigu, angered, kicked Vishnu in the chest, only to find that Vishnu welcomed him with a **gentle smile** and his chest, the seat of Lakshmi (goddess of wealth), was marked with the imprint of Bhrigu's foot. This act is said to have shown Vishnu's supreme quality of **forgiveness** and **compassion**, proving Vishnu's place as the highest deity in the Hindu pantheon. This act also set the stage for the **Vishnu Bhakti** movement that would dominate later centuries.

5.   **The Role in the Mahabharata**: In the Mahabharata, Bhrigu's importance is somewhat indirect but highly symbolic. His contributions are seen in his teachings on dharma, his association with various events, and his impact on the spiritual guidance of the **Kuru dynasty**. While Bhrigu himself does not play a direct role in the events of the Mahabharata, his teachings on **karma**, **astrology**, and the nature of **dharma** are critical in understanding the decisions and fates of characters like **Dhritarashtra**, **Bhishma**, and **Karna**.

6.   **Influence in the Adhyatma Ramayana**: Although primarily associated with the Mahabharata, Bhrigu also plays a role in other texts. In the **Adhyatma Ramayana**, a philosophical interpretation of the Ramayana, Bhrigu is depicted as a significant sage offering counsel to the royal families. His importance across texts demonstrates the broader spiritual and ethical contributions of Bhrigu's wisdom to Indian mythology.

Teaching and Preaching

Sage Bhrigu's teachings were profound, diverse, and focused on **spiritual wisdom**, **astrology**, and the **philosophical nature of the universe**. His preaching transcended conventional religious doctrines; but often involved direct engagement with kings, sages, and the general populace.

1.   **Astrological Teachings**: One of Bhrigu's most prominent contributions was his work on **astrology** and the **Bhrigu Nadi** system. His approach was based on the belief that **astrology**, in connection with one's **karma**, can reveal the true nature of an individual's life, helping to guide them in fulfilling their **life's purpose**. Bhrigu emphasized that the stars and planets had a significant influence on a person's life but did not define their destiny entirely. He believed that through spiritual practices and aligning oneself with **dharma**, an individual could change the course of their life, irrespective of astrological predictions.

2.   **Teaching of Karma and Dharma**: Bhrigu emphasized the importance of **karma** and its role in shaping the future. In his view, **dharma** (righteousness) should be practiced by rulers, sages, and common people alike, with a focus on spiritual awakening. Through his astrological predictions and spiritual counsel, he taught kings that their actions in accordance with dharma would ultimately lead to their **spiritual liberation**, regardless of their material successes or failures.

3.   **The Test of the Three Deities**: Bhrigu's famous test of the three major gods of Hinduism is a teaching in itself. The test shows that **selfless service**, **compassion**, and **forgiveness** are paramount virtues that elevate one's spiritual standing. His actions are a commentary on the **divine nature of the gods**, demonstrating that while power and glory may be revered, it is the qualities of **humility**, **forgiveness**, and **love** that define the ultimate divine being.

4.   **Sage of Compassion**: Despite his role in testing the three gods, Bhrigu himself was known to be a sage of great compassion and wisdom. His spiritual practice was based on the principle that one's **actions** should be guided by compassion and a desire to alleviate suffering. He often spoke about the nature of the soul, urging followers to see beyond material wealth and power and to focus on their **spiritual growth**.

5.   **The Role of a Guru**: Bhrigu taught that the role of a **guru** (spiritual teacher) is vital in guiding a person towards self-realization and understanding of the divine. His approach to teaching was deeply personal and experiential, as he would often mentor his disciples directly, allowing them to explore the mysteries of the universe through **meditation**, **penance**, and **self-discipline**.

Importance and Neglect

Sage Bhrigu, despite his immense contributions to spiritual and astrological wisdom, is often overshadowed by figures like **Vyasa**, **Brahma**, and

Krishna in the grand narrative of Indian mythology. His contributions, especially in the field of astrology, have been crucial in shaping the spiritual and philosophical practices of many Hindus, but his importance is often marginalized.

The **Bhrigu Samhita** is a crucial text for practitioners of astrology, yet it is not as widely known or studied as the Vedas or the Puranas. Similarly, his teachings on **karma, dharma**, and the divine qualities of compassion remain a cornerstone of spiritual practice but are often not given the same attention as those of other sages.

Despite this, Bhrigu's **astrological legacy** continues to impact modern-day **astrologers**, while his wisdom on the cosmic order remains a timeless source of guidance for those seeking deeper understanding.

Conclusion

Sage Bhrigu, through his contributions to **astrology**, **dharma**, and **spiritual wisdom**, remains one of the most profound figures in Hindu tradition. His teachings on **karma, self-realization**, and the nature of the divine continue to inspire followers today, even as his contributions are often overshadowed by other legendary figures in Indian mythology. Sage Bhrigu's **test of the gods**, his work in astrology, and his emphasis on **compassion** make him a sage who is deserving of greater recognition in the spiritual and philosophical spheres.

9. Sage Atri: Illustrious Carrier

Illustrious Career

Sage Atri is one of the **Saptarishis** and one of the most revered figures in Hindu mythology. Known for his deep spiritual wisdom and divine knowledge, Atri holds a significant place in the **Vedas, Upanishads, Mahabharata**, and various **Puranas**. He is renowned for his **penance** (tapas), **devotion**, and his extensive influence on the spiritual and cultural development of ancient Indian society.

Atri was born to **Brahma** and **Saraswati**. His **spiritual lineage** is considered pure and sacred, as his devotion and wisdom transcended even the highest levels of divine knowledge. Sage Atri is known for being a highly disciplined sage, whose focus was on the welfare of the world and the preservation of divine knowledge. He is also associated with the composition of a number of hymns in the **Rig Veda**.

Contributions to the Kingdom

1.   **Divine Insight for Rulers**: Sage Atri's profound wisdom was often sought by kings and rulers who desired to align their kingdoms with **dharma** (righteousness). His role was particularly notable in helping rulers understand the importance of **spiritual growth** alongside material prosperity. Atri's counsel helped maintain a balance between **administrative duties** and spiritual responsibilities, which laid the foundation for **ideal governance**. His emphasis on wisdom and compassion influenced various kings who

sought his guidance in matters of both governance and spiritual ethics.

2.   **The Family of Atri**: Atri's contributions were not confined to his teachings alone. His family, especially his wife **Anasuya**, was instrumental in shaping the ethical and moral landscape of the time. Anasuya's **selfless devotion** and role as a model of purity and righteousness were the embodiment of the teachings that Atri himself practiced. Together, Atri and Anasuya formed a **power couple** whose commitment to dharma and spiritual purity was unparalleled. Their story is an inspiration for generations of Hindus who look up to them for guidance in matters of devotion and righteous living.

3.   **Astrological and Spiritual Contributions**: Atri is said to have had a deep understanding of **cosmic order** and **astrology**, which made him a respected figure in both **spiritual** and **astronomical** circles. His profound knowledge of celestial bodies and their relationship to human affairs helped in predicting favorable moments for various religious and state functions. In addition to his studies in astrology, Atri also contributed significantly to the practice of **yajnas** (fire sacrifices) and rituals intended to uphold **cosmic balance**.

4.   **The Atri-Gautami Dynasty**: Atri's legacy extended to the formation of the **Atri-Gautami** lineage, which produced many scholars, sages, and great personalities who were instrumental in preserving the **Vedic traditions**. His descendants played

significant roles in guiding future generations and preserving the purity of spiritual and philosophical teachings.

5. **Role in the Mahabharata**: In the Mahabharata, Atri's presence is felt through his contributions to **spirituality** and his teachings on **dharma**. He is mentioned in several places where the **Kuru princes** seek advice and wisdom. Atri's role is not as prominent in the epic as other sages like Vyasa or Bhishma, but his influence is seen in the broader spiritual framework in which the Mahabharata is set. His emphasis on **self-realization**, **discipline**, and **devotion** helped in shaping the moral and ethical decisions of the characters in the epic.

Teaching and Preaching

Sage Atri's teachings were deeply rooted in the philosophy of **dharma**, which combined the principles of **truth**, **non-violence**, and **compassion**. His guidance was both spiritual and practical, as he worked to elevate the lives of those around him through both **personal discipline** and **service to society**.

1. **The Importance of Dharma and Non-Violence**: One of Atri's central teachings was the importance of **dharma**. He emphasized that righteousness should guide not only personal conduct but also political and social actions. Atri's teachings reflected a belief that a king, a ruler, or any individual must prioritize **spiritual practices** alongside fulfilling their worldly responsibilities. His focus on **non-violence** was profound, urging individuals to avoid

unnecessary harm to others, be it physical, emotional, or mental.

2.   **Meditation and Penance**: Atri is often depicted as a sage of great **penance**, and his teachings stressed the importance of spiritual discipline. He encouraged meditation and **introspection** as ways to purify the mind and soul. His teachings on **tapas** (spiritual austerities) and **self-control** inspired countless seekers of truth who adopted his practices to attain spiritual enlightenment.

3.   **Self-Realization and Humility**: Atri also stressed the importance of **self-realization**, teaching that true wisdom comes from understanding one's **inner nature** and the **divine presence** within oneself. Humility was a core element of Atri's teachings, and he often spoke of the importance of recognizing one's limitations and understanding that one must always strive to better oneself spiritually. His personal life was an example of this humility, as he led a simple life of devotion, even as he shared his wisdom with the world.

4.   **Teaching through Stories and Parables**: Like many ancient sages, Atri often used stories and parables to communicate profound truths. His most famous story is that of his wife **Anasuya**, whose purity and devotion to Atri led to divine rewards. The story of **Anasuya** and her interaction with the **Tridev** (Brahma, Vishnu, and Shiva) highlights the **importance of virtue, humility**, and **devotion**. This story is often told to illustrate the strength of **selfless devotion** and the power of a righteous woman.

Importance and Neglect

Despite his immense spiritual and philosophical contributions, **Sage Atri** is somewhat neglected in popular consciousness compared to other sages like **Vyasa, Vasistha**, or **Bhrigu**. His teachings are profound, yet they are often overshadowed by more widely known figures from the ancient Indian scriptures.

Atri's **astrological** and **spiritual knowledge** continues to influence the field of **Jyotisha** (astrology), yet his contributions are often relegated to the background. Additionally, his significant role in the formation of **dharmic governance** and his impact on rulers' decisions remain underappreciated in mainstream retellings of the Mahabharata and other texts.

Despite his profound influence on the **ethical governance** of kingdoms and his contributions to spiritual philosophy, Atri's teachings are not as celebrated in modern times. His life and philosophy represent an ideal balance between spiritual asceticism and worldly responsibilities, a wisdom that could greatly benefit the modern world.

Conclusion

Sage Atri's contributions to **spiritual philosophy, astrology,** and **dharma** have shaped Indian traditions profoundly. His emphasis on **penance, devotion**, and **self-realization** continues to guide many seekers of truth. Despite his underappreciation in popular culture,

Atri remains an important figure in Hinduism whose teachings on **humility, compassion,** and **spirituality** are timeless.

10. Sage Vashistha

Illustrious Career

Sage **Vashistha** is one of the most important and revered **rishis** in Hindu mythology. He is known as one of the **Saptarishis** (Seven Great Sages) and holds a key position in the **Vedas**, particularly in the **Rig Veda**, where his hymns form a significant portion. Vashistha's story is interwoven with **Brahmanic traditions**, and he is one of the few sages in Hindu texts who has achieved a remarkable **spiritual status**, being both a **teacher** and a **spiritual guide** to many generations of kings and spiritual seekers.

Vashistha's **lineage** is associated with the **Brahmanic tradition**, being the son of **Brahma** and **Varsha**. He is the spiritual master to **Lord Rama**, the central figure in the **Ramayana**, and his role as a teacher to the **Ikshvaku dynasty** makes him an incredibly influential figure in the epic.

His early life is filled with rich experiences in learning and acquiring wisdom. Vashistha is said to have possessed the knowledge of the **Brahman** (the Supreme Consciousness) and the **Vedic scriptures**. His wisdom extended beyond mere knowledge; he was known for his moral integrity, self-control, and devotion to **dharma** (righteousness). He was revered by kings, sages, and deities alike and his spiritual prowess earned him respect as one of the most revered figures in Indian history.

Contributions to the Kingdom

1. **Guiding Kings and Rulers**: Sage Vashistha's influence on rulers was profound. His teachings focused on the importance of **righteous rule** and **ethical governance**, a theme that is a common thread through much of his interaction with kings. Vashistha played a crucial role in guiding King **Dasharatha**, the father of Lord Rama, advising him on matters of **governance** and the **kingdom's welfare**. His counsel was often sought in times of moral and political confusion.

His wisdom was not only about the **material governance** of a kingdom but also about **spiritual** and **moral conduct**. His teachings were often about the balance between **worldly duties** (raja-dharma) and **spiritual practices** (Sadhana). He provided kings with knowledge of **justice**, **truth**, **love**, and **self-discipline** to ensure a kingdom's prosperity.

2. **Vashistha and the Royal Lineages**: Vashistha's role as a teacher and advisor extended to multiple generations. He was one of the key figures responsible for preserving the **moral code** and **spirituality** in royal families. His interactions with the **Ikshvaku dynasty** were crucial in shaping the ideals of kingship and **dharma**. His relationship with **King Dasharatha**, and by extension, **Lord Rama**, was one of deep mutual respect, and Vashistha was a pillar of strength and guidance in the royal court.

Notably, his support during Rama's **exile** demonstrated his firm belief in the principles of **dharma** over **personal loyalty**, an act that showcases his immense wisdom and impartiality.

3.   **Vashistha's Role in the Ramayana**: Vashistha's influence on the **Ramayana** cannot be overstated. He is seen as the spiritual guide to **Lord Rama**, whom he taught the ideals of **righteousness** and **duty**. Vashistha was not just a teacher but a father figure to Rama, helping him in his spiritual journey and preparing him for his role as the future king of **Ayodhya**. In the Ramayana, Vashistha is depicted as one who encourages adherence to **dharma**, even in the most testing times.

His teaching to Rama on how to act when faced with challenges and conflicts was crucial. Vashistha's role is emblematic of a teacher who does not give direct answers but guides his disciples to **self-realization**.

4.   **The Vashistha-Vishwamitra Conflict**: One of the more dramatic episodes in Vashistha's life is his **conflict** with the sage **Vishwamitra**, which had lasting repercussions on the balance between spiritual and material realms. This story highlights Vashistha's qualities of **restraint, wisdom**, and the power of **tapas** (austerity). The conflict arose due to Vishwamitra's attempt to claim Vashistha's divine cow, **Nandini**, and the resulting battle of **tapas**. Vashistha's ability to remain calm and uphold dharma in the face of such a confrontation shows his profound spiritual depth.

5.   **The Cow of Vashistha – Nandini**: A significant contribution of Vashistha's was his possession of the divine cow, **Nandini**, which was capable of fulfilling all desires. This cow symbolized **divine grace**, and its loss was a turning point in Vashistha's life. The cow, as a divine entity, allowed Vashistha to **maintain prosperity, peace**, and **spiritual wisdom** in his **ashram**. The cow also played a central role in his legendary feud with **Vishwamitra**, who was unable to overpower Vashistha's spiritual power, which ultimately led to his eventual submission.

Teaching and Preaching

Sage Vashistha's teachings were rooted in the **principles of dharma, tapas**, and **self-realization**. His profound wisdom has been passed down in various forms, including **Vedic hymns**, **Upanishadic teachings**, and stories that form the core of the **Ramayana**.

1.   **Dharma and Righteous Rule**: Vashistha's teaching emphasized the importance of **righteous rule** and **selfless service** for the greater good of the kingdom and its people. He strongly believed that a **king** or **ruler** must adhere to **justice, truth**, and **compassion**. In the Ramayana, the advice he gives to Lord Rama often centers on the balance between **personal duty** (Svadharma) and the universal duty (Svadharma) that a ruler has to society.

2.   **Teaching through Examples**: Sage Vashistha often used **practical wisdom** and **personal examples** to impart lessons. One of his key methods

of teaching was the use of stories, myths, and allegories. His role in teaching Rama, for example, was not through direct imposition of rules but through the spiritual example he set and the guidance he provided in understanding the **importance of dharma**.

3.   **The Power of Tapas**: Vashistha emphasized the importance of **tapas**—austerity, meditation, and self-discipline—as a way to connect with the divine. He taught that true power comes not from material wealth or force but from the internal strength that comes through deep spiritual practices. This teaching had a profound influence on the spiritual life of kings, warriors, and sages alike.

4.   **Humility and Service**: One of Vashistha's essential teachings is the importance of **humility** and **service** to others. His entire life serves as an example of how one can maintain power and influence without arrogance, and instead with a deep sense of service to the greater good. His calm demeanor in the face of adversity, especially during his conflict with Vishwamitra, serves as a powerful lesson on the importance of maintaining spiritual peace in moments of conflict.

Importance and Neglect

Despite his significant contributions, Sage Vashistha, like many of the great sages of Hindu mythology, has not always received the attention or focus that some of his counterparts have. The prominence of figures like **Vyasa**, **Bhishma**, or **Shiva** in Hindu tradition sometimes overshadows his own influence.

Vashistha's role as a spiritual and **philosophical guide** to key figures like Lord Rama is immense, yet his teachings often seem overlooked in modern times. His emphasis on the **balance between worldly duties** and **spiritual enlightenment** provides a unique **model for leadership** that is rarely explored in contemporary discussions on dharma. His legacy, however, remains deeply embedded in the **Ramayana** and **Vedic teachings**, ensuring that his wisdom continues to influence millions.

Conclusion

Sage Vashistha stands as a monumental figure in Indian spiritual and philosophical traditions. His **wisdom**, **spiritual discipline**, and **ethical governance** continue to guide both kings and commoners alike. Through his guidance to Lord Rama and his many contributions to Vedic literature, his legacy remains an essential aspect of India's ancient heritage. Though his significance may sometimes be overlooked in the modern age, his teachings on **dharma**, **self-discipline**, and **compassion** remain timeless and crucial for anyone seeking a righteous and spiritually fulfilling life.

Chapter Six - Two most neglected family members of the Pandavas

Nakula: The Epitome of Grace and Skill

1. Intellectual and Spiritual Strengths

Nakula's intellectual brilliance often goes unnoticed, but his abilities were indispensable to the Pandavas. Being the son of the Ashwini Kumar Nasatya, the divine physician, Nakula inherited exceptional knowledge of medicine and healing. His expertise in Ayurveda, particularly in veterinary science, earned him a reputation as a skilled caretaker of horses. During the exile, his ability to maintain the Pandavas' cavalry, despite limited resources, showcased his resourcefulness and dedication. This skill became crucial during the Kurukshetra war, ensuring the Pandavas' forces remained battle-ready.

Spiritually, Nakula symbolized calmness, discipline, and humility. Unlike his brothers, who were often embroiled in dilemmas or conflicts, Nakula adhered to his dharma without hesitation. His ability to maintain inner peace amidst adversity is a testament to his spiritual maturity. Nakula's reverence for dharma and his elders is evident in the Yaksha Prashna, where he chooses to revive his brother Sahadeva over others, valuing loyalty and fairness above all.

Nakula's spirituality also reflects in his acceptance of fate. Despite being equally royal and skilled, he never sought prominence, embodying the ideal of silent service. His character highlights the importance of balance and humility in achieving greatness.

2. Martial Abilities

Nakula was an exceptional swordsman, known for his agility and precision. During the Kurukshetra war, his combat skills were on full display. He defeated prominent warriors like Shakuni's brothers, showcasing his strategic prowess and bravery. His swordsmanship was marked by finesse rather than brute force, setting him apart from Bhima's overwhelming strength or Arjuna's mastery of archery.

Nakula was also trained in archery and combat techniques, making him a versatile warrior. During the exile, he practiced extensively, preparing for the inevitable conflict. His ability to adapt to different combat scenarios demonstrates his preparedness and tactical intelligence.

Though Nakula's battles are less detailed in the epic, his contributions were vital to the Pandavas' overall strategy. His presence in the battlefield added depth to the Pandavas' fighting force, proving that even overlooked warriors can play decisive roles.

3. Role in the Epic

Nakula's role in the Mahabharata might appear understated, but it was essential. He was the glue that held the Pandavas' army together, ensuring their cavalry and war animals were in top condition. His quiet competence complemented his brothers' strengths, creating a well-rounded team.

Nakula's humility also allowed him to take on supportive roles without resentment. For instance, during the exile, he never questioned Yudhishthira's leadership, even when it meant enduring hardships. His loyalty and dedication underscore the value of teamwork and selflessness in achieving collective goals.

In many ways, Nakula represents the unsung hero, whose contributions often go unnoticed but are critical for success. His character is a reminder that greatness is not always loud or visible; it often lies in silent service and unwavering commitment to one's duties.

Sahadeva: The Oracle and Strategist

1. Intellectual and Spiritual Strengths

Sahadeva, the youngest Pandava, possessed a rare blend of intelligence and spiritual insight. As the son of the Ashwini Kumar Dasra, he inherited extraordinary intellectual capabilities. Sahadeva was an expert astrologer, capable of predicting future events with accuracy. It is said that he knew the outcome of the Kurukshetra war but chose not to disclose it, adhering to his vow of silence and his commitment to dharma.

Sahadeva's strategic mind was evident in his advice during critical moments. His insights often shaped the

Pandavas' decisions, though his humility meant he rarely sought recognition. For instance, his understanding of time cycles and celestial movements helped determine auspicious moments for battles, giving the Pandavas an edge in the war.

Spiritually, Sahadeva embodied wisdom and restraint. Unlike his elder brothers, who often grappled with moral dilemmas, Sahadeva displayed a clarity of purpose and an unwavering commitment to dharma. His inner strength and ability to see the bigger picture made him a silent yet profound contributor to the epic's narrative.

2. Martial Abilities

Sahadeva was a skilled swordsman, trained in close combat techniques. His precision and agility made him a formidable opponent on the battlefield. During the Kurukshetra war, Sahadeva displayed his martial prowess by defeating Shakuni, avenging the latter's treachery in the dice game. This act not only demonstrated his bravery but also brought closure to one of the Pandavas' deepest grievances.

Sahadeva's contributions extended beyond direct combat; as a strategist, he played a key role in planning the Pandavas' war strategies. His ability to analyze situations and anticipate enemy moves made him an invaluable asset.

Though Sahadeva's battles are not as extensively described as those of Arjuna or Bhima, his skills and contributions were no less significant. He represented the silent warrior, whose actions often went unnoticed but were vital to the Pandavas' success.

3. Role in the Epic

Sahadeva's role in the Mahabharata is marked by his intellect, humility, and sense of duty. He served as a strategist, warrior, and counselor, providing guidance when needed. Despite his immense knowledge, he never sought the spotlight, embodying the ideal of selfless service.

Sahadeva's silence about the war's outcome reflects his deep understanding of dharma. He knew that revealing the future would interfere with the natural course of events, undermining the lessons of karma and dharma central to the epic. This restraint underscores his spiritual maturity and commitment to higher principles.

Like Nakula, Sahadeva represents the unsung heroes of the Mahabharata, whose contributions often go unnoticed but are critical to the epic's narrative. His character highlights the importance of wisdom, humility, and selflessness in achieving greatness.

Conclusion: Why Were They Sidelined?

Nakula and Sahadeva's sidelining in the Mahabharata reflects a narrative focus on conflict and drama. Their lack of personal vendettas or moral dilemmas made them less compelling in a story driven by complex characters like Arjuna, Bhima, and Yudhishthira. However, this does not diminish their importance.

Their roles as silent supporters underscore the value of teamwork and the unsung contributions that underpin great achievements. Nakula and Sahadeva remind us that true greatness lies not in seeking recognition but in fulfilling one's duties with humility and dedication. Their legacy, though often overlooked, remains a testament to the diverse strengths that shaped the Pandavas' journey and the epic's enduring appeal.

1. Narrative Focus on Conflict and Drama

The Mahabharata thrives on complex characters and dramatic conflicts. Figures like Yudhishthira, Arjuna, and Bhima embody archetypes—truth, heroism, and strength—that drive the narrative. Nakula and Sahadeva, with their balanced and composed personalities, lacked the dramatic arcs that make characters compelling in storytelling. Their adherence to dharma and their lack of internal conflicts made them less captivating in a tale rich with moral dilemmas and emotional struggles.

2. Thematic Priorities

The epic emphasizes themes of dharma, power, and destiny, often through the lens of characters who struggle with their responsibilities and choices. Nakula and Sahadeva's unwavering commitment to their duties meant they did not face the same moral quandaries as their brothers. This thematic simplicity, while admirable, relegated them to the background in a narrative that prioritizes moral complexity.

3. Cultural and Hierarchical Context

In the patriarchal and hierarchical structure of ancient Indian society, the eldest (Yudhishthira) and the most accomplished (Arjuna) brothers naturally commanded attention. Nakula and Sahadeva, as the youngest, were often seen as supportive figures rather than leaders. Their roles as the sons of Madri, a secondary queen, further contributed to their perceived secondary status in the Pandava lineage.

4. Lack of Personal Vendettas

While Yudhishthira, Bhima, and Arjuna had personal rivalries and vendettas driving their narratives, Nakula and Sahadeva were motivated solely by their loyalty to the Pandavas and their commitment to dharma. This lack of personal stakes made their stories less compelling in the epic's broader narrative framework.

Reevaluating Their Legacy

Nakula and Sahadeva represent the unsung heroes of the Mahabharata. Their intellectual brilliance, spiritual depth, and martial prowess underscore the diversity of strengths needed for collective success. Their sidelining reflects a narrative choice rather than a lack of significance. In the grand tapestry of the Mahabharata, they symbolize the virtues of humility, silent service, and unwavering dedication—qualities that often go unnoticed but are indispensable for true greatness.

Their legacy invites readers to look beyond the obvious and recognize the value of quiet competence in shaping history and destiny.

Chapter Seven - Three most important communicators in epic Mahabharata

1. Sanjaya: The Visionary Narrator

Sanjaya, King Dhritarashtra's charioteer and advisor, played a pivotal role as a communicator in the Mahabharata. His unique ability to narrate the Kurukshetra war with vivid detail, impartiality, and spiritual insight made him an extraordinary narrator. Sanjaya's communication skills were essential not only for informing Dhritarashtra but also for highlighting the moral and philosophical undertones of the epic.

Articulation and Eloquence

Sanjaya's words were not mere descriptions but immersive narratives that brought the battlefield to life for the blind king. His eloquence was unparalleled, as he conveyed the complexity of strategies, emotions, and heroics of the warriors. Sanjaya's descriptions enabled Dhritarashtra to visualize the events with clarity, even allowing him to experience the sights, sounds, and emotions of the battlefield. His narrative structure was logical and coherent, guiding Dhritarashtra step by step through the unfolding events.

Sanjaya's narration also included profound insights into the psychological and emotional states of the warriors. For instance, when Arjuna hesitated on the battlefield, Sanjaya vividly captured his turmoil, making it relatable to Dhritarashtra and the audience. His ability to translate complex situations into simple yet impactful words made his communication highly effective.

Impartiality

Despite his loyalty to Dhritarashtra, Sanjaya maintained impartiality in his narration. He did not sugarcoat the truth or manipulate events to suit the king's preferences. This neutrality ensured that his communication remained credible and trustworthy. Even when the narrative favored the Pandavas, Sanjaya presented it with fairness, emphasizing the importance of dharma over personal loyalties. His unbiased account of events like Abhimanyu's valor or Drona's tactics showcased his commitment to truth.

Spiritual Depth

One of Sanjaya's most remarkable moments as a communicator was his narration of the Bhagavad Gita. As he recounted Krishna's discourse to Arjuna, Sanjaya revealed a deep understanding of the philosophical and spiritual principles underlying the epic. His ability to convey these profound truths in a relatable manner made his narration not just a war report but a spiritual guide. This aspect of Sanjaya's communication elevated him from a mere storyteller to a medium of divine wisdom.

Impact

Sanjaya's communication had a profound impact on Dhritarashtra, offering him both insight and solace amidst the tragedy of the war. It also served as a timeless record for humanity, illustrating the power of clear, honest, and empathetic communication. Through his words, Sanjaya immortalized the Mahabharata, ensuring that its lessons resonate across generations.

2. Krishna: The Divine Orator

Krishna, the central figure of the Mahabharata, was not only a warrior and statesman but also a masterful communicator. His ability to blend wisdom, diplomacy, and persuasion made him one of the most impactful characters in the epic. Krishna's communication skills were pivotal in influencing key events and guiding individuals towards their dharma.

Persuasion and Diplomacy

Krishna's role as a peace envoy to the Kauravas is a testament to his skill as a communicator. Tasked with preventing the war, Krishna approached Dhritarashtra's court with logical arguments, moral reasoning, and a vision for harmony. His words were carefully chosen to appeal to the different personalities in the Kaurava court. For Dhritarashtra, he emphasized the long-term consequences of adharma. For Duryodhana, he highlighted the futility of arrogance and greed. Despite the rejection of his peace proposal, Krishna's diplomacy remains a shining example of how words can be used to advocate for peace.

Philosophical Guidance

Krishna's discourse to Arjuna on the battlefield, the Bhagavad Gita, is one of the most celebrated examples of effective communication in history. Faced with Arjuna's moral and emotional crisis, Krishna adapted his communication to resonate with his friend's doubts and fears. He used metaphors, analogies, and logic to explain complex philosophical concepts like karma, dharma, and the transient nature of life. Krishna's ability to simplify profound truths and present them in a relatable manner transformed Arjuna's hesitation into resolve, enabling him to fulfill his duty as a warrior.

Charisma and Relatability

Krishna's charisma was central to his communication. Whether addressing kings, warriors, or commoners, he tailored his words to suit the audience. His playful demeanor, combined with his profound wisdom, made him approachable and relatable. This adaptability ensured that his message resonated with everyone, regardless of their status or beliefs.

Impact

Krishna's communication had far-reaching effects, inspiring individuals to rise above their limitations and align with their dharma. His words shaped the course of the war, guided Arjuna through his struggles, and imparted timeless lessons on life and spirituality. Krishna's role as a communicator highlights the transformative power of words when combined with wisdom and empathy.

3. Vidura: The Wise Counselor

Vidura, the illegitimate yet morally upright son of Vyasa, was a beacon of wisdom in the Kuru court. As a counselor to Dhritarashtra, Vidura's words were a blend of clarity, prudence, and ethical guidance. Despite his limited authority, Vidura's communication often served as the moral compass for the Kuru dynasty.

Clarity and Wisdom

Vidura's counsel was marked by its clarity and directness. Unlike other characters who often spoke in riddles or veiled threats, Vidura communicated in a straightforward manner. He used logical reasoning to present his arguments, ensuring that they were understood by everyone, including Dhritarashtra. His teachings, later compiled as Vidura Niti, addressed topics such as governance, morality, and personal conduct, providing timeless lessons on ethical leadership.

Moral Courage

Vidura's communication was rooted in dharma, even when it put him at odds with Dhritarashtra and Duryodhana. He was unafraid to speak the truth, regardless of the consequences. For instance, Vidura repeatedly warned Dhritarashtra about the dangers of supporting Duryodhana's ambitions, emphasizing the long-term consequences of adharma. His willingness to confront authority with honesty reflects his moral courage and integrity.

Empathy and Prudence

Vidura's words were not only logical but also empathetic. He understood the emotions and motivations of others, tailoring his advice to address their concerns without compromising on ethics. His ability to balance honesty with compassion made him a trusted advisor, even if his counsel was often ignored.

Impact

Though Dhritarashtra rarely heeded Vidura's advice, his words left a lasting impression on the narrative of the Mahabharata. Vidura's communication highlighted the importance of wisdom, integrity, and empathy in leadership. His teachings continue to inspire, serving as a guide for navigating the complexities of life and governance.

Conclusion: The Power of Communication

Sanjaya, Krishna, and Vidura exemplify the transformative power of communication in the Mahabharata. Each of them, in their unique way, used words to enlighten, persuade, and guide others. Sanjaya's eloquence brought the battlefield to life, Krishna's charisma and wisdom transformed lives, and Vidura's prudence provided moral guidance. Together, they illustrate the enduring impact of effective communication in shaping destinies and upholding dharma.

Chapter Eight - Five Most selfless Krishna's friends in Mahabharata

1. Sudama (Kuchela)

Sudama, also known as Kuchela, is a name that often evokes images of a humble man who was both poor and pious. However, the depth of his friendship with Krishna, and the spiritual lessons drawn from their bond, are often not fully appreciated. Sudama was a Brahmin from a modest family and was a childhood companion of Krishna in their early years at the ashram of Sage Sandipani. What is lesser known is that Sudama's life, despite his poverty, was rich in spiritual values and humility. His unwavering devotion to Krishna and his simplicity made him not just a friend to Krishna, but a true reflection of the kind of love and faith Krishna holds dear.

Sudama's virtues were rooted in his complete lack of attachment to material wealth. He was never drawn to the fleeting nature of earthly riches, and unlike many others who sought Krishna's favor for personal gain; Sudama sought only Krishna's divine companionship. His most notable virtue was his **devotion to Krishna**, which surpassed all material concerns. He remained a constant and devout worshipper of Krishna even though he lived in poverty. This purity of devotion, devoid of any desire for material benefit, earned him Krishna's deepest affection. Sudama's humility and spiritual focus allowed him to avoid the distractions of the world and remain steadfast in his love for Krishna.

However, Sudama's life was not easy. Despite his humble nature, he struggled with poverty, and his family often went hungry. His wife, in desperation, one day sent him to Dwarka to seek help from Krishna, suggesting that he request something to alleviate their hardships. Sudama, however, was reluctant to ask for anything, having grown accustomed to living without desires. He left for Dwarka carrying nothing but a small offering of beaten rice, a token of his love for Krishna, which he had no intention of presenting as a plea for help.

When Sudama arrived at Krishna's palace in Dwarka, the sight was overwhelming, but Sudama remained unfazed, knowing that he had come to meet his old friend. Krishna, on seeing Sudama, immediately recognized him, even though Sudama had changed over the years. Krishna, with great love and affection, rushed to meet him, addressing him as his dear friend. He washed Sudama's feet, a gesture reserved only for the most honored guests. Krishna then invited Sudama into his private chambers, where they conversed like two childhood friends reconnecting after many years. What is less known in this story is that Krishna did not need Sudama's offering, nor did he ever expect him to bring anything. Yet, Krishna accepted the beaten rice, not as a gift, but as a symbol of Sudama's unwavering devotion and love.

Krishna's response to Sudama's visit reveals his true nature—Krishna's love is not conditional upon material gifts but is founded in the heart of the devotee. Krishna knew that Sudama's love was pure, and therefore, he blessed him abundantly. Krishna not only provided Sudama with riches but also ensured that his family would never want for anything again. The divine intervention was not just a material reward, but a transformation of Sudama's life, as Krishna's grace extended beyond wealth to the spiritual fulfillment of his soul.

Through Sudama's story, Krishna teaches a profound lesson about the nature of friendship, love, and devotion. Sudama's bond with Krishna exemplifies a relationship that is not built on what one can give or receive in worldly terms, but on the sincere, selfless love and faith that transcends all material concerns. Krishna maintained this friendship not through political or personal gain but through the purity of heart that Sudama demonstrated. The story of Sudama's devotion and Krishna's boundless grace remains a timeless lesson on humility, love, and the power of true friendship.

## 2.	Subala

Subala, the father of Shakuni, is a character in the Mahabharata whose complexities are often overshadowed by the actions of his infamous son. While Shakuni is remembered as a cunning and manipulative figure, Subala was a man of wisdom, political insight, and deep familial loyalty. His friendship with Krishna is less celebrated but is crucial in understanding the nuances of relationships in the epic.

Subala was the king of Gandhara, a region situated between the Indian subcontinent and the Iranian plateau, and it was here that Shakuni was born. Subala, like many kings of his time, was engaged in political maneuvering and alliances. Despite the tumultuous relationship between his kingdom and the Kuru family, Subala maintained a close relationship with Krishna's family. He was an ally of Krishna's father, Vasudeva, and his connection with Krishna, though not highlighted in many stories, is significant in its political and moral implications. Subala's virtues lie in his wisdom, his sense of duty, and his deep love for his family.

One of Subala's most important qualities was his **diplomacy and political acumen**. He understood the art of negotiation and alliances, which was essential for the survival and prosperity of his kingdom. Subala knew that Krishna, even though born in a Yadava clan, was a figure of immense power and influence. Subala, understanding Krishna's spiritual nature, respected him not just as a powerful ruler but as a wise and virtuous man. Subala's respect for Krishna was based on recognition of Krishna's divine qualities and his ability to uphold dharma (righteousness). Subala was well aware that his son Shakuni's actions were driven by vengeance and manipulation, yet he did not allow this to disrupt his relationship with Krishna.

The lesser-known aspect of their friendship is the deep **mutual respect** they held for one another. Subala never sought to exploit Krishna for political gain but instead appreciated Krishna's wisdom and sought guidance when necessary. Krishna, on his part, treated Subala with the same respect, recognizing him as a wise king who upheld the duties of governance and family. Krishna's efforts to maintain this friendship are subtle yet significant. While Krishna often dealt with the more aggressive and overt conflicts around him, he ensured that his bond with Subala remained intact, even as tensions with the rest of the Gandhara family, particularly Shakuni, increased.

Subala's family, particularly his son Shakuni, caused great strain in Krishna's relationships with the Kuru dynasty. Shakuni's manipulations led to the eventual war of Kurukshetra, but Subala's relationship with Krishna remained one of mutual understanding. Krishna did not let the misdeeds of Shakuni, who later became a prominent antagonist in the Mahabharata, affect his friendship with Subala. Despite the destructive influence of Shakuni on the Kuru dynasty, Krishna continued to honor the bond he shared with Subala, showing that true friendship transcends the misdeeds of one's kin.

Subala's story is an important reminder of the complexities of relationships in the Mahabharata. Krishna's treatment of Subala reveals his ability to separate the actions of individuals from their familial bonds. It also highlights Krishna's willingness to forgive and maintain relationships based on respect, wisdom, and mutual understanding, even in the face of betrayal and manipulation from other members of Subala's family.

3.   Shishupala

Shishupala, the king of Chedi, is a figure who embodies the complexities of friendship and enmity in the Mahabharata. His relationship with Krishna is often remembered for its dramatic turn from friendship to conflict, which ended with his death at the hands of Krishna. What is lesser known, however, is the depth of their friendship before it soured, and Krishna's patient efforts to maintain that bond despite Shishupala's flaws.

Shishupala was initially a cousin of Krishna and, like many other royal figures in the Mahabharata, shared a kinship with Krishna. He was a powerful and ambitious king, and during his early years, there was no reason to believe that their relationship would eventually deteriorate. Krishna, known for his magnanimity and grace, tried to maintain a cordial relationship with Shishupala, respecting him as a fellow ruler and relative. Shishupala, however, was plagued by jealousy, pride, and an inability to accept Krishna's superior position.

One of Shishupala's most significant virtues was his **bravery and strength** as a warrior. He was known for his valor in battle and his skill as a strategist. Despite his arrogance, Shishupala had the potential to be a great king, but his inability to control his temper and his jealousy of Krishna's success led to his eventual downfall. What is less often discussed is how Shishupala's envy of Krishna was not rooted in personal malice but rather in his deep insecurities. As Krishna's fame and power grew, Shishupala felt increasingly overshadowed, which led to a series of insults directed at Krishna.

Krishna, ever the patient friend, initially responded to Shishupala's insults with forgiveness. Krishna had vowed to forgive Shishupala up to a hundred times for his offenses. Each time Shishupala insulted Krishna, Krishna refrained from retaliating, offering him the benefit of the doubt and the chance to correct his ways. Krishna's willingness to forgive Shishupala demonstrated his divine patience and commitment to maintaining their friendship. However, despite Krishna's repeated pardons, Shishupala's insults became more frequent and severe, culminating in a public insult at the Rajasuya Yagna, where Shishupala mocked Krishna in front of a gathering of kings and sages.

Krishna, recognizing that Shishupala had crossed the line and could no longer be forgiven, finally took action. He killed Shishupala during the Yagna, but the manner in which he did so reveals the complexities of their relationship. Krishna did not take pleasure in Shishupala's

4.   Narakasura

Narakasura, a powerful and infamous demon king, is often remembered in the Mahabharata for his conflict with Krishna, culminating in his defeat at Krishna's hands. However, the deeper relationship between Krishna and Narakasura is much more nuanced, reflecting the dynamics of friendship, power, and redemption. Narakasura's story is one of arrogance and ultimate downfall, but it also offers a glimpse into Krishna's approach to justice, friendship, and compassion.

Narakasura was originally born to the Earth and the celestial being Bhudevi. However, his nature changed when he was raised by the demon king, and he soon became a tyrant. His strength, military might, and conquests led him to dominate vast territories, and he became infamous for his cruel reign. He ruled over the kingdom of Pragjyotisha and acquired immense power, but his arrogance grew with his strength, and he began to commit heinous acts against the gods and even his own people. He captured 16,100 daughters of kings and princes, keeping them captive in his palace.

Despite his tyrannical ways, Narakasura's story with Krishna is not entirely one of enmity. The bond between Krishna and Narakasura was rooted in the fact that Narakasura was the son of Bhudevi, Krishna's mother Earth, making him a part of Krishna's extended family. Krishna's maternal connection to Narakasura, although distant, is often overlooked in the broader narrative of their enmity. While Narakasura's actions were unforgivable, Krishna still felt a sense of responsibility to restore balance and to free those suffering under Narakasura's cruelty.

Krishna's effort to deal with Narakasura was driven by his deep sense of dharma and justice. Despite the demon king's transgressions, Krishna's approach was not to simply destroy him but to engage with him as an adversary in a battle of power. Krishna, in his divine wisdom, understood that Narakasura had become a symbol of unchecked power and corruption, and thus his defeat was necessary to restore order in the world. Krishna's victory over Narakasura was a direct consequence of his commitment to the principles of justice, but it also demonstrated Krishna's desire to restore Narakasura's kingdom to the rightful order, not merely as a triumph of good over evil.

When Krishna killed Narakasura, he not only liberated the captive princesses but also ensured that the demon king's mother, Bhudevi, was appeased. Krishna had a deep respect for the Earth, and in his final acts of compassion, he allowed Narakasura's soul to be freed from the cycle of sin. Krishna also granted Narakasura the boon of immortality, making him a symbol of redemption rather than just destruction. This final act of mercy reflects Krishna's approach to friendship and justice—while he would not tolerate evil, he was always willing to restore balance and show mercy when possible.

Narakasura's relationship with Krishna is a complex one that highlights Krishna's divine capacity for both justice and compassion. Although Narakasura was a bitter enemy of Krishna, the bond between them can be seen as a testament to Krishna's broad sense of duty, his understanding of familial connections, and his unyielding desire to bring peace, even when it involved confronting the most formidable of enemies.

5.   Uddhava

Uddhava, a cousin of Krishna and one of his closest confidants, is often seen as one of the most devoted and spiritually enlightened figures in the Mahabharata. His relationship with Krishna is profound, with Uddhava being depicted as a sage, a devoted friend, and an intermediary for Krishna's teachings. Uddhava's unwavering loyalty to Krishna and his role as a messenger and confidant reveals the depth of their friendship and the mutual respect they held for one another.

Uddhava was born to the Yadava clan, but his true connection to Krishna was forged not just through their familial ties but through deep spiritual understanding. He was a disciple of Brihaspati, the teacher of the gods, and was well-versed in the Vedic scriptures and the intricacies of dharma. His intellect and wisdom were revered by all, and he was known for his calm demeanor, strategic thinking, and unwavering faith in Krishna. What is less commonly known is that Uddhava's spiritual journey was profoundly shaped by Krishna's teachings, and their friendship was based on a foundation of mutual respect for knowledge, virtue, and the pursuit of dharma.

Uddhava's role in the Mahabharata extends beyond that of a mere companion to Krishna. Krishna often relied on Uddhava's counsel in delicate matters and trusted him to carry out important tasks. Uddhava's devotion to Krishna was unwavering, and he regarded Krishna not just as a cousin but as a divine teacher and guide. This devotion is best illustrated in Uddhava's conversations with Krishna, particularly in the **Uddhava Gita**, where Krishna imparts spiritual wisdom to him in the form of teachings on yoga, devotion, and the nature of the self. Uddhava, through these teachings, comes to realize the depth of Krishna's divinity and his role in guiding the world through dharma.

One lesser-known aspect of their friendship is Krishna's efforts to prepare Uddhava for the challenges ahead. In times of crisis, Krishna often sent Uddhava as an emissary, and Uddhava's role in the Mahabharata was that of a peacemaker and a communicator of Krishna's divine will. When the Yadava dynasty was nearing its end, Krishna sent Uddhava to deliver messages to the various kings and factions, urging them to adhere to dharma and avoid conflict. Krishna, knowing that Uddhava was a wise and compassionate figure, entrusted him with these difficult tasks to maintain peace and prevent further bloodshed.

One of the most significant moments in their relationship came when Krishna, before his departure from the mortal world, sent Uddhava to Vrindavan to console the gopis, the women who had been so devoted to Krishna during his childhood. Uddhava's journey to Vrindavan and his attempt to convey Krishna's teachings to the gopis are some of the most poignant moments in the Mahabharata. Uddhava, though deeply knowledgeable, was struck by the unparalleled devotion of the gopis, who loved Krishna without any expectation of reward or recognition. This experience deeply humbled Uddhava and further solidified his respect for Krishna, as he realized the purity of Krishna's devotees.

Krishna's friendship with Uddhava is marked by a sense of mutual respect, spiritual depth, and unwavering loyalty. While Krishna often guided Uddhava through his teachings, he also trusted him with the critical task of carrying out his divine will. Uddhava's devotion to Krishna was not based on material gain or power but on a profound understanding of Krishna's divinity and a deep sense of friendship that transcended worldly attachments. Their bond illustrates the ideal of spiritual friendship— one based on respect, wisdom, and a shared commitment to dharma. Through their relationship, Krishna demonstrates how true friendship is rooted in the pursuit of higher knowledge and the dedication to uplifting others through divine teachings.

Chapter Nine - Five most significant places mentioned in Mahabharata

1.   Kurukshetra

Historical Significance:

Kurukshetra, known as Dharmakshetra or the "Field of Righteousness," is central to the Mahabharata. It is where the 18-day war between the Pandavas and Kauravas unfolded. The place is immortalized for being the site of the Bhagavad Gita, the philosophical dialogue between Lord Krishna and Arjuna. This scripture encapsulates the essence of duty (dharma), morality, and the path to liberation, shaping spiritual thought across millennia. Kurukshetra's significance extends beyond the war, symbolizing the eternal battle between good and evil. It is also linked to other legends, such as King Kuru, after whom the land is named, emphasizing its importance as a center of ancient Aryan civilization.

Political Dynamics:

Kurukshetra was the battlefield for a political struggle that had grown over generations. It was the culmination of alliances, betrayals, and power struggles among the clans of Bharatavarsha. The participation of almost every kingdom in the region reflects the epic's portrayal of the subcontinent as a unified political entity. The Kauravas' ambitions and the Pandavas' quest for justice clashed here, making it a theater for exploring ethical governance and leadership.

Cultural Dynamics:

Kurukshetra's events highlight the cultural values of sacrifice, bravery, and devotion. Rituals, war customs, and dharma debates during the battle reveal ancient Indian societal values. Krishna's role as Arjuna's charioteer and guide also reflects the cultural integration of divine principles into human lives.

Emotional Dynamics:

The war in Kurukshetra was a tragedy, bringing grief to every participating family. The deaths of heroic figures like Bhishma, Karna, and Abhimanyu evoke profound sorrow, while Arjuna's moral conflict before the battle adds emotional depth. It also reveals the agony of dharma when family ties clash with justice.

Geographical Dynamics:

Kurukshetra is located in present-day Haryana, near the Sarasvati and Yamuna rivers. Its fertile land made it a significant agricultural area. The flat terrain and proximity to water sources made it a practical location for large-scale battles, underlining its strategic importance.

2. Dwarka

Historical Significance:

Dwarka, founded by Krishna, was the Yadava kingdom's capital. It symbolized a new beginning after Krishna led his people from Mathura to escape the repeated invasions by Jarasandha. Described in the Mahabharata as a magnificent city built with celestial assistance, Dwarka became a symbol of prosperity and advanced urban planning. The eventual submergence of Dwarka into the ocean, as prophesied by Krishna, marks the end of the Yadava lineage and a significant turning point in the epic's narrative.

Political Dynamics:

As Krishna's capital, Dwarka was a hub of diplomacy. Krishna mediated numerous conflicts from here, including his interventions in the Hastinapura-Kuru rivalry. Dwarka's political neutrality allowed Krishna to balance alliances without direct involvement in the Kuru succession disputes until absolutely necessary.

Cultural Dynamics:

Dwarka became synonymous with Krishna's legacy and devotion. Its vibrant cultural life revolved around Krishna's role as a divine figure, strategist, and statesman. Over time, Dwarka's stories inspired art, music, and literature, portraying Krishna as both god and protector.

Emotional Dynamics:

Dwarka provided Krishna's followers with security and a sense of belonging. However, it also became a place of sorrow when Krishna's dynasty met its tragic end due to internal strife. Krishna's departure and

Dwarka's submergence symbolize the fleeting nature of life and material success.

Geographical Dynamics:

Situated on the western coast of Gujarat, Dwarka's proximity to the Arabian Sea made it a vital center for trade and maritime activities. Its strategic location reflects Krishna's vision of building a thriving, defensible city.

3. Hastinapura

Historical Significance:

Hastinapura was the capital of the Kuru dynasty and the epicenter of the Mahabharata. As the ancestral seat of power, it witnessed critical events like the division of the kingdom, the dice game, and Draupadi's humiliation. It represents the intersection of history and mythology, encapsulating the grandeur and decline of a mighty dynasty.

Political Dynamics:

Hastinapura was a microcosm of political intrigue, with Dhritarashtra's indecision, Shakuni's manipulation, and Duryodhana's ambition driving the kingdom toward chaos. It highlights the challenges of leadership, the importance of dharma, and the consequences of misgovernance.

Cultural Dynamics:

As a royal city, Hastinapura reflected the grandeur of courtly rituals, governance, and societal norms. It was a hub of learning, where figures like Bhishma upheld ancient traditions while dealing with evolving challenges.

Emotional Dynamics:

Hastinapura's story is one of love, loyalty, betrayal, and loss. The familial bonds within the Kuru dynasty, strained by jealousy and ambition, created some of the most poignant moments in the epic, from the exile of the Pandavas to the anguish of Gandhari over the loss of her sons.

Geographical Dynamics:

Located near the Ganges in present-day Uttar Pradesh, Hastinapura was strategically positioned for agriculture, trade, and defense. Its central location made it a pivotal political hub in ancient India.

4. Indraprastha

Historical Significance:

Indraprastha, built by the Pandavas, represented their rise to power after a fair division of the Kuru kingdom. Constructed with celestial assistance, it was a testament to their capability and Krishna's guidance. Its splendor, especially the Maya Sabha, underscored the Pandavas' vision for a prosperous rule.

Political Dynamics:

Indraprastha symbolized a political resurgence for the Pandavas. However, it became a source of envy and hatred for the Kauravas, fueling the events that led to the Kurukshetra war. The dice game and the Pandavas' loss of their kingdom underscore the fragile nature of political alliances.

Cultural Dynamics:

The city showcased advanced architectural and governance practices. The Maya Sabha became a cultural icon, symbolizing prosperity, creativity, and divine blessings.

Emotional Dynamics:

Indraprastha was a place of joy and unity for the Pandavas, but its loss marked a turning point in their journey. The humiliation of Draupadi in Hastinapura deeply scarred them, emphasizing the emotional stakes tied to their kingdom.

Geographical Dynamics:

Located on the Yamuna's banks, Indraprastha's fertile land and central position made it a strategic choice for the Pandavas' capital. Its proximity to Hastinapura highlighted the enduring tensions between the two factions.

5. Panchala

Historical Significance:

Panchala, ruled by Drupada, was a kingdom renowned for its valor and scholarship. The birthplace of Draupadi and Dhrishtadyumna, it played a vital role in uniting the Pandavas and Drupada's lineage through marriage alliances, strengthening their position against the Kauravas.

Political Dynamics:

Panchala's alliance with the Pandavas through Draupadi's marriage was a game-changer in the epic. It showcased the importance of strategic partnerships in ancient politics. Drupada's enmity with Drona, a Kaurava ally, added complexity to the war's dynamics.

Cultural Dynamics:

Panchala was a center of martial and intellectual excellence. The swayamvara of Draupadi reflects the cultural emphasis on skill, valor, and choice in marital alliances. The kingdom's traditions highlighted ancient India's societal values.

Emotional Dynamics:

Panchala's emotional significance is tied to Draupadi, whose life became a symbol of resilience and dignity. Her humiliation in Hastinapura was not only personal but also a blow to her homeland's honor, motivating Panchala's active participation in the war.

Geographical Dynamics:

Situated in present-day Uttar Pradesh, Panchala's fertile plains and proximity to key regions made it a prosperous kingdom. Its location ensured its strategic importance in the political and military landscape of the epic.

Each place in the Mahabharata is deeply intertwined with the themes of dharma, power, and human emotions, making them integral to the epic's narrative.

Chapter Ten - Five characters of Mahabharata having extraordinary magical power

1. Krishna

• **Divine Incarnation**: As an avatar of Lord Vishnu, Krishna's actions reflected his divine essence.

o **Lifting Govardhana Hill**: To protect the people of Vrindavan from Indra's wrathful rains, Krishna lifted the Govardhana Hill with a single finger, sheltering everyone for seven days and nights.

o **Rescuing Draupadi**: During Draupadi's disrobing, Krishna miraculously provided an endless sari, showcasing his ability to bend reality.

o **Cosmic Vision to Arjuna**: On the battlefield, Krishna revealed his Vishwaroopa, displaying countless universes and terrifying forms. This act overwhelmed even Arjuna, who realized Krishna's divine omnipotence.

• **Manipulation of Time and Destiny**: Krishna's strategy during the Kurukshetra war was unmatched.

o **Bhishma's fall**: He advised Arjuna to use Shikhandi as a shield against Bhishma, exploiting the latter's vow not to fight against women or those born as women.

o   **Drona's Demise**: Krishna instructed Yudhishthira to use the ambiguous statement "Ashwatthama hathaha (is dead), kunjaraha (the elephant)," misleading Drona into abandoning his weapons.

2. Bhishma Pitamaha

•   **Iccha Mrityu (Death at Will)**: Bhishma was granted the boon of choosing the time of his death by his father, King Shantanu.

o   **Example**: Even after being grievously injured in the Kurukshetra war with hundreds of arrows piercing his body, Bhishma remained alive on a bed of arrows until the time he deemed appropriate to leave his mortal body.

o   He chose to die only after the war ended and the auspicious Uttarayana (northern solstice) began, showcasing his superhuman endurance and control over death.

•   **Unmatched Warrior**:

o   Bhishma defeated many great warriors in battle, including Bhima and Arjuna, proving his martial prowess. Despite his age, he was nearly unstoppable on the battlefield until Krishna's intervention led to his fall.

•   **Vow of Celibacy**:

o   Bhishma took a lifelong vow of celibacy to ensure his father's happiness. This vow granted him divine blessings, making him invincible and a symbol of immense willpower.

- **Strategic Wisdom**:

o   As the commander of the Kaurava army, Bhishma's strategies caused massive losses to the Pandava side. He could singlehandedly challenge the combined might of their warriors.

3. Karna

- **Celestial Gifts**: Karna's Kavacha (armor) and Kundala (earrings) rendered him invincible.

o   **Surviving Arjuna's Attacks**: In multiple battles, Karna's celestial armor protected him from deadly attacks, until he willingly donated them to Indra as an act of generosity.

- **Magical Weaponry**:

o   **Brahmastra Expertise**: Karna's mastery over this divine weapon allowed him to face Arjuna on equal footing during the war.

o   **Vasavi Shakti**: Karna possessed this one-time-use weapon granted by Indra. He used it to slay Ghatotkacha, demonstrating its immense destructive power.

- **Superhuman Strength**:

o   **Winning the Competition at Draupadi's Swayamvara**: Karna displayed unmatched skill in archery but was denied the chance to marry Draupadi due to his perceived lower status.

o   **Battle Prowess**: In individual duels, he defeated formidable warriors like Bhima and Yudhishthira, proving his extraordinary combat abilities.

4. Ashwatthama

- **Immortal Being**:

o   Ashwatthama's forehead gem protected him from illness and physical harm. He remained undefeated in battle until Krishna cursed him after the war.

- **Narayanastra's Devastation**:

o   During the Kurukshetra war, Ashwatthama unleashed the Narayanastra, a weapon that sought out enemies who resisted. Krishna instructed the Pandavas and their armies to lay down their weapons in surrender to survive its wrath.

- **Brahmashira Astra**:

o   After Drona's death, Ashwatthama used the Brahmashira Astra against Arjuna. Krishna intervened to prevent its full impact, redirecting its energy to avoid annihilating the world.

- **Night Massacre at the Pandava Camp**:

o   In a desperate act of vengeance, Ashwatthama used magical powers to enter the Pandava camp at night and slaughter their sons, further highlighting his superhuman abilities, albeit in a darker context.

5. Ghatotkacha

- **Peak Powers at Night**:

o   During the Kurukshetra war, Ghatotkacha's magical abilities caused havoc in the Kaurava army. He summoned illusions, created storms, and rained down fiery weapons on his enemies.

- **Shape-Shifting and Flight**:

o   Ghatotkacha changed his size and form at will, growing into a gigantic warrior during battle. He flew over the battlefield, raining terror from above.

o   **Destroying Kaurava Forces**: At night, he wiped out large sections of Duryodhana's army, demonstrating why Rakshasas were considered invincible in darkness.

- **Ultimate Sacrifice**:

o   His death was instrumental in protecting Arjuna. Karna was forced to use the Vasavi Shakti on him, which saved Arjuna and secured the Pandavas' eventual victory.

Chapter Eleven - The birth history of six brothers

1. Yudhishthira (Son of Dharma)

• **Parents**: Kunti and Dharma (the god of righteousness).

• **Birth History**:

o Kunti was granted a divine boon by Sage Durvasa to invoke any god and bear a child. After her marriage to King Pandu, she used this boon as Pandu had been cursed by Sage Kindama to die if he engaged in physical intimacy.

o To fulfill Pandu's desire for progeny, Kunti invoked **Dharma**, the god of righteousness, resulting in the birth of Yudhishthira.

o **Significance**: As the eldest Pandava, Yudhishthira symbolized truth, justice, and dharma. His birth marked the entry of dharma incarnate into the lineage.

2. Bhima (Son of Vayu)

• **Parents**: Kunti and Vayu (the wind god).

• **Birth History**:

o   Pandu desired a son with immense physical strength to defend their kingdom. Kunti invoked **Vayu**, the wind god, using Durvasa's boon.

o   Bhima was born with divine strength, blessed by Vayu to be unmatched in physical prowess.

o   **Incident at Birth**: As a child, Bhima fell from Kunti's lap onto a rocky surface, shattering the rock instead of being injured, showcasing his superhuman strength.

3. Arjuna (Son of Indra)

•   **Parents**: Kunti and Indra (the king of the gods).

•   **Birth History**:

o   Pandu wished for a son who would be a master archer and warrior. Kunti invoked **Indra**, the king of the Godheads, and Arjuna was born.

o   **Divine Favor**: Indra blessed Arjuna with exceptional skill in warfare, making him the most proficient archer of his time.

o   **Prophecy**: It was foretold that Arjuna would bring great glory to the Kuru dynasty and play a pivotal role in the Mahabharata.

4. Nakula (Son of Ashwini Kumaras)

•   **Parents**: Madri and Ashwini Kumaras (the twin celestial physicians).

•   **Birth History**:

o   Pandu, feeling guilty for not granting Madri a child, asked her to use Kunti's boon. Madri invoked the **Ashwini Kumaras**, and Nakula was born, embodying beauty, grace, and charm.

o   **Divine Traits**: Nakula was exceptionally handsome and skilled in swordsmanship and horse rearing, inheriting the Ashwini Kumaras' qualities of swiftness and agility.

5. Sahadeva (Son of Ashwini Kumaras)

* **Parents**: Madri and Ashwini Kumaras.

* **Birth History**:

o   At the same time as Nakula's birth, Madri gave birth to Sahadeva, also fathered by the Ashwini Kumaras.

o   **Divine Traits**: Sahadeva was wise, intelligent, and deeply knowledgeable in astrology. He became an exceptional warrior with expertise in battle strategy.

o   **Twin Connection**: Nakula and Sahadeva shared a special bond, reflecting their divine origin.

6. Karna (Son of Surya) - Half-Brother to the Pandavas

* **Parents**: Kunti and Surya (the sun god).

* **Birth History**:

o   Before her marriage, Kunti tested Sage Durvasa's boon and invoked **Surya**, the sun god, out of curiosity. Surya appeared and blessed her with a son born with natural armor (**Kavacha**) and earrings (**Kundala**) to protect him.

o   Fearing societal shame as an unwed mother, Kunti placed the infant Karna in a basket and set it afloat in a river. He was later found and adopted by a charioteer couple, Radha and Adhiratha.

o   **Divine Traits**: Karna inherited Surya's radiance, courage, and generosity, becoming one of the greatest warriors of the Mahabharata.

Key Connections and Themes:

1.   **Divine Intervention**: All six brothers were born with the blessings of gods, marking them as divine beings with extraordinary abilities.

2.   **Kunti's Role**: As the mother of five of the brothers, Kunti was instrumental in invoking divine forces for the Pandavas' births.

3.   **Sibling Rivalry**: Karna's abandonment and his later rivalry with the Pandavas added complexity to the epic, especially his conflict with Arjuna.

These divine origins not only set the stage for the Pandavas' extraordinary feats but also underscored the celestial influence on the epic's narrative.

Karna is considered the **half-brother** of the Pandavas because they share the same mother, **Kunti**, though they were born to different fathers.

How Karna is related to the Pandavas:

1.   **Kunti – The Common Link**:

o   Kunti, the mother of the Pandavas, gave birth to Karna before her marriage to Pandu. She had been blessed by Sage Durvasa with a mantra to summon any god and bear a child. Out of curiosity, she invoked the sun god, **Surya**, and Karna was born with celestial armor and earrings.

2.   **Different Fathers**:

o   Karna's father was **Surya**, the sun god.

o   The Pandavas were born to **different deities** through Kunti and Madri as follows:

▪   Yudhishthira: Son of Dharma (the god of righteousness).

▪   Bhima: Son of Vayu (the wind god).

▪   Arjuna: Son of Indra (the king of the gods).

▪   Nakula and Sahadeva: Sons of the Ashwini Kumaras (twin celestial physicians).

o   Hence, Karna and the Pandavas had different fathers, making Karna their **half-brother**, as only their mother, Kunti, was common.

3.   **Why the Relationship Was Hidden**:

o   Kunti, fearing societal shame as an unwed mother, abandoned Karna shortly after his birth. He was adopted by the charioteer couple **Radha** and **Adhiratha**, who raised him as their son. Karna grew up unaware of his true parentage.

o   Kunti revealed the truth to Karna only before the Kurukshetra war, begging him to join his half-brothers, the Pandavas. However, Karna, loyal to Duryodhana, refused to betray his friend.

Significance of Karna's Half-Brotherhood:

This hidden relationship added emotional and moral complexity to the Mahabharata:

o   Karna's rivalry with Arjuna gained poignancy when it was revealed that they were brothers.

o   Kunti's internal conflict and grief over Karna's fate highlighted the tragic dimensions of the epic.

o   Despite their blood connection, Karna remained on the Kaurava side due to his loyalty to Duryodhana, eventually meeting his demise at the hands of Arjuna.

Chapter Twelve - Ten true and unselfish friendship found in Mahabharata

1. Karna and Duryodhana: A Friendship Built on Loyalty and Mutual Respect

Karna and Duryodhana's friendship is one of the most profound and selfless bonds in the Mahabharata. This relationship transcended societal norms and personal ambitions, becoming a defining element of their lives. Karna, born as the eldest son of Kunti but abandoned at birth, was raised by a charioteer's family. This lineage subjected him to constant humiliation and exclusion, especially from the Kshatriya class. Despite Karna's unmatched skill and valor, his caste became a barrier to gaining recognition.

Duryodhana, the eldest Kaurava prince, saw in Karna a capable ally and a potential equal. When Karna was insulted by the Pandavas and others during the archery tournament, Duryodhana stood up for him, declaring him the king of Anga. This act of generosity and defiance not only elevated Karna's status but also forged an unbreakable bond between them. Karna, overwhelmed by Duryodhana's gesture, pledged his unwavering loyalty to him.

Throughout their lives, Karna and Duryodhana's friendship remained steadfast. Karna became Duryodhana's most trusted confidant and strategist. Despite learning his true identity as Kunti's son, Karna chose to remain loyal to Duryodhana, rejecting Kunti's request to join the Pandavas. This decision highlights Karna's sense of honor and gratitude, as he valued Duryodhana's trust and friendship above blood ties.

Duryodhana, too, was deeply respected Karna's abilities and character. He relied on Karna in the Kurukshetra war, often placing him in critical roles. Even as the odds turned against the Kauravas; their bond remained unshaken. Duryodhana's unwavering faith in Karna is evident when he names him the commander of the Kaurava army after Dronacharya's death.

Their friendship, however, was not without tragedy. Karna's loyalty to Duryodhana ultimately led to his downfall. Despite his heroic efforts on the battlefield, Karna was defeated by Arjuna, partly due to his adherence to dharma and curses placed upon him. Duryodhana, too, faced a bitter end, grieving the loss of his closest friend.

The friendship between Karna and Duryodhana serves as a poignant reminder of loyalty, gratitude, and the complexities of human relationships. It showcases how bonds forged in mutual respect and understanding can endure even in the face of overwhelming odds and societal prejudices. Their relationship remains a cornerstone of the Mahabharata, symbolizing the power of selfless friendship.

2. Kunti and Madri: Sisterhood Forged in Love and Shared Responsibility

Kunti and Madri, the co-wives of King Pandu, embody a unique bond of sisterhood in the Mahabharata. Their relationship transcended the traditional rivalries of polygamous unions, instead highlighting mutual respect, understanding, and selflessness. Despite the challenges of their shared marital life, they navigated their roles with grace and solidarity, setting an example of sisterly affection.

Kunti, the elder of the two, was blessed with a divine boon to invoke any deity and bear children. This gift became a cornerstone of their relationship. After Pandu was cursed by Sage Kindama to die if he engaged in marital relations, Kunti used her boon to bear three sons Yudhishthira, Bhima, and Arjuna thereby ensuring the continuation of Pandu's lineage. However, Kunti's most selfless act was sharing her boon with Madri, enabling her to bear Nakula and Sahadeva through the Ashwini Kumaras. This gesture demonstrated Kunti's magnanimity and commitment to familial harmony, as she willingly sacrificed exclusivity to uplift Madri's position.

Madri reciprocated this generosity with immense gratitude and loyalty. She supported Kunti as an equal partner in their shared responsibility of managing the household and raising their children in the forest exile.

However, their bond was most poignantly tested after Pandu's untimely death. Overcome by guilt and love for her husband, Madri decided to ascend his funeral pyre in the practice of sati. Before doing so, she entrusted the care of Nakula and Sahadeva to Kunti, affirming her trust in her elder co-wife's ability to nurture her sons as her own.

Kunti's fulfillment of this promise further highlights the depth of their relationship. Despite the challenges of raising five children under harsh conditions, Kunti never showed favoritism, treating Nakula and Sahadeva with the same affection and guidance she provided to her biological sons. This commitment to Madri's memory underscores Kunti's role as the emotional anchor of the family.

The bond between Kunti and Madri reflects a rare harmony in shared womanhood, where love and duty overcame jealousy or competition. Their story symbolizes the strength found in unity, the beauty of selflessness, and the enduring power of trust and shared purpose. Their relationship adds a profound emotional layer to the Mahabharata, emphasizing the importance of collective responsibility and sisterhood in sustaining family and legacy.

3. Draupadi and Bhanumati: Graceful Bonding across Rivalry

The relationship between Draupadi, the queen of the Pandavas, and Bhanumati, the wife of Duryodhana, is a lesser-explored aspect of the Mahabharata. Their friendship, though understated, reveals the possibility of grace and camaraderie amidst the intense enmity between their respective families. While the rivalry between the Pandavas and the Kauravas shaped the epic's central conflict, Draupadi and Bhanumati's bond stands as a quiet testament to human connection transcending political divisions.

One anecdote often recounted involves Draupadi inadvertently entering Bhanumati's chamber during a casual game between her and Duryodhana. As the story goes, Bhanumati was startled, and Duryodhana lost the game due to the interruption. Instead of reacting with hostility, Bhanumati laughed off the incident, demonstrating her gracious nature and an ability to separate personal relationships from political animosities. This interaction, though brief, became emblematic of mutual respect and understanding between the two women.

Their friendship is further highlighted by their shared experiences as royal women navigating immense pressure. Draupadi, often caught in the crossfire of power struggles, found solace in her ability to maintain dignity amidst adversity. Similarly, Bhanumati, though married to a man often criticized for his ambitions, managed her role with elegance and resilience. Their individual strength and poise became a common ground for mutual admiration.

This understated friendship also underscores the human side of the Mahabharata, often overshadowed by its grand narratives of war and dharma. It suggests that relationships, even among rivals, can foster empathy and shared respect. The moments they shared, even if limited, reflect the potential for unity and understanding in a world dominated by divisions.

In a broader sense, Draupadi and Bhanumati's interactions remind us of the importance of transcending enmity to recognize shared humanity. Their bond, though not a central theme of the epic, offers a refreshing perspective on the lives of women in the Mahabharata. It is a subtle yet powerful example of how personal grace and understanding can prevail even amidst the most divisive conflicts.

4. Krishna and Draupadi: The Eternal Bond of Divine Friendship

The relationship between Krishna and Draupadi is one of the most significant and celebrated friendships in the Mahabharata. It is a bond built on mutual trust, spiritual understanding, and unwavering support. Krishna, as the divine incarnation of Lord Vishnu, and Draupadi, born from the sacred fire, shared a unique connection that transcended ordinary human relationships. Their friendship is a cornerstone of the epic, demonstrating selfless love, loyalty, and the sanctity of true companionship.

Draupadi trusted Krishna implicitly and sought his guidance during her darkest moments. The most defining instance of their bond is the infamous dice game episode. When Draupadi was humiliated in the Kaurava court and subjected to the disrobing attempt, she called out to Krishna for help. Krishna responded immediately, miraculously extending her sari to protect her dignity. This act not only symbolized Krishna's divine intervention but also underscored his role as her protector and confidant. It also highlighted the spiritual aspect of their relationship, where Krishna embodied dharma and Draupadi symbolized faith and devotion.

Krishna, on his part, admired Draupadi for her resilience, intelligence, and unwavering adherence to dharma. He often acted as her guide and advisor, offering strategic counsel during critical moments of the Pandavas' journey. For example, during the Kurukshetra war, Krishna's plans often revolved around ensuring justice for Draupadi, who had suffered immensely at the hands of the Kauravas.

Their bond was not just limited to moments of crisis but extended to everyday life. Draupadi's interactions with Krishna reveal a deep emotional understanding. She confided in him, and Krishna, in turn, treated her with the utmost respect and empathy. Their conversations often carried profound spiritual and philosophical undertones, reflecting their intellectual compatibility and mutual regard.

Krishna's unwavering support for Draupadi highlights his role as a divine friend who stood by her without expecting anything in return. He saw in her a reflection of dharma and justice, and his actions were aimed at upholding these values. Draupadi, on the other hand, demonstrated unshakeable faith in Krishna, considering him her ultimate refuge.

The friendship between Krishna and Draupadi serves as an eternal example of selfless love, unwavering support, and spiritual connection. It underscores the idea that true friendship transcends gender, social norms, and worldly limitations, becoming a sacred bond rooted in mutual respect and shared purpose.

5. Krishna and Shiva: The Divine Alliance of Harmony and Balance

Krishna and Shiva represent two of the most revered deities in Hinduism, symbolizing two distinct yet complementary aspects of divinity. Their interactions in the Mahabharata illustrate an alliance of harmony, balance, and cosmic order. While Krishna is the preserver and a master strategist embodying love and compassion, Shiva is the destroyer and ascetic, representing transformation and detachment. Together, they personify the cyclical nature of creation, preservation, and destruction that sustains the universe.

In the Mahabharata, the bond between Krishna and Shiva is highlighted through several instances that showcase their mutual respect and cooperation. One of the most notable examples is Krishna's worship of Shiva to obtain the Pashupatastra, a powerful celestial weapon. Despite being an incarnation of Vishnu, Krishna approached Shiva with utmost humility and devotion, performing penance to seek his blessings.

This act underscores Krishna's recognition of Shiva's unparalleled strength and his role as a cosmic force.

Shiva, in turn, acknowledged Krishna's divine purpose and supported him in his mission to uphold dharma. By granting Krishna the Pashupatastra, Shiva demonstrated his trust in Krishna's ability to use the weapon responsibly and for the greater good. This mutual recognition of each other's roles reflects the spiritual synergy between them.

The Krishna-Shiva dynamic also carries profound philosophical significance. While Krishna represents the path of devotion and righteous action (karma), Shiva embodies the path of renunciation and self-realization (jnana). Together, they offer a holistic vision of life, emphasizing the importance of balancing worldly responsibilities with spiritual pursuits.

Their bond also highlights the principle of interdependence among divine forces. Krishna and Shiva, though different in their attributes and functions, worked together to maintain cosmic balance. This collaboration serves as a reminder of the unity underlying the diversity of divine manifestations, reinforcing the idea that all paths ultimately lead to the same truth.

The relationship between Krishna and Shiva is a testament to the coexistence of contrasting yet complementary forces in the universe. It exemplifies how cooperation, mutual respect, and shared purpose can harmonize differences to achieve a greater good. Their bond in the Mahabharata is not just a narrative element but a profound spiritual teaching, emphasizing the unity and interconnectedness of all aspects of existence.

6. Ashwatthama and Duryodhana: A Bond of Shared Vengeance and Loyalty

The friendship between Ashwatthama and Duryodhana stands out as a unique blend of loyalty, shared ambition, and mutual respect in the Mahabharata. Ashwatthama, the son of Dronacharya, was a formidable warrior and one of the few humans granted immortality (chiranjivi) by Lord Shiva. Duryodhana, as the eldest Kaurava prince, saw in Ashwatthama a steadfast ally and a reliable confidant. Their friendship was deeply rooted in their shared belief in the Kaurava cause and their personal grievances against the Pandavas.

Ashwatthama and Duryodhana bonded over their mutual dissatisfaction with the perceived injustices of the world. While Duryodhana harbored deep-seated jealousy and animosity towards the Pandavas due to their superior claim to the throne, Ashwatthama's grievances stemmed from his father's humiliation and eventual death at the hands of the Pandavas. These shared emotional wounds solidified their partnership, with Ashwatthama dedicating himself to Duryodhana's cause out of loyalty and a sense of personal vendetta.

Throughout the Kurukshetra war, Ashwatthama stood by Duryodhana as a loyal friend and warrior. He played a key role in several critical battles, showcasing his strategic acumen and martial prowess. However, his most notable act of loyalty occurred after Duryodhana's defeat. Devastated by the deaths of his brothers and allies, Duryodhana sought solace in Ashwatthama's companionship. In response, Ashwatthama vowed to avenge Duryodhana's suffering. This culminated in the infamous night raid on the Pandava camp, where Ashwatthama slaughtered the sleeping sons of the Pandavas, believing them to be his enemies.

Despite the questionable morality of his actions, Ashwatthama's loyalty to Duryodhana was unwavering. Even when cursed by Krishna for his heinous act, Ashwatthama's regret was more for his failure to secure Duryodhana's ultimate victory than for his own suffering. This highlights the depth of his commitment to their friendship.

The bond between Ashwatthama and Duryodhana is a complex and tragic narrative. While their shared vengeance brought them close, it also led them down a path of moral compromise and destruction. Their friendship serves as a cautionary tale about the dangers of unchecked loyalty and the consequences of allowing personal grievances to dictate one's actions. Nevertheless, it is a poignant example of selfless devotion, showcasing the lengths to which true friends might go for one another, even at great personal cost.

7. Shishupala, Salva Naresh, Kashiraj, and Dantavakra: A Quartet of Political Alliances and Shared Animus

The alliance among Shishupala, Salva Naresh, Kashiraj, and Dantavakra is one of the most intriguing examples of selfless camaraderie rooted in shared opposition to Krishna. Despite their individual differences and personal ambitions, these four kings united in their animosity towards Krishna and the Yadavas, creating a bond that transcended political rivalry.

Shishupala, the king of Chedi, was Krishna's cousin but nurtured a lifelong hatred towards him due to a prophecy predicting his death at Krishna's hands. Salva Naresh, the ruler of Saubha, bore a grudge against Krishna for defeating him in battle and destroying his flying city. Kashiraj, as the ruler of Kashi, shared similar enmity stemming from Krishna's military interventions, while Dantavakra, another cousin of Krishna, harbored personal grievances against him.

This quartet found common ground in their opposition to Krishna's growing influence, both politically and spiritually. Their bond was characterized by mutual respect and strategic cooperation rather than personal affection. For instance, Shishupala's defiance during Yudhishthira's Rajasuya Yajna was supported by these allies, demonstrating their united front against Krishna. Similarly, Salva Naresh's attempts to wage war against Dwaraka were bolstered by the moral and logistical support of this alliance.

While their friendship was primarily driven by their shared hatred, it also reflected a deeper sense of loyalty and mutual dependence. They recognized each other's strengths and weaknesses, pooling their resources to challenge Krishna's dominance. However, their combined efforts ultimately fell short, as Krishna's divine prowess and strategic brilliance outmatched their plans.

The camaraderie among these kings highlights the complexities of political alliances in the Mahabharata. It underscores how shared goals, even if negative, can foster strong bonds among individuals. Their relationship, though adversarial in nature, was marked by selflessness and a willingness to support one another unconditionally.

Ultimately, their downfall serves as a reminder of the futility of opposing dharma and divine will. While their friendship remains an interesting aspect of the Mahabharata, it also emphasizes the limits of human ambition and the inevitability of justice. Their bond, though rooted in negativity, showcases the power of unity and cooperation, even among individuals driven by animosity.

8. Virat Raj and Yudhishthira: A Friendship of Mutual Trust and Strategic Alliance

The bond between Virat Raj, the ruler of Matsya, and Yudhishthira, the eldest Pandava, stands as a testament to trust, hospitality, and political foresight. This friendship played a crucial role during the Pandavas' final year of exile, where they had to live incognito to fulfill the terms of their agreement with the Kauravas. Virat Raj unknowingly provided the Pandavas sanctuary in his kingdom, enabling them to navigate this challenging period successfully.

When the Pandavas entered Matsya in disguise, Yudhishthira, taking the role of a courtier and dice player named Kanka, won the favor of Virat Raj through his wisdom and impeccable conduct. Despite being unaware of Yudhishthira's true identity, Virat Raj trusted him deeply, often seeking his counsel in matters of state and governance. Yudhishthira's composed demeanor, intellectual sharpness, and moral integrity strengthened this bond, making him an indispensable advisor to the king.

The friendship between Virat Raj and Yudhishthira highlights the concept of mutual respect. While Virat Raj unknowingly protected the exiled Pandavas, his relationship with Yudhishthira was not merely transactional. Yudhishthira's loyalty to his temporary role as Kanka and his efforts to uphold the kingdom's welfare demonstrated his gratitude and integrity. This dynamic reflected the ethos of dharma, where alliances are nurtured through selfless service and unwavering commitment to shared ideals.

This friendship also had significant political implications. After the Pandavas revealed their identities following the successful defense of Matsya against the Kauravas, Virat Raj realized the magnitude of his decision to shelter them. His alliance with the Pandavas became a cornerstone of their preparations for the Kurukshetra war. By marrying his daughter Uttara to Arjuna's son Abhimanyu, Virat Raj solidified his kingdom's loyalty to the Pandava cause, providing them with a strategic advantage.

Emotionally, Virat Raj's trust in Yudhishthira represents the resilience of human relationships, even under deceptive circumstances. Despite the Pandavas' need for secrecy, their virtuous conduct ensured that their bond with Virat Raj was founded on genuine respect and mutual benefit.

The friendship between Virat Raj and Yudhishthira showcases the importance of trust and integrity in forging alliances. It serves as an example of how selflessness, wisdom, and moral conduct can transform a temporary association into a lasting partnership that shapes the course of history.

9. Nand and Vasudeva: A Relationship of Parental Devotion and Shared Responsibility

The friendship between Nand, the head of the Gokul community, and Vasudeva, the father of Krishna, is a profound example of trust, selflessness, and shared responsibility. Their bond is marked by the ultimate sacrifice and unwavering loyalty, as Nand risked his life and the safety of his family to protect Krishna during his infancy, fulfilling a divine purpose.

When Vasudeva, imprisoned by Kansa, received a divine revelation that his eighth child, Krishna, would be the slayer of Kansa, he turned to his trusted friend Nand for help. In a night filled with divine intervention and danger, Vasudeva carried the newborn Krishna across the flooded Yamuna River to Gokul, entrusting him to Nand and Yashoda's care. This act underscored Vasudeva's faith in Nand's devotion and his ability to protect Krishna from Kansa's wrath.

Nand and Yashoda accepted Krishna as their own child without hesitation, raising him with unconditional love and care. Their selflessness is evident in the way they shielded Krishna from Kansa's numerous attempts to kill him, often putting their community at risk. Nand's steadfast loyalty to Vasudeva and his divine mission demonstrates the depth of their friendship and his commitment to dharma.

Vasudeva, on the other hand, remained grateful to Nand, recognizing the immense sacrifice he made. Their bond extended beyond personal friendship, rooted in their shared responsibility to nurture and protect Krishna, who was destined to restore cosmic order.

This relationship also carries significant emotional depth. Nand's unwavering love for Krishna, despite knowing the truth of his parentage, reflects the purity of a father's devotion. For Vasudeva, entrusting his child to Nand was an act of immense faith and emotional resilience. Their mutual understanding and respect transcended familial boundaries, creating a bond that symbolized the unity of purpose and the power of selflessness.

The friendship between Nand and Vasudeva is an enduring narrative of shared sacrifice and trust. It highlights the strength of relationships forged in the crucible of divine purpose and personal hardship. Their bond serves as a reminder of the transformative power of selflessness and the enduring impact of true friendship in fulfilling higher responsibilities.

10. Lakshmana and Vrishasena: A Friendship of Youthful Innocence and Warrior Spirit

Lakshmana, Duryodhana's beloved daughter, and Vrishasena, Karna's eldest son, shared a friendship that is often overlooked in the Mahabharata. This bond, formed during their childhood, was marked by youthful innocence, mutual admiration, and the shared legacy of their fathers' camaraderie.

Both Lakshmana and Vrishasena grew up in the opulent yet volatile atmosphere of Hastinapura, surrounded by the ambitions and conflicts of their families. As the children of two of the Kaurava camp's most influential figures, their friendship symbolized the unity and loyalty within the Kaurava fold. Despite the impending doom of the Kurukshetra war, Lakshmana and Vrishasena maintained a bond rooted in simplicity and shared experiences, away from the complexities of adult politics.

Vrishasena, inheriting his father's valor and skills as a warrior, became an integral part of the Kaurava army during the Kurukshetra war. Lakshmana, though not a warrior herself, admired Vrishasena's courage and dedication, often serving as a moral support. Their friendship reflected the untainted ideals of loyalty and mutual respect, even in the shadow of conflict.

Tragically, both Lakshmana and Vrishasena's lives were cut short during the war, symbolizing the futility of generational enmity and the loss of youthful potential. Vrishasena was killed by Arjuna, fulfilling his vow to avenge Abhimanyu's death, while Lakshmana's fate remains uncertain, though her grief over the war's devastation is a poignant reminder of the human cost of conflict.

Their friendship is a testament to the innocence and purity that can exist even amidst chaos and destruction. It highlights the unifying power of personal relationships, offering a stark contrast to the divisive ambitions of their elders. While their bond is a minor narrative in the epic, it serves as a poignant reminder of the lives and relationships overshadowed by the grander schemes of history.

Chapter Thirteen - Three unwavering Bhakti towards Krishna

1. Vidura: The Embodiment of Selfless Devotion

Vidura, the wise counselor of Hastinapura, exemplifies unwavering Bhakti in every facet of his life. Born to a maidservant and Sage Vyasa, Vidura was denied royal privileges but was blessed with extraordinary wisdom and insight. His devotion was not expressed through rituals or chants but through his lifelong adherence to Dharma. Vidura viewed Dharma as the very embodiment of the divine, and his actions reflected his deep spiritual connection with Lord Krishna.

One of the most illustrative moments of Vidura's Bhakti is his interaction with Krishna during the latter's peace mission to Hastinapura. Despite being a minister, Vidura lived modestly, away from the indulgences of the royal palace. When Krishna chose to stay at Vidura's humble abode instead of the grand accommodations prepared by Duryodhana, it reflected the purity of their relationship. Vidura welcomed Krishna with great affection, offering him simple food. Legend has it that in his nervous devotion, Vidura accidentally peeled bananas and offered Krishna the peels instead of the fruit. Krishna, delighting in Vidura's sincerity, accepted the offering without hesitation. This moment is celebrated as an example of how true devotion transcends material offerings—it is the purity of intention that matters.

Vidura's Bhakti extended beyond personal devotion; it was intertwined with his duty as a guide and protector of righteousness. During the events leading to the Kurukshetra war, Vidura tirelessly warned Dhritarashtra and Duryodhana against their unjust actions. He reminded them of the divine presence in Krishna and urged them to uphold Dharma. His unwavering moral stance made him a lone voice of reason in a court driven by greed and ambition. Despite facing ridicule and isolation, Vidura remained steadfast, knowing that his allegiance was to Krishna and Dharma.

In the aftermath of the war, Vidura chose to renounce worldly life and retreat to the forest, dedicating himself entirely to meditation and spiritual pursuits. He sought to merge with the divine essence he had served all his life. Vidura's Bhakti, rooted in wisdom and selflessness, teaches us that true devotion lies in living a life of integrity, even when faced with adversity. His life serves as a timeless example of devotion expressed through righteous action.

2. Kunti: A Mother's Devotion to Krishna

Kunti, the matriarch of the Pandavas, exemplifies devotion born from faith and surrender. Her life was a tapestry of trials, from her early widowhood to her struggles as the mother of five exiled sons. Yet, Kunti's unwavering Bhakti in Krishna became her anchor through every storm. Her devotion was not just emotional; it was rooted in her deep understanding of the divine plan and her role in it.

One of the most illustrative examples of Kunti's Bhakti is her interaction with Krishna after the Kurukshetra war. Despite having lost all her sons except Arjuna, Kunti did not complain or curse her fate. Instead, she expressed gratitude to Krishna for protecting her family and asked for continued adversities in her life. This surprising request, recorded in her famous prayer, reflects her profound spiritual wisdom. She believed that challenges kept her mind focused on Krishna, ensuring her liberation from worldly attachments. This prayer highlights the depth of her devotion Kunti saw suffering as a blessing that brought her closer to the divine.

Kunti's faith in Krishna's guidance was evident throughout the Mahabharata. When the palace of wax was set ablaze by Duryodhana's conspirators, it was Kunti's quick thinking and faith in divine protection that saved the Pandavas. Later, during the exile, she encouraged her sons to remain steadfast in their adherence to Dharma, even in the face of immense hardship. Kunti's Bhakti was not passive; it was a source of strength and resilience for her family.

Her relationship with Krishna was deeply personal. She addressed him as her savior and nephew, blending familial affection with spiritual reverence. In moments of despair, she turned to Krishna, trusting his divine wisdom to guide her through. Even when faced with the heartbreak of Karna's death, Kunti found solace in her faith that Krishna's plan was ultimately for the greater good.

Kunti's Bhakti teaches us to view life's challenges as opportunities for spiritual growth. Her unwavering faith in Krishna, even in the darkest times, serves as an inspiring example of how devotion can provide strength and clarity in life's most difficult moments.

3. Draupadi: Devotion in the Face of Adversity

Draupadi, the queen of the Pandavas, is one of the most vivid examples of unwavering Bhakti in the Mahabharata. Her devotion to Krishna was born out of a deep faith in his divinity and an unshakable trust in his protection. Draupadi's life was a series of trials, each more harrowing than the last, yet her faith in Krishna never wavered.

The most iconic illustration of Draupadi's Bhakti is her appeal to Krishna during the dice game incident. After Yudhishthira gambled away everything, including Draupadi, she was dragged into the Kaurava court and humiliated. When Dushasana attempted to disrobe her, Draupadi turned to Krishna with complete surrender, crying out for his help. In that moment of utter helplessness, Krishna answered her call, miraculously extending her sari to an endless length and protecting her dignity. This event is a cornerstone of Bhakti literature, symbolizing the power of complete surrender and trust in the divine. Draupadi's plea was not just a cry for help; it was a declaration of her unyielding faith that Krishna would never abandon her.

Draupadi's Bhakti went beyond moments of crisis. She shared a deep, personal bond with Krishna, who often referred to her as Sakhi (friend). This relationship was marked by mutual respect and understanding. During the exile, Krishna visited the Pandavas and reassured Draupadi of his support, giving her strength to endure the hardships. When Krishna provided the Akshaya Patra, a magical vessel that ensured endless food, it was a testament to his care for her and her unwavering faith in him.

Even during the Kurukshetra war, Draupadi's faith in Krishna remained unshaken. She believed that he was the ultimate orchestrator, guiding the Pandavas to victory while upholding Dharma. Her devotion was not passive; she actively encouraged her husbands to fight for justice, embodying the strength of a devotee who stands firm in righteousness with the divine as her anchor.

Draupadi's life teaches us that Bhakti is not limited to rituals or prayers—it is an unshakable trust in the divine, especially during life's most challenging moments. Her devotion to Krishna, marked by both surrender and resilience, remains an enduring inspiration for generations.

The unwavering Bhakti of Vidura, Kunti, and Draupadi serves as a testament to the power of faith and devotion in navigating life's challenges. Each of these characters expressed their devotion uniquely—Vidura through his adherence to Dharma, Kunti through her surrender to Krishna's divine plan, and Draupadi through her trust in Krishna's protection. Their lives illustrate that true Bhakti transcends rituals and manifests in the way one lives, guided by faith, integrity, and a deep connection to the divine. These stories continue to inspire us, reminding us that devotion, rooted in sincerity and resilience, can transform even the most difficult circumstances into paths of spiritual growth.

Chapter Fourteen - Five significant contradictions in Mahabharata

Intricacies and moral ambiguities of decision-making in the Mahabharata offering valuable insights into its timeless relevance

1. Draupadi's Swayamvara and Rejection of Karna

The Swayamvara of Draupadi stands as one of the most significant events in the Mahabharata, but it also reveals a glaring contradiction in her decision-making. The contest required a suitor to string a mighty bow and pierce the eye of a moving fish by only looking at its reflection in water an impossible feat for all but the most skilled warriors. Among those who attended were the greatest princes and warriors of the time, including Arjuna, Karna, Duryodhana, and Krishna.

When Karna, the mighty archer and Duryodhana's close ally, stepped forward, he effortlessly strung the bow and prepared to complete the challenge. However, before he could shoot the arrow, Draupadi intervened, declaring that she would not marry a suta putra (the son of a charioteer). This decision shocked the audience, including Karna, whose talent and skill were unquestionable. Draupadi's proclamation denied him a fair chance to win her hand, contradicting the swayamvara's promise of impartiality and meritocracy.

Draupadi's rejection of Karna is often interpreted as a conflict between her feelings and societal norms. Some versions of the Mahabharata hint that Draupadi admired Karna's prowess and may have had feelings for him, but her loyalty to social expectations overrode personal preferences. Her decision aligned her with the Pandavas, as Arjuna ultimately won the contest, but it also sowed the seeds of Karna's deep resentment toward Draupadi and the Pandavas.

This act had far-reaching consequences. It strengthened Karna's bond with Duryodhana, as the rejection reaffirmed his outsider status in the royal circles. It fueled Karna's animosity toward Draupadi, leading to his role in her public humiliation during the dice game. Additionally, her decision highlighted the caste prejudice prevalent even among the noblest characters in the epic, contradicting the ideals of dharma and fairness.

Draupadi's rejection of Karna demonstrates the complexity of her character—strong-willed and principled but also bound by societal constraints. It reflects the moral ambiguities of the Mahabharata, where even seemingly righteous decisions have consequences that ripple far beyond the moment of choice. This contradiction underscores the tension between individual merit and societal norms, making it one of the most debated episodes in the epic.

2. Bhishma's Vow of Celibacy

Bhishma's vow of lifelong celibacy is one of the most celebrated yet contradictory decisions in the Mahabharata. Born as Devavrata, he was the son of King Shantanu and Goddess Ganga, destined to be a great ruler of the Kuru dynasty. His life took a pivotal turn when Shantanu fell in love with Satyavati, a fisherwoman. Her father, Dasaraj, demanded that her offspring inherit the throne, even over Devavrata, the crown prince.

To fulfill his father's wishes, Devavrata renounced the throne, a sacrifice that earned him the name "Bhishma" (the one who undertakes a terrible vow). However, Dasaraj was still unsatisfied, fearing that Bhishma's descendants might challenge Satyavati's line. In response, Bhishma took an extraordinary oath of lifelong celibacy, ensuring that he would neither marry nor father children, eliminating any potential rival heirs.

While this act of selflessness is celebrated as an ultimate display of loyalty and duty, it created a glaring contradiction. By taking this vow, Bhishma unintentionally jeopardized the very future of the Kuru dynasty. Without him as a successor, the throne was passed to less capable rulers like Vichitravirya and later, Dhritarashtra and Pandu. This lack of strong leadership eventually led to the disintegration of the dynasty and the catastrophic Kurukshetra War.

Bhishma's decision also contradicted his responsibility as a prince to prioritize the stability of the kingdom over personal sacrifice. Though his intentions were noble, his vow indirectly caused political instability, as the Kuru throne lacked capable heirs for generations. Additionally, his celibacy distanced him emotionally from the family's internal struggles, limiting his ability to intervene effectively in resolving conflicts, especially between the Kauravas and Pandavas.

The consequences of Bhishma's vow were profound. It led to Satyavati summoning Vyasa to father children through niyoga, an act that perpetuated discord within the family. Moreover, Bhishma's inability to relinquish his loyalty to the throne, even when Duryodhana acted unjustly, further amplified the conflict.

Bhishma's sacrifice reflects the complex nature of dharma in the Mahabharata, where personal righteousness can clash with broader responsibilities. His vow, while heroic, highlights how even the most virtuous choices can have unintended and devastating consequences, making him a tragic figure in the epic.

3. Drona's Partiality Towards Arjuna

Dronacharya, the revered teacher of the Pandavas and Kauravas, is a figure marked by wisdom and skill but also by contradictions in decision-making. His unwavering partiality towards Arjuna stands out as a defining paradox, challenging his role as an impartial guru.

Drona's preference for Arjuna became evident early in their training. While all the princes received equal lessons, Drona ensured Arjuna received extra attention, recognizing his exceptional talent and devotion. He promised to make Arjuna the greatest archer in the world, a vow that dictated many of his decisions.

This favoritism culminated in a controversial episode involving Ekalavya, a tribal boy who surpassed Arjuna in archery. Denied formal training due to his lower caste, Ekalavya practiced in front of a statue of Drona, achieving extraordinary skill. When Arjuna expressed insecurity about Ekalavya's abilities, Drona demanded Ekalavya's thumb as guru dakshina (teacher's fee), knowing it would cripple his archery skills. This decision, made to fulfill his promise to Arjuna, contradicted Drona's duty as a teacher to nurture talent impartially.

The consequences of this act were profound. It highlighted the systemic injustice of caste discrimination, alienating Ekalavya and others like him from the mainstream. Drona's partiality also set a dangerous precedent, demonstrating that merit could be sacrificed for personal bias and promises.

Furthermore, Drona's favoritism towards Arjuna clashed with his loyalty to the Kauravas, particularly Duryodhana, who was instrumental in Drona's appointment as royal teacher. While Drona's heart lay with the Pandavas, his dependence on the Kauravas for livelihood forced him to train both factions, ultimately fueling the rivalry that led to the Kurukshetra War.

Drona's decisions illustrate the complex moral dilemmas faced by individuals bound by competing loyalties. While his preference for Arjuna stemmed from admiration for his dedication, it revealed the human flaws of a man hailed as a symbol of wisdom. His actions emphasize the recurring theme in the Mahabharata: that even the most righteous individuals are susceptible to contradictions when navigating the intricate web of duty, loyalty, and morality.

4. Yudhishthira's Gamble

Yudhishthira, the eldest Pandava and a paragon of dharma, made a decision during the dice game that starkly contradicted his moral principles. Known for his sense of justice and adherence to truth, Yudhishthira willingly gambled away his kingdom, wealth, brothers, and even Draupadi in a game of chance, undermining his responsibilities as a king and protector of his family.

The dice game was orchestrated by Shakuni, Duryodhana's uncle, who manipulated the event to exploit Yudhishthira's weaknesses. Despite knowing that Shakuni was an unscrupulous player, Yudhishthira agreed to play, driven by a misplaced sense of honor and obligation to accept challenges. As the game progressed, he fell into a spiral of greed and desperation, staking everything he held dear.

Yudhishthira's decision to gamble Draupadi, a sentient being, was a glaring contradiction to his values as a just ruler. This act not only degraded Draupadi but also exposed his inability to uphold dharma in moments of personal weakness. Furthermore, his choices disregarded the collective welfare of the Pandavas and their shared responsibilities.

The consequences of Yudhishthira's actions were devastating. Draupadi's humiliation in the Kaurava court, where Dushasana attempted to disrobe her, became a turning point in the epic, escalating the feud between the Kauravas and Pandavas. The Pandavas' subsequent exile and the Kurukshetra War were direct outcomes of this event.

Yudhishthira's gamble reveals the vulnerability of even the most virtuous individuals when confronted with temptation and manipulation. It underscores the Mahabharata's central theme of dharma being a fluid and often contradictory concept, challenging individuals to navigate its complexities in real-time decisions.

5. Krishna's Role in Abhimanyu's Training

Krishna, known for his divine wisdom and strategic brilliance, made a seemingly contradictory decision in Abhimanyu's training. While Abhimanyu learned the intricate strategy of entering the Chakravyuha (a complex, multi-layered battle formation), he was never taught how to exit it. This gap in his knowledge became fatal during the Kurukshetra War, when Abhimanyu, unable to escape the formation, was trapped and killed by the Kauravas.

Abhimanyu's partial training raises questions about Krishna's motives and foresight. As an omniscient being and protector of the Pandavas, Krishna could have ensured that Abhimanyu was fully equipped for battle. Some interpretations suggest that Krishna deliberately withheld this knowledge to ensure

Abhimanyu's heroic death, which would rally the Pandavas and justify their cause in the war.

The consequences of this decision were profound. Abhimanyu's death deeply affected the Pandavas, especially Arjuna, who vowed to avenge his son. It also intensified the war's moral stakes, exposing the Kauravas' ruthlessness in attacking a single warrior en masse.

Krishna's decision highlights the Mahabharata's complex portrayal of dharma, where even divine figures must make choices that appear morally ambiguous for the greater good. It reflects the recurring theme of sacrifice, where individual losses are seen as necessary for collective victory.

Chapter Fifteen - Five sinister and treacherous moves during Kurukshetra war

These episodes showcase the complexities of dharma, strategy, and morality that define the Mahabharata, where every action carried profound consequences. Mahabharata teaches us to be submissive but not surrender if you are in righteous path. If war is inevitable despite several submissive attempts then the target shifts to winning. It may be a tectonic shift from so called moral and ethical values. Values must be followed and preserved by all stakeholders and not just one party.

1. The Tragic Killing of Abhimanyu in the Chakravyuha

On the thirteenth day of the Kurukshetra War, the battlefield witnessed one of its most heart-wrenching moments—the death of Abhimanyu, Arjuna's 16-year-old son. Dronacharya, the Kaurava commander, devised the Chakravyuha, a complex circular battle formation designed to entrap and decimate the Pandava forces. With Arjuna and Krishna occupied elsewhere, Abhimanyu volunteered to break into the formation, showcasing his bravery and determination.

Abhimanyu, having learned only the entry technique of the Chakravyuha but not the method to exit, fought valiantly as he penetrated the formation. Single-handedly, he defeated several great warriors, including Duryodhana's brothers. However, as he advanced deeper, the Kaurava warriors—Drona, Karna, Ashwatthama, and others—gathered to corner him. Jayadratha, using his divine boon from Lord Shiva, blocked the Pandavas from coming to his rescue.

As Abhimanyu's weapons were gradually destroyed, he continued to fight with whatever he could find, including the wheel of a chariot. His courage was unmatched, but the Kauravas, disregarding the code of war, attacked him collectively. Stripped of his weapons and surrounded by enemies, the young warrior was finally killed in a tragic and unfair manner.

This incident broke all ethical principles of warfare, which traditionally mandated one-on-one combat. Abhimanyu's death not only marked a turning point in the war but also demonstrated the erosion of dharma in the pursuit of victory. His sacrifice deeply affected the Pandavas, particularly Arjuna, who vowed to kill Jayadratha before sunset the next day—a promise that further escalated the stakes of the war.

2. Bhishma's fall through the Use of Shikhandi

Bhishma, the grand patriarch of the Kuru dynasty and commander of the Kaurava forces, was a warrior of unparalleled skill and integrity. His boon of choosing the time of his death made him nearly invincible, and his presence on the battlefield resulted in heavy losses for the Pandavas. Krishna, understanding Bhishma's principles, devised a strategy to counter him by using Shikhandi.

Shikhandi, born as Amba in a previous life, had a personal vendetta against Bhishma for denying her marriage and indirectly causing her humiliation. Reborn as Shikhandi, she vowed to be the cause of Bhishma's death. Krishna advised Arjuna to place Shikhandi in front during their attack, knowing Bhishma would not raise his weapons against someone he perceived as a woman.

On the tenth day of the war, with Shikhandi leading the charge, Arjuna showered Bhishma with arrows, immobilizing him and causing him to fall from his chariot onto a bed of arrows. Despite his fall, Bhishma accepted his fate with grace, acknowledging that his time had come. However, the use of Shikhandi in this manner was viewed by some as a tactical but morally ambiguous move.

Bhishma's fall was a turning point in the war, symbolizing the sacrifices required to uphold dharma. His willingness to submit to his destiny also reflected the complexities of duty, honor, and morality in the epic.

3. Drona's Death through the Ashwatthama Lie

Dronacharya, the revered teacher of both the Pandavas and Kauravas, was a formidable warrior and the commander of the Kaurava forces after Bhishma's fall. As long as Drona held his weapons, he was invincible, and his tactical brilliance continued to inflict heavy losses on the Pandavas. Krishna, understanding Drona's emotional attachment to his son, Ashwatthama, devised a strategy to exploit this bond.

Bhima killed an elephant named Ashwatthama and loudly proclaimed its death. When Drona heard the news, he was skeptical but sought confirmation from Yudhishthira, the epitome of truthfulness. Bound by his principles but urged by Krishna to prioritize the greater good, Yudhishthira reluctantly stated, "Ashwatthama is dead," adding under his breath, "the elephant, not your son."

Distraught by the supposed death of his son, Drona abandoned his weapons and entered meditation. Seizing this opportunity, Dhrishtadyumna, son of Drupada and Drona's sworn enemy, beheaded the unarmed commander. While this act fulfilled Dhrishtadyumna's vow of vengeance, it also raised questions about the ethics of killing a defenseless opponent.

Drona's death was both a strategic necessity and a deeply tragic event, underscoring the moral dilemmas faced by the Pandavas in their pursuit of justice.

4. Ashwatthama's Nocturnal Attack on the Pandava Camp

After the war had formally ended, with the Pandavas emerging victorious, Ashwatthama, the son of Dronacharya, was consumed by grief and anger over the loss of his father and the Kauravas. Seeking vengeance, he launched a surprise attack on the Pandava camp at night, violating the traditional rules of warfare, which prohibited combat after sunset.

Guided by his fury, Ashwatthama used the celestial Narayanastra and infiltrated the sleeping camp. He killed Dhrishtadyumna, the commander of the Pandava forces, and the five sons of the Pandavas (the Upapandavas). His actions were driven by a sense of duty to avenge his father and Duryodhana but were widely condemned for their breach of ethical conduct.

Ashwatthama's actions reflected the destructive power of unchecked emotions and the cycles of vengeance that plagued the war. His use of the Brahmastra to target Uttara's unborn child further highlighted the tragic consequences of anger and hatred.

5. The Sacrificial Death of Ghatotkacha

On the fourteenth night of the war, Ghatotkacha, the rakshasa son of Bhima, emerged as a key figure in the Pandava strategy. His supernatural abilities made him a formidable opponent, especially during nighttime battles. Under Krishna's guidance, Ghatotkacha launched a ferocious attack on the Kaurava forces, causing significant damage and demoralizing the enemy.

As Ghatotkacha's assault intensified, Duryodhana, in desperation, urged Karna to use the Vasavi Shakti, a divine weapon gifted by Indra. This weapon, which could be used only once, was Karna's trump card against Arjuna. Karna, reluctant but compelled by the situation, deployed the weapon, killing Ghatotkacha instantly.

Ghatotkacha's death, though heroic, was a calculated sacrifice orchestrated by Krishna to ensure the Vasavi Shakti was expended, thus protecting Arjuna. This event highlighted the difficult choices made in war, where even allies had to be sacrificed for the greater good.

Chapter Sixteen - Five moral and ethical interventions of Krishna

While Krishna's actions in these instances were ultimately aimed at ensuring the victory of the Pandavas, they often stretched the boundaries of ethical conduct in war. Krishna's divine wisdom and strategies, though effective, were sometimes employed in ways that manipulated emotions, bypassed traditional norms, and exploited vulnerabilities, raising questions about the morality of winning at any cost. These instances reflect the complexity of dharma in the Mahabharata, where even divine intervention in the name of righteousness could be seen as ethically controversial.

In the Mahabharata, Krishna plays a pivotal role in ensuring the success of the Pandavas, but some of his actions during the Kurukshetra War raise moral and ethical questions. While Krishna is revered for his divine wisdom and guidance, there are several instances where his interventions could be considered unethical by conventional standards of dharma. Here are five such instances:

1. The Use of Shikhandi to Defeat Bhishma

Bhishma, the grandsire of both the Pandavas and Kauravas, was a warrior of immense stature, and his boon of choosing the time of his death made him nearly invincible on the battlefield. The Pandavas, particularly Arjuna, found it impossible to defeat him. To overcome Bhishma, Krishna advised Arjuna to place Shikhandi, who had a personal vendetta against Bhishma due to her past life as Amba, in front of him.

Bhishma, bound by his vow not to raise arms against a woman or someone who had been a woman in a past life, refrained from fighting Shikhandi. Arjuna, guided by Krishna, then shot arrows at Bhishma, ultimately leading to his fall. This tactic, while effective, can be seen as ethically questionable, as Bhishma's restraint due to his moral code was exploited in a way that bypassed a direct confrontation, highlighting a strategic manipulation of his vow.

2. The Deception with the Killing of Drona

Drona, the teacher and commander of the Kaurava army, was an extraordinary warrior who could not be defeated unless he was disarmed. Krishna, knowing that Drona's emotional attachment to his son Ashwatthama was his greatest vulnerability, suggested a strategy to deceive Drona into laying down his weapons.

On the fifteenth day of the war, Bhima killed an elephant named Ashwatthama, and Yudhishthira, who was known for his commitment to truth, was pressured into saying the words, "Ashwatthama is dead." However, he muttered "the elephant, not your son," in a whisper. Drona, hearing Yudhishthira's declaration, believed his son was dead and, overcome by grief, relinquished his weapons. At this moment,

Dhrishtadyumna, son of Drupada and Drona's sworn enemy, killed him.

While the deception was a strategic necessity, it raised serious ethical concerns as it manipulated Drona's emotions, exploiting the truth and causing his downfall based on a lie.

3. The Killing of Karna When He Was Defenseless

Karna, one of the greatest warriors on the battlefield and a key figure on the Kaurava side, had a deep sense of honor and was bound by the rules of war. In a moment of vulnerability, when Karna's chariot wheel became stuck in the mud and he was defenseless, Krishna urged Arjuna to take advantage of the situation and kill Karna.

Karna, in a desperate plea, requested Arjuna to wait until he had freed his chariot wheel and mounted his weapon. However, Krishna, knowing that Karna was a formidable adversary and that the Pandavas could not afford to let him live any longer, pressed Arjuna to kill Karna while he was vulnerable. Arjuna, though reluctant, followed Krishna's advice and shot Karna with a fatal arrow.

This act, while within the context of war, can be seen as an unethical tactic because it violated the established code of conduct that forbade killing an opponent who was defenseless, asking for time to regain their strength.

4. The Use of the Brahmastra against Ashwatthama

In the final stages of the war, after Duryodhana's defeat, Ashwatthama, filled with rage and grief, decided to launch a deadly attack on the sleeping Pandava camp. He used the Brahmastra, a powerful celestial weapon, to target the Pandava's unborn grandchildren in Uttara's womb. In response, Arjuna, with Krishna's guidance, invoked the Brahmastra as well.

While both Brahmastras were neutralized, Krishna played a significant role in ensuring the safety of the Pandavas. However, Krishna, knowing the immense destructive potential of the Brahmastra, encouraged Arjuna to use it, even though it was supposed to be invoked only under extreme circumstances and with the consent of the gods. This, in a way, led to the potential destruction of an entire lineage, and Krishna's direct influence in the matter blurred ethical boundaries in favor of strategic success.

5. The Incitement to Kill Duryodhana through Bhima's Oath

Throughout the war, Krishna guided the Pandavas with a moral compass that emphasized the importance of dharma, but his guidance sometimes involved questionable methods. Before the final battle, Krishna advised Bhima to take an oath to kill Duryodhana in a particular way. Bhima vowed to kill Duryodhana by striking him on the thigh, a move that was considered below the standards of warrior conduct.

Duryodhana, due to a curse from his mother, had vulnerability in his thigh, and Krishna used this information to ensure the Pandavas had an advantage.

During the final duel between Bhima and Duryodhana, Bhima struck Duryodhana's thigh, thus violating the traditional rules of warfare that prohibited such attacks. Krishna, however, remained silent, allowing Bhima to fulfill his vow.

This act, while satisfying the Pandavas' desire for justice, was seen as an unethical strategy because it involved using a physical flaw to secure a victory, bypassing the established rules of fairness in battle.

Chapter Seventeen - Five Kings who were never in limelight in Mahabharata

1. Shalya: King of Madra

Kingdom: The kingdom of Madra, situated in the northwestern region of present-day Punjab, was among the most affluent and culturally advanced states of ancient India. Renowned for its opulence, skilled warriors, and diplomatic traditions, Madra upheld unique customs like Kanyashulka (dowry paid to the groom), which influenced many royal alliances. Shalya, the ruler of this kingdom, epitomized the grace, refinement, and valor of his land. His kingdom's wealth and traditions set it apart, and its strategic location made Madra an essential ally in the Great War.

Contribution:
Shalya's role in the Mahabharata was pivotal and complex. Known for his unparalleled skill as a charioteer and warrior, Shalya initially intended to side with the Pandavas due to his familial ties with Nakula and Sahadeva, his nephews. However, Duryodhana cunningly intercepted him on his way to the Pandavas' camp and lavished him with hospitality, securing his reluctant allegiance.

Despite fighting for the Kauravas, Shalya's heart often remained with the Pandavas. As Karna's charioteer, Shalya employed his wit and sarcasm to undermine Karna's confidence during his critical duel with Arjuna. His psychological tactics, though seemingly destructive for his own side, subtly weakened the Kaurava cause.

Towards the war's end, Shalya was appointed the commander-in-chief of the Kaurava army after Karna's death. His leadership, though formidable, failed to turn the tide of the war. His final battle against Yudhishthira demonstrated his valor and skill, but he ultimately fell, marking the collapse of the Kaurava resistance.

Shalya's dual loyalties and nuanced role highlight the moral dilemmas faced by many characters in the epic. As a warrior, he fulfilled his obligations, but his internal conflict and ultimate downfall emphasize the futility of war and the human cost of alliances made under duress. His contribution as a master strategist and warrior was instrumental, yet his legacy is often overshadowed by the more prominent figures of the Mahabharata.

Shalya's story reflects the complexities of duty, loyalty, and personal conviction, adding depth to the grand narrative of the Mahabharata. His kingdom and his role stand as testaments to the diverse cultural and moral fabric of ancient India.

2. Drupada: King of Panchala

Kingdom:

The kingdom of Panchala, located in the fertile plains

of northern India near the Ganges, was one of the most powerful and culturally rich regions of the Mahabharata era. Divided into Northern Panchala and Southern Panchala, the kingdom was renowned for its military strength, wealth, and scholarly traditions. Its capital, Kampilya, was a hub of learning and governance, home to great sages and warriors. Under King Drupada's rule, Panchala flourished as a center of Vedic culture and military prowess.

Contribution:

Drupada's life was marked by his rivalry with Drona, a conflict that became a cornerstone of the Mahabharata. During their youth, Drupada and Drona were close friends. However, when Drupada ascended the throne, he dismissed Drona, considering him unworthy of friendship due to his humble background. This insult fueled Drona's desire for revenge. Years later, Drona, aided by his Kuru disciples, defeated Drupada and seized Southern Panchala, deepening their enmity.

To avenge this humiliation, Drupada performed a yajna (sacred sacrifice), seeking a son who would kill Drona. This ritual brought forth Dhrishtadyumna, a warrior destined to fulfill this purpose, and Draupadi, who became central to the Pandavas' rise. Drupada's contributions to the Pandavas' cause were profound. By organizing Draupadi's swayamvara, he forged an alliance with the Pandavas, strengthening their claim to power and providing them with a staunch ally.

In the Kurukshetra War, Drupada fought valiantly for the Pandavas, using his strategic acumen to fortify their position. Though overshadowed by his children, Drupada's role as a king, father, and ally was crucial. His actions influenced the trajectory of the Mahabharata, particularly through Dhrishtadyumna's slaying of Drona and Draupadi's unwavering support for the Pandavas.

Drupada's character embodies the complexities of pride, revenge, and redemption. His kingdom, a beacon of Vedic culture and military strength, played a pivotal role in shaping the epic's events. Though often he was remembered for his enmity with Drona; Drupada's legacy lies in his unwavering commitment to justice and his pivotal role in aligning Panchala with the Pandavas' cause.

3. Bhagadatta – King of Pragjyotisha

Kingdom:

Pragjyotisha, ruled by King Bhagadatta, was located in the easternmost regions of ancient India, corresponding to present-day Assam. This kingdom was known for its dense forests, rich biodiversity, and immense natural wealth. Pragjyotisha was a stronghold of Shiva worship, with traditions deeply rooted in mysticism and spirituality. Bhagadatta's kingdom was also famed for its expertise in elephant warfare, with Supratika, his war elephant, being one of the mightiest beasts of its time. The strategic location of Pragjyotisha ensured its independence and prominence in the epic era.

Contribution:

Bhagadatta's allegiance to the Kauravas during the Kurukshetra War was an extension of his longstanding ties with Dhritarashtra. Despite his age, Bhagadatta was an active participant in the war, showcasing the resilience and strength of Pragjyotisha. His decision to fight for the Kauravas reflected the diverse alliances that characterized the epic.

Bhagadatta's most significant contribution was his prowess in elephant warfare. Mounted on his colossal war elephant, Supratika, he unleashed havoc on the Pandava army. Supratika was no ordinary elephant; its sheer size and ferocity made it a living weapon. Bhagadatta used the elephant to overpower numerous warriors, including Bhima, who narrowly escaped death during one encounter.

One of the most dramatic moments involving Bhagadatta occurred during his duel with Arjuna. Bhagadatta unleashed the Vaishnavastra, a powerful celestial weapon, against Arjuna. However, Krishna, acting as Arjuna's charioteer, intervened to neutralize the weapon, ensuring Arjuna's survival. This incident highlighted Bhagadatta's formidable capabilities as a warrior while also underscoring Krishna's divine intervention in favor of the Pandavas.

Bhagadatta eventually fell to Arjuna, marking a significant loss for the Kauravas. His death symbolized the diminishing strength of their allies and the nearing end of their campaign.

Bhagadatta's role in the Mahabharata is a testament to the inclusion of distant and culturally distinct kingdoms in the epic. His kingdom, Pragjyotisha, and his use of elephant warfare add a unique dimension to the narrative, showcasing the diverse martial traditions of ancient India. Despite his defeat, Bhagadatta's bravery and loyalty to his allies remain an enduring part of his legacy.

4. Kritavarma: Commander of the Yadava Army

Kingdom:

Kritavarma was a key figure in the Yadava dynasty, a clan known for its advanced governance and maritime prowess. The Yadavas, based in Dwaraka (modern Gujarat), were led by Lord Krishna, whose capital was a magnificent city built on the western coast. Kritavarma, though not as prominent as Krishna, was a skilled warrior and a respected commander in the Yadava forces. The Yadava kingdom was a beacon of prosperity, diplomacy, and military strength, renowned for its naval fleet and cultural contributions.

Contribution:

Kritavarma's role in the Mahabharata reflects the complex dynamics within the Yadava clan. After Krishna declared neutrality in the Kurukshetra War, Kritavarma joined the Kauravas, taking half the Yadava forces with him. His decision was based on the principle of honoring alliances, as the Kauravas had long-standing ties with the Yadavas.

During the war, Kritavarma distinguished himself as a commander and warrior. His strategies and disciplined approach bolstered the Kaurava army, particularly during critical phases of the battle. However, his most infamous act occurred after the war. Along with Ashwatthama and Kripacharya, Kritavarma participated in the massacre of the sleeping Pandava camp, killing Draupadi's sons and other key warriors. This act, though carried out in vengeance, was condemned as unethical and cast a shadow over Kritavarma's legacy.

Kritavarma's post-war life was marked by the Yadava clan's eventual downfall. After Krishna's death, the internal strife within the Yadavas led to their destruction, and Kritavarma, like other members of the clan, met a tragic end.

Kritavarma's story reflects the moral ambiguities and complex loyalties of the Mahabharata. His kingdom and his role as a Yadava commander underscore the epic's exploration of duty, allegiance, and the consequences of war.

5. Virata: King of Matsya

Kingdom:

The Matsya kingdom, ruled by Virata, was located in the fertile plains of present-day Rajasthan. Its capital, Viratanagara, was a thriving city known for its agriculture, trade, and military strength. Matsya held a strategic position, acting as a buffer state between the Kurus and other kingdoms. Under King Virata's rule, Matsya was a prosperous and peaceful kingdom, characterized by its economic stability and strong governance.

Contribution:

Virata's role in the Mahabharata was instrumental during the Pandavas' final year of exile, where they lived incognito in his court. Unaware of their true identities, Virata employed Yudhishthira as his advisor, Bhima as his cook, Arjuna as a eunuch dance instructor for his daughter, and the rest of the Pandavas in various roles.

Virata's court became the stage for key events, such as Bhima's killing of Kichaka, the kingdom's corrupt and lecherous commander, and Arjuna's display of valor during the cattle raid by the Kauravas. These incidents highlighted the Pandavas' prowess and loyalty to their cause, even in anonymity.

After the exile, Virata allied with the Pandavas, offering his son Uttara as a groom for Abhimanyu, Arjuna's son. This marriage solidified Matsya's alliance with the Pandavas, strengthening their position in the Kurukshetra War. Virata himself participated in the war, leading sections of the Pandava army and providing critical support.

Virata's kingdom and his role in sheltering the Pandavas were pivotal to their survival and resurgence. His contributions underscore the importance of alliances and the influence of lesser known rulers in the grand narrative of the Mahabharata.

Chapter Eighteen - Five most sinister minded characters in Mahabharata

1. Duryodhana: The Embodiment of Jealousy and Ego

Background and Personality:

Duryodhana was the eldest of the 100 Kaurava brothers and heir to the throne of Hastinapura by virtue of birth. However, his claim was constantly overshadowed by the virtues, strength, and leadership of his cousins, the Pandavas. This inferiority complex fermented jealousy within Duryodhana, who saw the Pandavas as usurpers of his rightful position.

Key Moments of Cruelty:

• **Lakshagriha (House of Lac):** Duryodhana plotted to eliminate the Pandavas by setting fire to a highly inflammable palace built specifically to trap them. This was one of his earliest displays of malicious intent.

• **Dice Game and Draupadi's Humiliation:** Duryodhana's most heinous act was orchestrating the dice game that led to Draupadi's disrobing in the Kaurava court. He mocked Draupadi openly, even slapping his thigh as an obscene invitation to her.

- **War Strategy:** During the Kurukshetra war, Duryodhana ordered the unethical killing of Abhimanyu and continued to disregard the rules of dharma yuddha (righteous warfare).

Ego and Rejection of Offers:

Duryodhana's ego was colossal. Krishna's offer to give the Pandavas just five villages to avoid war was met with scorn. Duryodhana famously declared, "I will not give them even a needlepoint of land." His inability to compromise stemmed from his belief that he was the rightful ruler of Hastinapura and his refusal to accept the Pandavas' moral superiority.

Intentions:

Duryodhana's ultimate goal was absolute dominance. His hatred for the Pandavas drove every decision, and his ambition blinded him to the consequences of his actions. For him, annihilating the Pandavas was not merely a political move but a deeply personal vendetta.

2. Shakuni: The Mastermind of Deception

Background and Personality:

Shakuni, the prince of Gandhara (modern-day Kandahar), entered Hastinapura with vengeance in his heart. After his family suffered humiliation and imprisonment at the hands of Dhritarashtra and Bhishma, Shakuni swore to destroy the Kuru dynasty. Despite his charming demeanor, he was a master manipulator who harbored deep hatred.

Key Moments of Cruelty:

- **Dice Game:** Shakuni was the architect of the dice game where he used loaded dice to cheat Yudhishthira repeatedly, leading to the Pandavas losing their kingdom, wealth, and Draupadi.

- **Instigation of Duryodhana:** Shakuni continuously fueled Duryodhana's hatred toward the Pandavas, ensuring that reconciliation was never an option.

- **War Tactics:** During the war, Shakuni played a pivotal role in unethical strategies, including using deceit to trap Abhimanyu in a chakravyuha (military formation).

Ego and Rejection of Offers:

Shakuni's rejection of Krishna's peace mission was rooted in his desire for vengeance. Peace would have thwarted his lifelong mission to destroy the Kuru dynasty. He manipulated Duryodhana into seeing Krishna's proposal as a sign of weakness and capitulation.

Intentions:

Unlike others on the Kaurava side, Shakuni's intentions were not rooted in loyalty to Duryodhana. His ultimate goal was to dismantle the Kuru lineage, even if it meant sacrificing the Kauravas in the process. His machinations ensured perpetual discord between the Pandavas and Kauravas.

3. Karna: The Tragic Antihero

Background and Personality:

Karna, born to Kunti before her marriage, was abandoned at birth and raised by a charioteer. Despite his extraordinary skills and virtues, Karna was often humiliated for his lowly social status. This sense of rejection and injustice made him fiercely loyal to Duryodhana, who recognized his worth and crowned him the king of Anga. Karna's loyalty, however, led him down a morally ambiguous path.

Key Moments of Cruelty:

• **Draupadi's Humiliation:** Karna mocked Draupadi during her disrobing, calling her unchaste and suggesting she belonged to all five Pandavas. His words added to her trauma.

• **Killing of Abhimanyu:** Karna played a key role in the unethical killing of Abhimanyu, knowing the young warrior was trapped and defenseless.

• **Battle with Bhima's Sons:** Karna mercilessly killed the sons of Draupadi, including the brave Ghatotkacha, who was a major threat to Duryodhana's forces.

Ego and Rejection of Offers:

When Krishna revealed Karna's true identity as Kunti's son and offered him the chance to join the Pandavas, Karna's ego and sense of loyalty to Duryodhana prevailed. He rejected the offer, stating that he would not betray the man who gave him dignity when the world scorned him.

Intentions:

Karna's intentions were complex. While he sought to prove his worth and gain recognition, his loyalty to Duryodhana made him complicit in the Kauravas' atrocities. His inner conflict between dharma (righteousness) and loyalty ultimately led to his downfall.

4. Dushasana: The Face of Barbarism

Background and Personality:

Dushasana, Duryodhana's younger brother, was a cruel and arrogant prince who blindly followed his elder brother's commands. While not as cunning as Shakuni or as skilled as Karna, Dushasana's actions often embodied the Kauravas' worst traits.

Key Moments of Cruelty:

• **Draupadi's Disrobing:** Dushasana dragged Draupadi by her hair into the court and attempted to disrobe her, showing utter disregard for her dignity. This act of barbarism became the Pandavas' primary motive for vengeance.

• **Mockery of the Pandavas:** Throughout the dice game and exile, Dushasana mocked and ridiculed the Pandavas, adding to their humiliation.

• **Battlefield Savagery:** Dushasana fought fiercely in the war, embodying the Kaurava desire for dominance, but his arrogance and lack of strategic thinking led to his downfall.

Ego and Rejection of Offers:

Dushasana, like Duryodhana, saw Krishna's peace mission as an affront to Kaurava pride. He believed that their vast army and alliances rendered the Pandavas' claims irrelevant.

Intentions:

Dushasana's intentions were rooted in his blind loyalty to Duryodhana and his desire to uphold Kaurava supremacy. His cruelty and arrogance, however, made him a symbol of adharma (unrighteousness).

5. Dhritarashtra: The Blind King of Moral Cowardice

Background and Personality:

Dhritarashtra, though physically blind, was also metaphorically blind to justice and morality. His love for Duryodhana overshadowed his duties as a king and father figure to the Pandavas. This moral weakness made him complicit in the Kauravas' actions.

Key Moments of Cruelty:

•   **Tacit Approval of Draupadi's Humiliation:** Despite being present in the court, Dhritarashtra failed to intervene during Draupadi's disrobing.

•   **Support for Duryodhana's Schemes:** Dhritarashtra often turned a blind eye to Duryodhana's malicious plots, including the Lakshagriha and the dice game.

- **Inaction during the Peace Mission:** Dhritarashtra's failure to endorse Krishna's peace mission highlighted his inability to act decisively.

Ego and Rejection of Offers:

Dhritarashtra's rejection of Krishna's proposals was driven by his attachment to Duryodhana. He feared that conceding to the Pandavas would undermine his son's position and reflect poorly on his reign.

Intentions:

Dhritarashtra's primary intention was to secure Duryodhana's legacy. However, his moral cowardice and failure to uphold dharma ultimately led to the destruction of his family and kingdom.

Conclusion

The five sinister characters on the Kaurava side Duryodhana, Shakuni, Karna, Dushasana, and Dhritarashtra played pivotal roles in driving the Mahabharata toward its tragic conclusion. Each was guided by personal flaws, such as jealousy, vengeance, ego, loyalty, and moral weakness. Their collective refusal to accept Krishna's peace proposals underscores how ambition, hatred, and pride can lead to catastrophic consequences. The Kurukshetra war was not merely a clash of armies but a culmination of these characters' moral failings, which serve as timeless lessons on the importance of dharma and self-awareness.

Chapter Nineteen - Five most suffered women in Mahabharata

1. Draupadi: The Embodiment of Resilience

The Depth of Her Suffering

1.   **Dice Game Humiliation**: Dragged to the Kuru court, her dignity trampled by Dushasana and Duryodhana as the elders watched silently.

2.   **Attempt to Disrobe**: Dushasana tried to strip her in public, an act prevented only by Krishna's divine intervention.

3.   **Unique Marital Arrangement**: Sharing five husbands created emotional struggles, especially as Arjuna married Subhadra.

4.   **Exile Hardships**: Accompanying the Pandavas into the forest, she faced the loss of her royal comforts and endured harsh living conditions.

5.   **War's Emotional Toll**: Witnessed her sons' deaths in the Kurukshetra war, further deepening her anguish.

Who Was Responsible?

•   **Duryodhana and Dushasana**: Orchestrators of her humiliation.

- **Karna**: For calling her unchaste and supporting the disrobing attempt.

- **Yudhishthira**: For staking her in the dice game.

- **Society**: For failing to protect her honor and dignity.

Draupadi's suffering was a result of the combined actions and inactions of several key figures. Duryodhana and Dushasana bore direct responsibility for her humiliation during the dice game, as their relentless pursuit of power blinded them to basic decency. Karna's cruel words, branding her unchaste and justifying her disrobing, further deepened her wounds, reflecting his misplaced loyalty to Duryodhana. Yudhishthira's decision to stake her in the dice game, despite knowing it was morally wrong, betrayed his duty as her husband and protector. The silence of the elders, Bhishma, Drona, and Vidura added to her anguish, as their failure to speak out implied complicity. Above all, the societal norms that dictated a woman's worth based on her husband's status and allowed such atrocities to go unchallenged were equally culpable, amplifying her torment and stripping her of justice.

Coping Mechanisms

1. **Channeling Anger**: Her rage became a driving force for justice, urging her husbands to avenge her.

2.   **Faith in Krishna**: Turned to Krishna during her most vulnerable moments, believing in divine justice.

3.   **Resilience**: Despite her suffering, she emerged as a strong queen, supporting the Pandavas throughout their trials.

2. Gandhari: The Silent Sufferer

The Depth of Her Suffering

1.   **Marriage to Dhritarashtra**: Entered a union with a blind man due to political circumstances, blindfolding herself in solidarity.

2.   **Loneliness in the Kuru Court**: Faced isolation as her husband's focus remained on the throne.

3.   **Motherhood Woes**: Helplessly watched Duryodhana's moral decline and the seeds of destruction sown in her family.

4.   **Loss of Her Sons**: Witnessed the deaths of her 100 sons during the war.

5.   **Living with Consequences**: Endured the pain of knowing her silence and inaction contributed to the tragedy.

Who Was Responsible?

•   **Bhishma and Shakuni**: For engineering her politically motivated marriage.

•   **Dhritarashtra**: For his inability to correct Duryodhana's flaws.

- **Duryodhana**: For his obstinacy and arrogance.

Gandhari's suffering stemmed from a series of systemic failures and individual betrayals. Bhishma and Shakuni's decision to marry her off to Dhritarashtra, a blind prince, purely for political gain, denied her agency in her own life. Dhritarashtra, though blind physically, was blinded by his ambitions and attachment to his son, Duryodhana, failing to uphold dharma or provide her emotional support. Duryodhana's unchecked arrogance and obsession with power plunged her into constant worry and helplessness as a mother. The elders of the Kuru dynasty, including Bhishma and Vidura, were complicit in enabling Duryodhana's destructive path, leaving Gandhari to witness the disintegration of her family. Ultimately, the patriarchal structure of the Kuru court, which devalued her voice as a woman and queen, deepened her isolation and suffering.

Coping Mechanisms

1.   **Blindfold as a Symbol**: Represented her sacrifice and acceptance of suffering.

2.   **Moral Anchor**: Often guided Dhritarashtra and lamented the loss of dharma in her family.

3.   **Faith in Dharma**: Turned to spirituality and dharma as solace.

4.   **Expression of Grief**: Cursed Krishna, showcasing her raw emotions and humanity.

3. Kunti: The Mother Torn by Choices

The Depth of Her Suffering

1.   **Unwed Motherhood**: Secretly bore Karna and abandoned him due to societal stigma.

2.   **Widowhood**: Raised the Pandavas alone in a politically charged environment.

3.   **Conflict of Loyalties**: Her secret about Karna left her torn as he fought against the Pandavas.

4.   **Loss in War**: Endured the deaths of Karna and other loved ones during the war.

5.   **Guilt**: Carried lifelong guilt for her decisions, especially her silence about Karna's identity.

Who Was Responsible?

•   **Her Father and Society**: For forcing her into Durvasa's service and the societal stigma surrounding unwed mothers.

•   **Dhritarashtra and Duryodhana**: For their hostility toward the Pandavas.

•   **Karna's Fate**: Resulted from her abandonment under societal pressure.

Kunti's suffering was rooted in societal pressures, family expectations, and her own decisions shaped by these influences. Her father and society bore initial responsibility, sending her to serve the sage Durvasa as a young girl, where she was bestowed with a boon that later became a curse. Karna's abandonment was a direct consequence of societal stigma against unwed motherhood, forcing Kunti to suppress her maternal instincts and prioritize her reputation. Pandu's premature death left her alone to raise the Pandavas in a hostile political environment. Dhritarashtra and the Kauravas further fueled her struggles by creating constant threats to her sons' survival. Finally, Kunti's own choice to conceal Karna's identity, driven by fear and loyalty to the Pandavas, created a tragic rift that added layers of guilt and sorrow to her already burdened soul.

Coping Mechanisms

1.   **Wisdom and Leadership**: Guided the Pandavas through challenges with her intelligence and pragmatism.

2.   **Faith in Divine Justice**: Trusted dharma and divine will to justify her actions.

3.   **Revealing the Truth**: Confessed Karna's identity to the Pandavas, seeking closure.

4.   **Spiritual Solace**: Turned to spiritual practices later in life, accepting her suffering as karmic consequences.

4. Amba: The Woman Who Lived for Revenge

The Depth of Her Suffering

1.   **Abduction by Bhishma**: Forcefully taken from her swayamvara with her sisters, losing her autonomy.

2.   **Rejection by Shalva**: Spurned by the man she loved, leaving her humiliated and abandoned.

3.   **Bhishma's Refusal**: His oath of celibacy barred her from seeking redress.

4.   **Social Ostracism**: Found no place in society, with her honor and future destroyed.

5.   **Obsession with Revenge**: Became consumed by hatred, dedicating her life to destroying Bhishma.

Who Was Responsible?

•   **Bhishma**: For disregarding her consent and personal feelings.

•   **Shalva**: For rejecting her out of ego.

•   **Society**: For not supporting her as a wronged woman.

Amba's plight can be attributed to the arrogance and rigidity of Bhishma and the cowardice of Shalva. Bhishma, bound by his vow to secure a bride for Vichitravirya, abducted Amba without her consent, treating her as an object of political convenience. When Amba revealed her prior love for Shalva, Bhishma's refusal to release her from her predicament displayed a lack of empathy and a rigid adherence to his celibacy vow. Shalva, on the other hand, rejected Amba out of wounded pride, blaming her for circumstances beyond her control. The Kuru court and society also failed her, offering neither protection nor justice, pushing her into a state of despair and obsession. This chain of betrayals stripped Amba of agency, dignity, and a place in society, leaving revenge as her only solace and purpose.

Coping Mechanisms

1. **Quest for Revenge**: Dedicated her life to penance, seeking power to destroy Bhishma.

2. **Rebirth as Shikhandi**: Her reincarnation fulfilled her vow, as she caused Bhishma's downfall.

3. **Determination**: Her unwavering focus on vengeance gave her purpose.

4. **Divine Assurance**: Gained confidence from Lord Shiva's boon, driving her resolve.

5. Uttara: The Young Widow

The Depth of Her Suffering

1. **Loss of Abhimanyu**: Witnessed her young husband brutally killed in the Chakravyuha, leaving her widowed while pregnant.

2. **Ashwatthama's Attack**: Targeted by a Brahmastra, which aimed to kill her unborn child, Parikshit.

3. **War's Aftermath**: Lived in a world ravaged by war, with most male relatives dead.

4. **Burden of Legacy**: Entrusted with raising Parikshit, the last hope of the Kuru dynasty.

5. **Isolation**: Faced a life of widowhood and loss at a young age.

Who Was Responsible?

• **Duryodhana and Kauravas**: For waging the war that led to Abhimanyu's death.

• **Ashwatthama**: For his cruel attack targeting her unborn child.

• **Society**: For glorifying war and neglecting the suffering of women.

Uttara's suffering was a consequence of the larger Kuru war, orchestrated by Duryodhana and the Kauravas, whose unyielding greed and ego sparked the conflict. Abhimanyu's untimely and brutal death in the Chakravyuha was the direct result of unethical warfare tactics, as seven warriors ganged up on a single young warrior. Ashwatthama's attack on her unborn child with a Brahmastra was a vile act of vengeance, showing complete disregard for innocence or dharma. The elders in the Kuru court, including Bhishma, Drona, and Dhritarashtra, also shared indirect responsibility, as their inaction and partiality allowed the seeds of the war to grow unchecked. Lastly, the societal glorification of war and its dismissal of women's suffering perpetuated Uttara's pain, leaving her to navigate widowhood and single motherhood in isolation.

Coping Mechanisms

1. **Focus on Motherhood**: Channeled her energy into raising Parikshit, ensuring the survival of the Kuru lineage.

2.   **Krishna's Support**: Gained strength from Krishna's intervention, which saved her child.

3.   **Inner Resilience**: Found purpose in preserving her husband's legacy.

4.   **Spiritual Growth**: Turned to spirituality to endure her immense grief.

Illustration Summary

Each woman in the Mahabharata illustrates different aspects of suffering and resilience. Draupadi embodies fiery resilience and the pursuit of justice, Gandhari symbolizes stoic acceptance of destiny, Kunti represents wisdom burdened by secrets, Amba personifies the destructive power of unresolved anger, and Uttara showcases quiet determination in the face of loss. Together, they reveal the silent strength and complexity of women in a patriarchal world, each rising above their torment to leave an indelible mark on the epic.

Chapter Twenty - Description of Five Conch shells used by different personalities in Mahabharata

The conch shells, or **Shankhas**, played a significant symbolic and functional role in the Mahabharata, particularly in the context of war. Each conch carried unique significance and was associated with specific personalities, reflecting their character, role, or divine powers. Here is an account of the prominent conches used by various characters in the Mahabharata:

1. Krishna's Panchajanya

- **Name**: Panchajanya

- **Meaning**: "Born of the Five" or "One of Five."

- **Origin**: Krishna's conch was said to be made from the bones of a demon named Panchajana, whom Krishna defeated while retrieving his guru's son.

- **Significance**:

  o   Represented divine will and dharma.

o   When blown, its sound was believed to strike fear into the hearts of adharma (unrighteousness) and inspire dharma (righteousness).

- **Role in the Mahabharata**:

o   Krishna blew the Panchajanya to signal the start of the Kurukshetra war.

o   It resonated with divine power, symbolizing Krishna's support for the Pandavas and righteousness.

2. Arjuna's Devadatta

- **Name**: Devadatta

- **Meaning**: "God-given."

- **Significance**:

o   Represented Arjuna's divine connection and valor.

o   Its sound echoed Arjuna's unmatched focus, skill, and dedication as a warrior.

- **Role in the Mahabharata**:

o   Arjuna used Devadatta to instill confidence in the Pandava army and to announce his readiness to uphold dharma.

3. Yudhishthira's Anantavijaya

- **Name**: Anantavijaya

- **Meaning**: "Endless Victory."

- **Significance**:

o   Symbolized Yudhishthira's steadfast commitment to dharma and his aspiration for victory through righteous means.

o   Represented the enduring nature of moral and ethical success.

- **Role in the Mahabharata**:

o   It was a reminder of Yudhishthira's role as a dharmic king and leader of the Pandavas.

4. Bhima's Paundra

- **Name**: Paundra

- **Meaning**: Named after its low and booming sound.

- **Significance**:

o   Reflected Bhima's immense physical strength, power, and indomitable spirit.

o   Its deep, thunderous sound symbolized fear and chaos for enemies.

- **Role in the Mahabharata**:

o   Bhima's conch often announced aggressive battle movements and instilled terror in the Kaurava ranks.

5. Nakula's Sughosha

- **Name**: Sughosha

- **Meaning**: "Melodious Sound."

- **Significance**:

o   Represented Nakula's grace, elegance, and strategic acumen in warfare.

o   Its clear and melodious sound was said to boost morale among the Pandavas.

- **Role in the Mahabharata:**

o   It reflected Nakula's calm yet steadfast presence in the battlefield.

6. Sahadeva's Manipushpaka

- **Name**: Manipushpaka

- **Meaning**: "Jewel Flower."

- **Significance**:

o   Symbolized Sahadeva's wisdom, tactical knowledge, and his ability to stay composed under pressure.

o   Its sound was soothing for allies but unsettling for enemies.

- **Role in the Mahabharata:**

o   Played a role in reinforcing the disciplined and strategic efforts of the Pandavas.

7. Duryodhana's Conch

- **Name**: Not explicitly named in the Mahabharata.

- **Significance:**

o   Represented his arrogance and misplaced confidence.

o   The conch symbolized the Kaurava claim to power, though it lacked divine favor.

- **Role in the Mahabharata**:

o   Duryodhana's conch was often blown to assert dominance, though it could not inspire the same reverence as those of the Pandavas.

8. Karna's Conch

- **Name**: Not specifically named in most versions of the Mahabharata.

- **Significance**:

o   Represented Karna's valor, generosity, and tragic destiny.

o   Its sound resonated with Karna's unmatched skill as a warrior and his dedication to loyalty.

- **Role in the Mahabharata**:

o   Its sound was both a challenge to the Pandavas and a proclamation of Karna's unyielding spirit.

9. Bhishma's Conch

- **Name**: Not explicitly named, but part of his war gear.

- **Significance**:

o   Represented Bhishma's role as the eldest warrior and his commitment to the Kaurava cause, even against his moral compass.

o   Symbolized the duty of a Kshatriya to fight, irrespective of personal relationships.

- **Role in the Mahabharata**:

o   Announced his leadership and the immense challenge he posed for the Pandavas.

Symbolism of Conch Shells in the Mahabharata

The conches were not just war instruments; they were symbolic of the deeper cosmic battle between **dharma (righteousness)** and **adharma (unrighteousness)**. Each conch's sound represented the character, role, and divine connection of its owner, reinforcing the spiritual and moral undertones of the epic.

Chapter Twenty One - Significance of Animals in Mahabharata

1. Cows

- **Role**: Symbols of wealth, purity, and dharma.

- **Key Events**:

o   **Pandavas' Generosity**: Cows were given as gifts during rituals, reflecting their importance in dharma and prosperity.

o   **Virata Parva**: The Kauravas attempt to seize the cattle of King Virata, which leads to Arjuna's revelation of his identity. This event underscores the importance of cows as a measure of wealth and power in ancient society.

2. Horses

- **Role**: Integral to chariots, they symbolized speed, power, and prestige.

- **Key Events**:

o   **Divine Horses of Arjuna's Chariot**: The celestial horses pulling Arjuna's chariot were gifted by Agni during the burning of the Khandava forest. These horses were invincible and added to the chariot's mystique.

o   **Ashvamedha Yajna**: After the Kurukshetra war, Yudhishthira performed the Ashvamedha Yajna, wherein a sacrificial horse roamed freely to assert the supremacy of the ruler.

3. Elephants

•   **Role**: Symbols of strength, royalty, and destruction in war.

•   **Key Events**:

o   **Supratika**: Bhagadatta, the king of Pragjyotisha, fought on his mighty elephant Supratika during the Kurukshetra war. Supratika wreaked havoc in the Pandava army until Bhima defeated Bhagadatta.

o   **Ashwatthama and the Elephant Trick**: To mislead Dronacharya, Yudhishthira declared that Ashwatthama was dead, referring to an elephant of that name. This led to Drona's surrender and subsequent death, marking a critical turning point in the war.

4. Snakes (Nagas)

•   **Role**: Represented power, vengeance, and wisdom, often tied to divine or cosmic forces.

•   **Key Events**:

o   **Takshaka's Revenge**: Takshaka, a prominent Naga, sought revenge for the destruction of the Khandava forest, which was set ablaze by Arjuna and Krishna.

o   **Arjuna's Grandson Parikshit**: Takshaka later killed King Parikshit, the grandson of Arjuna, through a venomous bite, fulfilling a long-standing grudge against the Pandava lineage.

5. Dogs

• **Role**: Symbols of loyalty, companionship, and dharma.

• **Key Events**:

○ **Yudhishthira's Final Journey**: During the Mahaprasthanika Parva, a dog accompanied Yudhishthira on his journey to the gates of heaven. When asked to abandon the dog, Yudhishthira refused, stating that loyalty should not be forsaken. The dog later revealed itself as the god Dharma in disguise, testing Yudhishthira's adherence to dharma.

6. Peacock

• **Role**: Symbol of beauty and divinity.

• **Key Events**:

○ Though not a central figure, the peacock's feathers adorned the crests of divine figures like Krishna, symbolizing grace, beauty, and auspiciousness in the Mahabharata.

7. Birds (Crows, Eagles, and Sparrows)

• **Role**: Omens, messengers, and symbols of divine or cosmic warnings.

• **Key Events**:

○   **Crows as Omens**: Before the Kurukshetra war, unusual behavior of birds, including crows, was interpreted as ominous signs of impending destruction.

○   **Eagles (Garuda)**: The banner on Arjuna's chariot bore the image of Garuda, the celestial eagle and mount of Vishnu. It symbolized divine protection and victory for the Pandavas.

8. Deer

•   **Role**: Represented innocence and served as instruments in moral dilemmas.

•   **Key Events**:

○   **Pandavas' Exile**: During their exile, the Pandavas encountered a situation involving a deer. A deer took a Brahmin's fire sticks, prompting the Pandavas to retrieve them. This event led to the encounter with the Yaksha and Yudhishthira's test.

9. Rats

•   **Role**: Symbols of destruction and subtle warning signs.

•   **Key Events**:

○   Rats are indirectly mentioned in metaphors and teachings as creatures that undermine stability, emphasizing vigilance and preparedness.

10. Boars

•   **Role**: Represented wild strength and challenges.

- **Key Events**:

o   Boars appear in the context of forest life during the Pandavas' exile. Hunting boars was a common activity for warriors to demonstrate their skill and assert their dominance over nature.

Symbolism of Animals in the Mahabharata

- **Represent Dharma and Adharma**: Animals often reflect moral dilemmas or test characters' adherence to dharma.

- **Instruments of War**: Horses and elephants played a direct role in battles, while birds like Garuda and crows carried symbolic meanings.

- **Divine Messengers**: Nagas and dogs represented cosmic and divine interventions, influencing key events.

In the Mahabharata, animals are not merely passive participants; they actively shape narratives, influence outcomes, and serve as symbols of deeper truths.

Epilogue

The Mahabharata, vast as the cosmos it seeks to encompass, defies singular interpretations. It is a tale of contradictions and harmony, where heroes falter, villains redeem, and choices ripple across eternity. This narrative, revisited through diverse perspectives, offers more than a retelling—it is a testament to the timelessness of human aspirations, conflicts, and dilemmas.

Through the voices of seemingly insignificant characters, we have glimpsed the silent yet profound impact of the unnoticed, proving that even the smallest of players contribute to the grandeur of destiny. The friendships of Krishna, the bonds of sages, and the invisible threads binding lives together remind us that history is seldom shaped by solitary figures; it is a confluence of countless stories interwoven into a singular epic.

The disastrous decisions, the moral ambiguities, and the lessons from the past echo the fragile nature of human choices. They caution us against hubris, emphasize the value of dharma, and illuminate the perennial struggle to balance justice with compassion.

This book is an invitation to delve deeper into the complexities of the Mahabharata and find fragments of ourselves within its eternal narrative. As we close these pages, we are reminded that every voice—be it of a king, a sage, or a forgotten soul—matters. Together, they form the essence of this timeless saga.

May we carry forward the wisdom, the questions, and the reflections, allowing the Mahabharata to continue guiding us in the ever-evolving journey of life.

The Mahabharata, in its essence, is not merely a chronicle of the past; it is a mirror to the present and a guide for the future. Its relevance transcends time, for it captures the eternal drama of the human condition—our joys, sorrows, ambitions, and frailties. As we interpret its myriad layers, we realize that its true power lies not in offering definitive answers but in provoking thought, introspection, and dialogue.

Through this retelling, we have sought to explore the unsung dimensions of its characters, the overlooked intricacies of its relationships, and the understated consequences of its pivotal events. By focusing on the so-called insignificant characters, we have discovered that their stories, too, are imbued with profound lessons, often more relatable and inspiring than those of the central figures. The uncelebrated devotion of Ekalavya, the hidden virtues of Shalya, the wisdom of Vidura—all these tales compel us to reconsider our definitions of greatness and contribution.

The friendships of Krishna and the sages' counsel reveal the strength found in unity and wisdom, even amidst chaos. These bonds remind us that relationships are the foundation of life, influencing destinies and shaping history. Meanwhile, the consequences of disastrous decisions serve as cautionary tales, warning against the perils of unchecked ambition, unbridled anger, and blind allegiance.

As we part ways with this narrative, the Mahabharata leaves us with more questions than answers:

- What is the true meaning of dharma in an ever-changing world?

- How do we balance individual aspirations with collective well-being?

- Can we ever truly escape the consequences of our actions, or are we forever bound by the cycles of karma?

These questions are not meant to be resolved; rather, they are meant to accompany us, shaping our perspectives and guiding our choices. The Mahabharata is not a book to be finished; it is a companion to be revisited throughout life, offering new insights with every reading.

As the echoes of its stories fade, they leave behind an enduring truth: the Mahabharata is not just the story of a distant past but a living epic, resonating in the hearts and minds of those who dare to listen. Let us carry its wisdom with us, cherishing the light it provides and embracing the shadows it illuminates. In the end, we are all participants in the great narrative of life, each of us a character in the unfolding epic of existence. May this journey inspire us to live with greater awareness, compassion, and purpose, ensuring that our stories, too, become worthy of remembrance.

About the Author

Aurobindo Ghosh

Dr. Aurobindo Ghosh, a distinguished academic with an M.Sc., M.Phil., and dual Ph.D.s in Statistics and Economics, is a teacher, trainer, and research guide. Beyond academia, he is an accomplished author and artist.

His first poetry collection, *Lily on the Northern Sky*, won an award from Ukiyoto Publishing and has been translated into French, German, Spanish, and Arabic. Dr. Ghosh is a regular contributor to Ukiyoto Publishing's anthologies, with notable works including *Fairy and the Queen*, *Youngest Freedom Fighter Baji Raut*, *Make a Wish*, *Pinky Mehra Became an Astronaut*, *Yudh Shastra*, *Nagoa Beach*, *Unity in Diversity: Unification of Germany*, *Mahakaal*, and *Upanishad*. Among these, *Unity in Diversity* has been translated into German.

His recent solo fiction, *Bimladadi's Dreams*, published by Ukiyoto, has garnered significant acclaim. It was awarded *Best Fiction Book of the Year* and adapted into an audiobook. The book is now available in Italian, Turkish, and Nepali. Other solo works by Dr. Ghosh include *Mystical Honeymoon*,

Deception Redefined, and *Chronicles of Detective Subroto Deb Barman*, all published by Ukiyoto.

In addition to writing, Dr. Ghosh explores visual art, creating works in acrylic, Warli, and Madhubani styles. Proficient in multiple languages, he writes in English, Bengali, Hindi, Gujarati, and Marathi. His other books include *Insight Outsight*, *Mejoder Golpo*, and *Chhondo Hole Mondo Ki*.

www.ingramcontent.com/pod-product-compliance
Lightning Source LLC
La Vergne TN
LVHW091658190726
843493LV00001B/61